"I'm very sorry to tu  **you, sir," Faye blurt** **had closed.**

"I made it obvious when you were last here that I like being bothered by you, Miss Shawcross." Slowly he straightened and turned to face her. "In fact, I'm hoping you've saved me the journey to Mulberry House to speak to you. If you're back to tell me you feel the same way about me, I can suggest what we can do about it."

The irony in his voice couldn't quite disguise the fact that he meant every word. And heaven only knew she did crave having his strong arms about her again. She knew if he bruised her mouth with his own as he had before, his fiery passion could eradicate every worry from her head as easily as sunlight dissolved snow.

"I deduce from your silence that you're of two minds on it. Perhaps I should help you decide." He plunged his hands into his pockets and pinned her with a dangerously challenging stare.

Faye put down her untasted tea in a rattle of crockery. "I bid you to be serious, sir, if you will."

"I've never been more serious in my life," he returned.

His vivid, unsmiling eyes tangled with hers before traveling over her body in a way that caused icy heat to streak through her veins.

"And neither was I more serious than when I told you I will soon be married." Slashes of bright color accented Faye's cheekbones. "You shouldn't have kissed me, Mr. Kavanagh, and I shouldn't have..." Unable to explain herself, she snatched up her hat and gloves from the sofa.

"You shouldn't have betrayed your fiancé by liking it?"

Author Note

In my new Regency, *Rescued by the Forbidden Rake*, the heroine is known to be a *good* young woman. Everybody says so. Faye Shawcross has cared for her younger half siblings since their feckless widowed mother abandoned them to chase after her lover. Faye's also been a constant fiancée to her seafaring future husband.

But sometimes the temptation to stray from the path of righteousness is too strong to resist. Especially when it becomes obvious that duty and selflessness are not appreciated by those benefiting from it. Faye might be sweet natured but she is nobody's doormat!

For years Faye has been content to settle for the quiet life of a country lady, surrounded by pastoral beauty and good friends. When Viscount Ryan Kavanagh turns up in the neighborhood, gossip immediately starts about the handsome Irishman's licentious ways. The things that Faye hears about Valeside Manor's new squire can't possibly be true...can they? He seems to be the perfect neighbor, helping her out of one tricky situation after another when her younger sister falls in love with a wanderer lad. But does Kavanagh have an ulterior motive where she's concerned that proves his devilishness isn't simply a rumor? And who is he *really*, anyway?

Faye wants to believe her rescuer sincere, but how can she trust him when he is reluctant to tell her about himself? Should she jeopardize everything she holds dear and take a chance on a future with the wicked Irishman?

I hope you enjoy reading about how Faye and Ryan battle their way through lies and deceit to discover peace and happiness for themselves and their families.

MARY BRENDAN

---

*Rescued by the
Forbidden Rake*

6672

HARLEQUIN HISTORICAL

Recycling programs
for this product may
not exist in your area.

ISBN-13: 978-0-373-63197-1

Rescued by the Forbidden Rake

Copyright © 2017 by Mary Brendan

This edition published by arrangement with Harlequin Books S.A.

For questions and comments about the quality of this book, please contact us at CustomerService@Harlequin.com.

Printed in U.S.A.

Mary Brendan was born in North London, but now lives in rural Suffolk, England. She has always had a fascination with bygone days, and enjoys the research involved in writing historical fiction. When not at her word processor she can be found trying to bring order to a large overgrown garden, or browsing local fairs and junk shops for that elusive bargain.

Books by Mary Brendan

Harlequin Historical

Rescued by the Forbidden Rake

Linked by Character

Tarnished, Tempted and Tamed
Compromising the Duke's Daughter

Society Scandals

A Date with Dishonor
The Rake's Ruined Lady

The Hunter Brothers

A Practical Mistress
The Wanton Bride

The Meredith Sisters

Wedding Night Revenge
The Unknown Wife
A Scandalous Marriage
The Rake and the Rebel

Visit the Author Profile page
at Harlequin.com for more titles.

Chapter One

'Our business is concluded, sir. I have made my decision.'

Faye Shawcross abruptly stood up. The sauce of the man! Not only had he advised her to invest in a financial plan that had failed dismally, but he wanted to persuade her to plough what money remained to her into another of his schemes. When she had received his note yesterday, requesting an audience, she had believed he intended to come and beg forgiveness for letting her down so badly. She had even harboured a hope that he might speak of recompense. Not so much of it! Barely had he settled on a chair before proffering a new parchment for signature as though she were a gullible fool.

'I do not want to seem dictatorial, Miss Shawcross, but I beg you will reconsider my proposal. I'm sure your fiancé would direct you to listen to me, were he here.'

'But he is not, and neither is his presence required. I need no further time, or advice, sir. I have clearly said I have made my decision and have terminated my contract with you. Goodbye.'

A moment ago Faye had employed the small brass bell

on the table by her side; her housekeeper had promptly appeared and was now hovering, awaiting an instruction.

'Mr Westwood is leaving, Mrs Gideon.'

A barking cough from the servant reminded the man she was ready to show him out.

Westwood had sprung to his feet as Miss Shawcross did, an angry blush burning in his cheeks at her curt dismissal; but he managed to jerk a bow. 'As you wish; but I make no apology for striving to assist you in restoring your fortunes.'

'Perhaps you might instead like to apologise for having depleted them in the first place,' Faye replied coolly, anger and impatience sparking green fire in her eyes.

'I mentioned to you there was a risk attached,' he intoned piously.

'But not quite as fulsomely as you bade me to pay no heed to it. Had I an inkling that my money might disappear within a short while of you handling it, sir, I would not have listened to a word you uttered.'

Westwood's eyes popped, but Faye was not intimidated by his display of fury. She indicated he should leave with a nod.

Barely had the parlour door closed on his ramrod-straight back when it again opened and a boy hurtled over the threshold.

'Are we poor?'

'Of course not, my dear.' Faye held out her arms to her half-brother, catching Michael into her embrace. 'We are just not quite as well off as once we were.'

'I can still go to school in Warwick?'

'Indeed you can! And I hope to have some better reports from your headmaster when you return in the autumn, young man.'

Michael looked sheepish at the reminder of his misbehaviour. 'I know I shouldn't have got into that fight.'

'No you shouldn't…but neither should you allow those boys to bully you.' Faye ruffled her half-brother's fair hair. She felt guilty that Michael had been mocked by some older pupils when the news circulated about his overdue school fees. The headmaster's letter had been one of the first indications that all was not well. She had accepted Westwood's explanation that the matter was just an oversight. How she regretted having been so naive!

But now she had terminated the lawyer's contract the periodic sum the charlatan had charged to nurture her investments would again be available for essentials. They weren't poor…but neither were they rich, nor even comfortably off as they had once been. Faye bitterly regretted having employed Westwood; but he had come recommended by the man she was to marry and thus she'd trusted the fellow to deliver what he'd promised. Now she suspected he was incompetent at best and corrupt at worst, but she had no proof that he'd done anything underhand. She'd willingly signed the documents, handing him control of half her father's bequest. Fighting Westwood in court and losing the battle would certainly end in her destitution. With her younger siblings relying on her she couldn't afford any such action…and no doubt Mr Westwood was aware of that fact.

At twelve years old Michael had many more years at school; further economies would need to be made if her half-brother were to stay in Warwick. Yet she must be even-handed; she also had her half-sister's future to consider. As though that young lady were aware of Faye's reflection she skipped into the room.

'May we go out this afternoon?' Claire asked excitedly. 'I saw the caravans from my window. There are crowds gathering already on the village green.'

'I saw them, too! May we go?' Michael interrupted his sister to add his own plea to be allowed to visit the local midsummer fair. The Romanies arrived annually and stayed for a few days to entertain the locals before moving on to another town.

'Yes, indeed, we shall go and enjoy ourselves; only a few pennies each to spend, though,' Faye cautioned. She sighed happily; a break from the unpleasant anxiety that had beset them all would be very welcome.

Just a few days ago at breakfast she'd unsuspectingly opened the letter from Westwood, finally admitting the truth. From her spontaneous gasp of dismay the children had learned something was amiss. Faye had been tempted to shield them from the dreadful news. But what use was procrastination when they must know immediately that savings had to be made.

'I'm going to fetch my new bonnet and stitch some ribbon on it.' Claire skipped towards the door.

'Bill Perkins won't be going, so you're wasting your time wearing it for him,' Michael ribbed.

'I'm not bothered about him anyway…' his sister retorted.

'No bickering, if you please,' Faye reprimanded wryly.

Claire had developed a crush on Bill Perkins after the young farmer rescued her from a ditch. Following a heavy bout of rain she'd lost her footing and slipped down into the sludge. The fellow had a fiancée, but always stopped to pass the time of day with them all.

'I have been thinking about that trip to town we spoke of.' Faye's thoughts had jumped from nice Bill Perkins to another worthy gentleman: a faceless, nameless person her sister—God willing—was yet to meet.

'*Must* we go to London for my debut?' Claire asked with a pronounced lack of enthusiasm. 'It'll be an expensive trip and I'm not sure I want to bother.' A private smile curved her lips. 'I might find a husband hereabouts.'

'Your dowry is still safe and as you are so pretty you will need no costly embellishment like some of the plain misses.' Faye tried to encourage her sister with a jocular comment. But the praise was justified. Claire was indeed a beauty and regularly drew attention from the lusty youths in Wilverton, the small town about a half-mile distant. Claire had never shown interest in having a local beau before. Yet, oddly, Faye had just seen her sister look like the cat with the cream when talking of finding a mate in the neighbourhood.

It was said that Claire resembled her; Faye believed that her half-sister took after Deborah Shawcross in looks. But they rarely spoke about her late father's second wife. Even before Deborah absconded to Ireland to join her lover the woman had been an embarrassment.

'You *should* have your Season in London, because I know you *will* have a wonderful time and meet a splendid fellow and fall in love.' Faye's confident tone barely lifted Claire's frown. But it amused Michael and he made much of patting at his yawning mouth, chortling.

'Aunt Agatha has invited us to stay with her in Hammersmith,' Faye continued. 'I'll write and let her know that we would be pleased to accept her hospitality in the spring.'

'I'd sooner stay here,' Michael piped up.

'You will be safely out of the way at school, young man.'

'Might I go and stay with Stanley Scott?'

'I don't think so, Michael,' Faye said apologetically. 'The cost of the fare to Scotland is rather a lot.' Her brother had received an invitation from his school chum's parents to holiday with them in Edinburgh until the autumn term.

'Shall I ask him to come here?' Michael asked, but not very optimistically.

'You know we don't really have the room for guests.' Faye gave her brother a rueful smile. Mulberry House *was* small—nothing like the castle in which the Scotts lived—but, that apart, another mouth to feed would be an additional financial burden. Despite her logic and prudence Faye felt mean denying her brother a friend for the holidays.

'Now if we are to spend an hour or two at the fair later I must get on.' Faye briskly clapped her hands. 'I want to catch the post and the shopkeepers in Wilverton must be paid. Mr Gideon warned of rain this evening; we'll want to be home from the fair before then.' Their housekeeper's husband was invariably accurate with his weather forecast.

Having sealed the note to her aunt about preparations for Claire's debut, Faye counted out the money owed to merchants and put it into her reticule. She was determined to carry on paying bills on time. But news of her reduced circumstances would eventually circulate and she hated the idea of being tattled over or pitied. The Gideons were aware of what had occurred and were as fiercely loyal to Faye and her half-siblings as they had been to her father. But it was an odd truth that no matter how conscientiously confidences were guarded, rumours spread.

* * *

A ride into town on Mr Gideon's dog cart was always a revelation. As they moved along at a steady pace the elderly fellow kept up a one-sided conversation past the clay pipe clenched between his teeth. Not that Faye was unwilling to add a comment; it was hard to get a word in edgeways. Mr Gideon had employment with several neighbours and was up to date with what went on in the hamlets that encircled Mulberry House, the Shawcrosses' residence for over one hundred years. By the time the elderly mare pulling the dog cart was drawn to a halt at Wilverton Green's turnpike, Faye had learned that there was a bad case of scarlatina in Moreton, to the south, that had resulted in one burial so far, and that twins had been born last week in Fairley, to the east. Having expressed her gladness that mother and babies were all doing well, Faye sprang nimbly down to the dusty ground.

'Shall I wait for you to finish your business and take you back, Miss Shawcross? It be no trouble.' Bert Gideon had removed his pipe to make that enquiry.

'It's kind of you to offer, but I shall have time enough to walk home, thank you.' Faye shook her light cotton skirts to remove the creases from them and retied the strings of her bonnet. She glanced up at the angle of the sun, judging it to be close to noon. A ride back would have been helpful as she'd promised the others an excursion in a few hours' time, but she didn't want to delay Mr Gideon getting to his next job.

'Don't be forgetting now that rain's due.' Bert clucked his tongue at the mare.

'Not before we've returned from the fair, I hope,' Faye said, half to herself.

Mr Gideon raised a hand in farewell as the vehicle creaked away and Faye set off to do her errands.

'And a very good day to you, Miss Shawcross.'

'And to you, sir. I have come to settle up and place my order for next week, Mr Bullman.' Had she imagined a look of relief in the butcher's eyes as he'd pounced on the cash in her hand?

'I have some mutton for stewing that you might like for a change and some beef suet that'll make you a nice dumpling.' Mr Bullman wiped his bloodied hands on his apron before pocketing his cash.

Had he sounded different…pitying? Faye noticed that he'd certainly collected up the notes she'd put down with unusual zeal. She glanced at his expression and, yes, he did seem to be avoiding her eyes.

'I won't have the mutton, thank you. I'll take my usual order and an extra two pork chops, if you please,' Faye said crisply.

'So Mr Collins is back and paying a visit, is he?' The butcher sounded jolly. 'I recall you told me your fiancé's partial to a chop for dinner.'

'He isn't calling until next week. I'll take the chops with the kidneys in them, please. Those will go nicely with fresh beans from the garden and some baked potatoes.'

'Of course, Miss Shawcross. I'll have the boy deliver the usual order and two extra chops on Thursday.'

Outside the shop Faye paused, giving herself a talking to. Mr Bullman was a good soul and she was being too sensitive because of her guilt and regrets over allowing Mr Westwood free rein with her money. She glanced back into the shop and saw the butcher deep in conversation with his wife. There was nothing unusual about that, but the way the couple darted surreptitious glances her way caused Faye's heart to sink. She sighed and walked on. So, news of her losses *had* circulated, but she wouldn't answer questions about it.

A few minutes later she had changed her mind. Her friend Anne Holly hailed her, trotting over the rutted road to her side.

'Oh, my dear, how are you?' Anne hugged Faye. 'Is it true you've suffered a setback?'

'How did you find out, Anne?' Faye huffed a resigned little laugh. 'Tongues are wagging, are they?'

'Not maliciously, I assure you; people are sympathetic and Mr Westwood has come in for some very harsh criticism,' Anne said gently. 'He has scuttled off quickly back to London.'

'I'd sooner people let the matter drop. Westwood will only prolong the gossip in defending his part in it all. Who spread the news?'

'I imagine it came from Westwood's office. I know the verger and several others travel to London and use that particular firm.'

Faye gave a faintly acid smile. 'I hadn't imagined it would happen so soon.'

'Derek was going to come over and see you this afternoon to condole, but I've persuaded him not to.'

'Thank you…' Faye said wryly. 'I will be less prickly about it in a day or two. I feel a fool for wanting to earn more than the bank paid while my money was safe in a vault.'

'Any person would seek the best return on a deposit,' Anne protested. 'You have your brother and sister depending on you so you need to be astute.'

'I don't mind providing for them.'

'Well, if it were me, I'd mind their mother shirking her duty so abominably.' Anne frowned an apology, knowing she'd said too much.

Faye was niggled by her friend's comment despite recognising the truth in what Anne had said. Not wanting to bicker, she changed the subject. 'We're going to the fairground this afternoon, so your husband would not have found us in. Are you going to come? You're welcome to join us in eating buns and throwing balls at skittles.'

'I'd like to, but Derek's mother has arrived on a visit with his sister and his niece. Sarah is a nice girl, a little older than your Claire, I'd say. She's making her come out in the spring. The family is well connected; they know some of the *ton's* hostesses. My mother-in-law is friendly with Lady Jersey, you know.' Anne sounded proud.

'As Claire is coming out next year, too, perhaps the girls could get together before Sarah returns to Essex.'

'I'm sure she'd like that…' Anne's enthusiastic response tailed away and her eyes narrowed on something over Faye's shoulder. 'Now there are some people who really *have* started tongues wagging,' she whispered. 'I have heard tales about *him* that would make your hair stand on end.'

Discreetly, Faye glanced around. A sleek curricle drawn by matching greys had stopped by the drapery shop. The tiger took the reins while the driver jumped down and helped his passenger alight.

'Who is *that*?' The town of Wilverton was off the beaten track for high society and the handsome couple looked to be top notch.

'That, my dear, is the new master of Valeside Manor.'

Anne inclined closer to her friend to murmur, 'And the young woman with him is rumoured to be his paramour.'

Faye looked suitably shocked. 'Well, she is very pretty…if barely out of her governess's care by the look of her.' She peeked again at the slender young lady, her raven hair cascading in ringlets to her shoulders. Even at some distance, Faye could tell that her summer gown was of exquisite style. And she was very possessive of her beau, judging by the way she clung to his arm. But the gentleman was watching her and appeared amused by her interest. Quickly Faye averted her face, regretting having stared for so long.

'He is a bachelor named Ryan Kavanagh and he's Irish, but nobody is sure of the lady's identity.' Anne shielded her moving lips with her gloved fingers. 'Apparently he has a mistress each end of London, who both drip jewels and drive about in swish carriages.'

'He is a wealthy fellow then.' Faye still felt warm from having the stranger's mocking eyes on her.

'Indeed, he is. A rich reprobate, Derek's mother called him.' Anne tilted her head at the newcomers. 'That young lady actually *lives* with him, you know, *at the Manor.*' The shocking information was ejected in a hiss.

Faye's small teeth nipped her lower lip, suppressing a scandalised laugh. 'Perhaps I should be grateful to Mr Kavanagh: in comparison to his affairs my sorry business barely merits a mention.'

The couple had entered the shop and Faye clasped her friend's hands in farewell. 'I must get home and freshen up and change my shoes for the trek over the fields.'

'Does your fiancé know of your bad news?' Anne asked hesitantly.

'He does not… Peter has docked at Portsmouth, but

he is not due to visit for a week or so.' Faye imagined
her seafaring future husband would take it very personally, knowing that the lawyer he had recommended had
failed her. But Peter had only done what he thought best.

With a wave, Faye set off back the way she had come.
As she passed the dusty curricle the smartly uniformed
tiger gave her a polite nod. Faye ran her eyes over the
fine horseflesh, then speeded up her pace towards home.
For some reason she didn't want to see Mr Kavanagh and
his concubine again. She felt a little *frisson* pass over
her. She regretted having humoured the man by staring
at him in such a vulgar fashion.

Once out of sight of townsfolk, Faye grabbed her
skirts and began to trot along the meadow path, feeling
quite joyous as she concentrated on the treat of an afternoon spent at the fair on such a glorious afternoon. The
ground beneath her flying feet had been worn in places
to bare soil where the locals took short cuts to and from
their cottages on the outskirts of Wilverton.

Having spied Mulberry House rising on the horizon,
Faye slowed down to appreciate her pretty home and re-
lieve the stitch in her side. It was a whitewashed building
topped with russet-coloured clay tiles and the sturdy iron
porch was smothered with scarlet roses that had climbed
as far as the eaves. Cecil Shawcross had always loved
his abundantly planted garden and the scented blooms
that rambled on the front of the house and spilled over
the trellises to the rear of the property had been his pride
and joy.

Her eyes prickled with tears as she thought about
him. Her half-siblings missed their father, too, but being
younger had not had the benefit of his company for as
long as she had when he passed away. Her father could

be a difficult man; without a doubt he would be angry
that part of his bequest had disappeared in a poor investment. But it would be towards Peter Collins that
he'd unleash his temper. Peter had proposed to her when
she was twenty-one, but another two years had passed
before her father eventually agreed to the match. It had
been a sadness to her that her father and her fiancé had
never really got on.

Drawing in a deep breath, she set off again, trotting
towards the side gate that led through the kitchen garden and into the house.

Chapter Two

'Ah, so you're back at last.' Mrs Gideon frowned as her rosy-cheeked mistress entered the kitchen. She put down on the floury table the pastry cutter she'd been using. 'I can see you've been dashing about again.' She poured a glass of lemonade from a metal jug. 'That'll help cool you off.'

Gratefully Faye took the tumbler, closing her eyes while relishing the refreshing brew. 'I have been running, and indeed it wasn't wise. It is very sultry today... perhaps a storm is on its way.' Faye brushed a hand beneath the damp blonde curls clinging to her nape.

'There's some warm water in the kettle for a wash.' Mrs Gideon filled a copper pitcher, then found a muslin cloth in a drawer. 'Your sister is still unpicking her stitching, so I reckon you've time enough to take a bath waiting for her to be satisfied with prettifying that hat.' The woman tutted. 'Miss Claire's had that piece of blue ribbon on and off the straw at least thrice.'

Faye took another sip of lemonade, intending to take the drink upstairs with her and finish it while she changed her clothes.

'Did anybody upset you while you were in town, miss?'

Faye turned back to see Mrs Gideon looking quite severe while forcefully rolling out pastry.

'Everybody was very polite, Mrs Gideon.' Faye gave a faint smile. 'Not a word spoken out of place by the shop-keepers, but I saw Anne Holly and she was kind enough to be blunt and tell me people know what has happened.' Untying her bonnet, she let it hang on its ribbons, then forked her fingers through her thick blonde tresses. So far Mr and Mrs Gideon had kept their own counsel on the business with Westwood; Faye feared they were too kind and loyal to openly say what they must privately be thinking: that her father would be spinning in his grave at her ineptitude with his money. If the couple were concerned over their employment at Mulberry House since she'd made losses, they'd not brought it up.

'I meant to say, Mrs Gideon, that I haven't come to such a sorry pass that I cannot afford to keep you on.'

'Oh, I know, Miss Shawcross.' The housekeeper's eyes held a sheen of tears. 'And much as I want to say I'd keep coming every day if you paid me or not, I won't upset you by doing it.' Nelly Gideon wiped her eyes on her rolled-up sleeve. 'Neither will Mr Gideon, but we wanted to let you know that we won't hear a word against you or the children.'

'I know I can rely on you both,' Faye said huskily.

Mrs Gideon nodded vigorously and set about cutting pastry cases.

Faye suddenly remembered something that might lighten the atmosphere; Mrs Gideon was frowning fiercely while running the rolling pin this way and that.

'Anne Holly told me that Valeside Manor has acquired a new owner.'

'Him!' The housekeeper gave a loud tut. 'A vicar's wife had no right bringing *that* fellow into a decent conversation.'

'You knew about Mr Kavanagh and his lady friend being at Valeside Manor?' Faye sounded surprised.

'Indeed, I did! I hope he'll soon take himself off to London where the likes of him and her are sure to be better received.' Mrs Gideon returned her attention to the tartlets she was filling with blackcurrants. 'What with those Romanies turning up as well we've got more than our fair share of rogues in the neighbourhood lately.'

Faye remained quiet for a moment. From her housekeeper's strong reaction she took it that her friend Anne had not overstated Mr Kavanagh's ill repute.

'Apparently he is very affluent. Local people might benefit from his patronage.' Faye felt an odd compulsion to find something good to say about the new master of Valeside. 'The manor has been empty for quite some time, it's sure to need repairs and additional staff. Mr Kavanagh might call on villagers to fill vacancies.'

'No decent woman would enter that house no matter what pay he offered. The only females likely to benefit from *his* patronage are those working in the room above the Dog and Duck.' The housekeeper turned florid, regretting having let her tongue run away with her.

Faye picked up her lemonade and took a gulp. She knew that a couple of harlots entertained clients above the taproom in the Dog and Duck. The hostelry was situated on the outskirts of Wilverton and was shunned by decent folk who supped in the White Hart tavern on the green instead.

Still, Faye felt an odd inclination to give the benefit of the doubt to Mr Kavanagh. 'He had a very well-behaved team of horses and his servant was nicely turned out, and polite, too. The boy made a point of raising his hat to me as I passed by.'

'You managed to get quite a good long look at Mr Kavanagh, did you, miss?' Nelly Gideon asked. 'Did you see the scar on his face?'

'He was too far away for me to see more than that he is a tall gentleman with very dark hair. I was talking to Anne across the road and he'd disappeared inside the drapery with his companion by the time I passed his curricle.'

Nelly put down a spoon stained with blackcurrant juice. 'Got a scar from here to here, he has…' She striped one side of her face from cheekbone to lip with a forefinger. 'Duelling over a woman, so I heard. Killed a man.' She shook her head. 'It makes me wonder what else might yet come out about his wickedness.'

Faye's eyes widened, but still she was reluctant to condemn too quickly. Today she'd had a taste of what it was like to be the butt of gossip and it wasn't pleasant. Despite what her friend Anne Holly had said about people's sympathy for her, there would doubtless be some private sniggering at her lack of judgement.

'You'd better keep your distance from the new master of Valeside Manor, miss,' Nelly said over a shoulder, sliding the tarts into the oven. 'Your fiancé won't want you associating with such a rogue.'

'Who is a rogue?' Claire had just entered the kitchen, eyes alight with interest at what she'd overheard.

'The new master of Valeside Manor,' Mrs Gideon informed darkly. 'Big handsome chap Mr Kavanagh may be, but he's got a black heart, so you all stay clear of that place.'

'Show me your hat then.' Faye changed the subject, thinking Mr Kavanagh had been a topic of conversation for long enough.

'What do you think?' Claire held aloft the bonnet, twirling it on her fingers so the blue ribbons flew out like flags.

'Very pretty…' Faye said, picking up the jug of washing water. 'I won't be long getting ready, then we'll get going. A storm's brewing for this evening and we won't want to be out in the thunder and lightning.'

Walking through long, murmuring grass with the warmth of late June on one's shoulders was one of life's wonderful pleasures, Faye thought as she picked seeds from her cotton skirts. She watched her brother and sister, chasing to and fro and throwing grassy darts at one another. Faye smiled wryly; her sister was still a child at heart and it was a shame to think of hurrying her to womanhood with a premature debut.

Claire wouldn't be seventeen until the middle of next year. She'd already said she was eager to be launched before her next birthday rather than wait until the following Season. Faye had worried that her half-sister might not be ready for such an important milestone at sixteen. But things had changed for them all. She could no longer afford to be so finicky.

Faye was obliged to tighten the purse strings on the family kitty and there was no denying that Claire might be better off now under a husband's protection than her sister's.

Turning her face up to the golden sunbeams, Faye

sighed, loosening her straw bonnet to let the breeze cool her skin. It was easy to feel lulled by the pastoral melody of birdsong and bees swarming nearby.

'That man's staring at you. Who is he?'

Faye's eyes flicked open and she saw her brother, flushed from his game of chase, ambling at her side.

'His name is Mr Kavanagh,' Faye said hoarsely, feeling rather shocked to see him again so soon. And at much closer quarters. Mrs Gideon had called him a big handsome man, and indeed he was broad of shoulder and very good looking. She could also see the thin pale mark dissecting his bronzed cheek that her housekeeper had spoken of.

'We mustn't have anything to do with him,' Claire whispered, having joined them. 'He's a black-hearted rogue, Mrs Gideon said so, and she knows everything.'

'What has he done?' Michael asked, agog.

'You're not old enough to know,' Claire replied, hoping to sound mysterious and knowledgeable.

'Hush…that's enough gossip.' Faye tore her eyes away from a steady, narrowed gaze. She was quite sure that *the black-hearted rogue* knew they were talking about him.

'Perhaps he's a highwayman or a smuggler.' Michael turned to Faye, eyes dancing with glee. 'He might be delivering kegs of brandy at dark of night or he might be like Dick Turpin with his own Black Bess.'

'He is probably quite an ordinary character in reality,' Faye interrupted, attempting to dampen down Michael's excitement. She wouldn't put it past her half-brother to dash across the field and quiz Mr Kavanagh about his dastardly exploits. But she doubted that her description of the man as ordinary was any more valid than were her brother's fanciful imaginings. Ryan Kavanagh might not be a model villain, but neither was he a tame fellow. She set a brisker pace, hoping the children would run ahead again and forget about their intriguing new neighbour.

'He must be rich,' Michael said, content to dawdle. He glanced over a shoulder at the fellow propped against an oak with a magnificent black stallion tethered to a branch by his side. 'He has a fine horse.' He frowned. 'I remember Papa had a similar beast.'

'He *is* a beast…' Claire hissed, determined to shock her younger brother.

'For goodness sake, turn around and stop staring, you two. Look…there's a juggler.' Faye distracted Michael's attention to the harlequin entertaining a group of youngsters.

They were now close to the fairground and the noise and appetising aromas caused the children to finally lose interest in Mr Kavanagh. But Faye had not. The need to take a peep over her shoulder was undeniable. He had sunk down to the grass with his back against the tree, one knee raised and supporting an elbow. He was smoking a cheroot, she realised as a faint scent of tobacco reached her on the breeze. He turned his head in her direction and Faye quickly whipped her face away, not wanting him to catch her staring at him for the second time that day.

Claire waved at her friend Peggy, their housekeeper's niece, and with a quick promise not to be gone long dashed away to talk to her. Michael had also spotted a group of chums and loped off in the opposite direction. Left alone, Faye became aware of her heart thudding beneath her embroidered bodice. An odd thrill was shooting iced fire through her veins. When their eyes had fleetingly met Mr Kavanagh had appeared aware of the unsettling effect he was having on her. His subtle smile had annoyed Faye as well as intrigued her. Yet there had been nothing in his behaviour that declared him to be the reprobate he'd been painted. His demeanour alone proclaimed him to be of wealth and status, and he was quietly minding his own business. But why was he here at all? He didn't seem interested in the fair—in fact, he seemed bored. And then Faye spotted the reason for him idling on the grass. He was waiting for his mistress to finish browsing the fairground stalls.

The lovely young lady was just ahead, making purchases from a vendor and handing over the packages to her maids. Yes, not one but two bombazine-clad servants were dancing attendance on her while her beau waited patiently at a distance for her to sufficiently enjoy herself.

For a moment Faye couldn't drag her eyes from Ryan Kavanagh's paramour. She was struck by the young woman's exquisite and rather exotic looks; the profound darkness of her hair and eyes were set off by the pale gold colour of the fine day dress that encased her perfectly proportioned figure. Her clear olive complexion was protected from the sun by her bonnet brim and a lacy parasol that one of the maids was diligently holding aloft and tilting to and fro. Aware that she had been standing quite still, staring, Faye propelled herself in the opposite direction, determined to forget all about the new master of Valeside and his entourage!

'Tell your fortune, my lady?' The voice was pleasantly accented. A weather-beaten face, with sharp dark eyes, was turned up to Faye's. The woman had plaited tresses resembling a sable snake on her crown and she was extending a hand to take Faye's palm in hers.

Ruefully Faye shook her head. 'Thank you, but I'm not sure I'm brave enough to know it.'

The crone gave a gap-toothed smile and grasped Faye's fingers so she couldn't escape. The abrupt movement set her hoop earrings dancing against her leathery neck. 'This isn't the hand of a coward, though you've hurdles in front of you and no denying. You're certainly of an age to be wed, but aren't.' She grinned. 'And I didn't know that from your bare fingers as I've not seen them yet.' She pulled off the cotton glove covering Faye's right hand and examined her palm. 'But you'll be happy and loved and give back those feelings to your man. Marriage and children are written for you here.' She traced a dirty fingernail on a zigzagging path across Faye's soft skin. Then she paused, frowning before raising her almond-shaped eyes. 'And your lover is very close by today. He's here with you…a good man…'

Faye's fingers curled to conceal her palm and she jerked free. Quickly she handed over some coins got from her pocket. Usually she would have chuckled at such fanciful nonsense and it confused her why she had not. She swiftly moved on, keeping her brother and sister in sight as they mingled with their friends in the crowd. But the gypsy's words were haunting her mind, urging her to glance back. The old woman had turned to watch her and nodded in a portentous and oddly reverential way. When Faye next tried to find her brother and sister, she found she couldn't locate either of them in the throng.

Determined to enjoy herself, Faye marched up to a stall and bought some lemon ribbon and pearl buttons for a favourite, but well-worn, gown that would benefit from being spruced up. She wandered on, feeling tempted to

purchase a meat pie from a woman carrying a tray laden
with pastries. The savoury aroma was appetising, but she
decided to resist and wait until the children came back
so they could all sit together on the grass and enjoy a
picnic. She examined some pretty gewgaws on another
stall, then selected a hair comb crafted in tortoiseshell
that she thought Claire might like. A pewter inkstand
also caught her eyes and she purchased that, too, for Michael to take back to school. She was placing the gifts
in her reticule when she sensed a looming figure close
by, then a heavy hand was on her arm.

'Mrs Gideon said I'd find you here...'

Faye spun about at the familiar baritone, then gasped
in surprise and pleasure.

'Peter! I had no idea you were coming. Why did you
not write and let me know to soon expect you?' She
chuckled. 'Had you sent word I would have given you
pork chops for dinner, you know. As it is, the butcher's
not due until Thursday.'

Peter Collins grasped her outstretched fingers and
brought them to his lips. 'I wanted to surprise you, my
dear.'

'You have certainly done that.' She paused. 'Although
I had my fortune read a moment ago and the woman did
say my sweetheart was close by... I thought it all nonsense, too.'

'It is nonsense,' Peter dismissed, top lip curling. 'You
should avoid such people.'

'That is easier said than done at a summer fair.' Faye
chuckled. 'You will stay and dine with us later?' She
smiled up into his hazel eyes.

'Of course, I'd be glad to, pork chops or no.' Again
his mouth brushed her knuckles. 'I'm putting up at the

White Hart in Wilverton for a few days.' Peter drew Faye
to a quieter spot so they might promenade and chat more
easily on the edge of the crowd.

Slipping her hand through her fiancé's arm, Faye discreetly hugged him, feeling oddly relieved as well as
happy to have his company. But there was one thing niggling at her: she had expected some notice of his arrival
so she might get straight in her mind how to tell him of
her meeting with Westwood. She didn't want Peter to
feel guilty for having put her in touch with the lawyer,
yet he was bound to feel disappointed that the best part
of her dowry had gone. The Collins family were well-
connected gentry, but Peter had told her that his mother
complained they were poor as church mice.

'What is it?' Peter looked down at her, his smile fading on noticing her frown.

'Oh…nothing that can't wait till later. Let's enjoy ourselves while the sun's shining. It might storm later, according to Mr Gideon.'

'Where are the scamps?' Peter asked, referring to
Faye's siblings.

'Oh, they've gone off to see their friends,' Faye answered as they began to promenade arm in arm. She
nodded to a spot where Michael and a chum were now
throwing balls at skittles. Even at a distance she could
hear the boys' whoops of glee.

'And where is Claire?' Peter turned his head, seeking her.

Faye also looked about. She came to a halt and pivoted
on the spot, but still she couldn't spot a blue-beribboned
bonnet anywhere. She realised it had been some time
since she'd last caught a glimpse of her sister.

'She was chatting with Mrs Gideon's niece earlier.

I expect they have found a shady spot to sit down. It is very hot…' Despite her explanation, Faye felt a *frisson* of uneasiness. Claire had said she would only be gone a short while. 'Michael might know where she's gone.'

'There she is!' Peter drew Faye's attention to a copse; Claire and Peggy were emerging from between two brightly painted caravans.

Slipping her hand from Peter's arm, Faye set off towards them, her heartbeat accelerating in alarm. They had the furtive look of people who feared being spotted doing something they shouldn't.

'I have been looking for you. Where have you been?'

Claire spun about with a guilty gasp, her cheeks reddening. 'I…we have only been looking at the ponies.'

Faye glanced at the squat piebald animals tethered to the low branches of trees, sedately cropping grass. 'You should have said you were going off the beaten track.' She hadn't really believed Claire might come to harm on this sunny afternoon, yet still uneasiness prickled at her. As she glanced at Peggy the girl averted her eyes, then excused herself, running back to the stalls with her fiery red tresses flying out behind her.

'I see Lieutenant Collins has turned up.' Claire sounded unenthusiastic at the forthcoming reunion with her future brother-in-law. Faye knew that Michael would react similarly. Peter had a lukewarm relationship with her half-siblings, believing them to be obstacles to his marriage. But Faye wouldn't hear of her brother and sister being nudged aside before they were of an age to be independent.

'I expect you've had your fill of the fair if you're feeling bored enough to pet the ponies.' Faye linked arms with Claire. 'Let's set off home. While we wait for Mrs

Gideon to cook dinner I'll show you what I've bought you today.'

'You've got me a present?' Claire sounded delighted. Then her expression drooped. 'Is Lieutenant Collins coming home with us?'

'Of course! He's putting up in Wilverton…but will dine with us first.'

Faye was walking ahead with Claire along the narrow earthy track towards Mulberry House. Her fiancé and brother were bringing up the rear and they had been strolling for little more than ten minutes when she noticed Mr Kavanagh and his party descending the hill towards Wilverton.

'Who is that with Mr Kavanagh?' Claire whispered, her eyes widening on the sight of the lovely young woman sitting atop the black stallion. The two maids were marching one either side of the fine animal, led by its master.

'Umm…the young lady is a friend of his I believe,' Faye said diplomatically, then turned to glance over a shoulder at Peter. He, too, had caught sight of the people descending towards the valley, travelling on a parallel course to their own.

'Do you know that fellow?' Peter had noticed the gentleman's head turn in their direction.

'We've not been introduced. I have it from the vicar's wife, though, that he is the new master of Valeside Manor…an Irishman, I believe.' Faye had noticed that the two men were staring at one another in the way fellows did when summing one another up.

'Mrs Gideon said he's a black-hearted rogue.' Claire followed her pronouncement with a mischievous smile. 'He's very handsome though.'

'Is he now?' was all Peter said, striding ahead and whipping aside the entangling grass with a twig he'd found on the ground.

Faye glanced across the meadow, but Kavanagh and his entourage had disappeared into the valley that led towards Wilverton.

Chapter Three

'I've put the chicken and vegetables on the dining table, Miss Shawcross. I'll be in the kitchen with Bertram, doing mending. Just ring, if you need me.'

'Thank you, Mrs Gideon.'

Faye and Peter had been idling in the parlour, waiting for their dinner while examining their fairground gifts.

'Mrs Gideon and her husband could surely go home now the meal is prepared,' Peter murmured close to his fiancée's ear, as he helped her to be seated. 'I'll gladly assist in clearing away the crockery if it means I get more time alone with you.'

'You know Nelly's a stickler for etiquette,' Faye whispered a rueful reply, unfolding her napkin. Her housekeeper took pains to ensure that her mistress's reputation was protected even if that meant returning home late, after visitors had left. Mr Collins might be Miss Shawcross's future husband, but in Nelly Gideon's mind one observed rules until vows were taken.

As Peter carved the chicken and helped hand around the dishes of vegetables Faye felt a twinge of melancholy that he couldn't always show such tolerance to her brother and sister. Soon, he would want them out of the way as well so that he could have his fiancée to himself. When it was just the two of them Faye enjoyed his kisses and caresses although sometimes she wondered why she didn't crave their privacy as passionately as he did.

'When must you return to your ship?' Faye asked when the children had left the table and she had also eaten her fill.

'In less than a week, I'm afraid.' Peter put down his pudding spoon and patted his stomach. 'Your Mrs Gideon always turns out a decent dinner.'

'She is a boon and I don't know what I'd do without her or her husband helping us out.' Faye rang the little bell to let Mrs Gideon know that she could clear the table. 'If you have finished, we can go and sit in the parlour.'

'I'd certainly like a little comfort before being ejected by your virtuous housekeeper to the frugal offerings of the White Hart.' His hazel eyes darkened with desire as he pulled out her chair, then teased her nape with his fingers. 'I can't wait much longer for us to be husband and wife.' His voice sounded rough. 'Have you contacted that woman yet to advise her you are to be married and she must send for her children?'

'I have not; as I have said, I've no idea whereabouts in Ireland my stepmother is.' Faye felt a niggling exasperation tighten her insides. Despite her reply never altering, Peter regularly asked her the same question about 'that woman' as he called Deborah Shawcross. Faye truthfully did not know her whereabouts and, even if she did, she would not force her brother and sister to go and live with an adulteress who had rejected her own flesh and blood in favour of her lover.

At the time her brother had been just six years old and although Michael had been distraught for a while he now avoided speaking of his mother. Claire, at ten years old, had comprehended what had occurred between her parents and had been so hurt by her mother's abandonment that she'd professed to hate her.

Humiliated by his wife's betrayal Cecil Shawcross had dealt with it as best he could, but when it became apparent Deborah was not coming home he had banned any mention of her. They had all sensed that their father's snapping and snarling was the outcome of him being deeply wounded and had obeyed his wishes. But none of them had forgotten that Deborah Shawcross had turned their lives upside down.

Peter's frustration that his fiancée had been burdened with caring for her siblings was understandable, but in other ways Faye thought him unreasonable. She would happily marry immediately, but Peter had made it clear that the children could not have a permanent home beneath his roof. Even had Faye not promised her late father that she would see the children safely settled, she loved them too much to ever reject them as their mother had.

'May I?' Peter had picked up the decanter on the sideboard in the parlour.

'Oh, do help yourself,' Faye replied, settling on the sofa. The children had gone to their rooms as they always did when Lieutenant Collins paid a visit. Now that they were alone Faye knew she had a perfect opportunity to broach the unpleasant subject of her meeting with Westwood. But she was reluctant to spoil their harmony on Peter's first day back and decided to wait until tomorrow to break news that was likely to create a bad atmosphere. But know about it he must.

'So, the new fellow at Valeside has moved in lock, stock and barrel with his wife, has he?' Peter made himself comfortable beside Faye, an arm slung negligently along the sofa's velvet back as he sipped his port.

'Oh, you mean Mr Kavanagh. I don't think the lady we saw with him is his wife.' Faye gave a tiny laugh. She had not expected the conversation to turn in that direction. 'According to Anne Holly she is his *chère amie.*'

'Is she indeed?' Peter snorted amusement and took a gulp of his drink. 'Deuced brass neck of the fellow taking her about with him like that. Ryan Kavanagh, you say, is his name?' Peter put down his goblet and turned his attention to his fiancée. 'Never mind about him... I'd sooner think about you and how much I shall miss you when I set sail.' He leaned forward, brushing his lips against Faye's. His hands travelled to her slender waist, shifting her closer to him on the sofa as his kiss deepened.

'Actually, there is something I should say to you, Peter...' Faye held him off a little. She'd had a change of heart and wanted to get the bad news over with, but he again hungrily captured her mouth with his own.

'Oh...sorry... I should have knocked...' Claire garbled out, having burst into the parlour. 'Michael is unwell; Mrs Gideon is with him. She said to tell you to come and see him.'

Peter cursed angrily beneath his breath and surged upright. 'I'll be on my way. I'll call tomorrow, if I may. Then I shall be in London for a day or two before returning to Portsmouth.'

'Yes, please do come tomorrow.' Faye gave her fiancé an apologetic smile. 'Would you like a nightcap before you go?' She was also disappointed that his visit had been abruptly curtailed.

Out in the hallway she heard the unmistakable sound from upstairs of Michael being sick. With a resigned sigh and a quick farewell peck on her fiancé's cheek, she let Peter see himself out.

'He's got the bellyache and headache; it's not the chicken I cooked,' Mrs Gideon announced bluntly, holding a basin under the invalid's chin.

'He's been scrumping today, he told me so,' Claire said, wrinkling her nose in distaste before adding, 'I'm off to bed.'

'Scrumping, eh? Apples aren't ripe yet...no wonder he's got the bellyache.' Mrs Gideon snorted.

'I'll see to him, Mrs Gideon; you and your husband will want to get to your own beds now.'

'I'll fetch Master Michael a powder to settle his stomach before I leave.'

'Have you been scrumping?' Faye asked when Nelly had left the room.

Michael nodded, screwing up his face as a cramp tightened his belly. 'Claire shouldn't have told on me. I don't tell on her.'

'What's to tell?' Faye asked mildly. She glanced at her brother, but he turned his face away on the pillow.

'Nothing...' he mumbled.

'There now. Get that down you. And stay away from sour apples; you've probably taken in a maggot as well,' Mrs Gideon scolded, handing over a tumbler of milky liquid. She picked up the bowl. 'I'll dispose of this and be by tomorrow as usual.'

'Thank you, Mrs Gideon.'

Meekly Michael did as he was bade, sipping the brew with a grimace before allowing his sister to tuck him up.

Faye was still mulling over what Michael had said about telling tales on Claire. Before quitting his chamber, she asked, 'Is there something going on that I should know about, Michael?'

'I'm tired,' her brother said, pulling the covers right up and closing his eyes.

'You can rest in bed tomorrow to get over this.'

'I was going to meet my friends at the fairground.' Michael made to sit up but fell back, exhausted, against the pillow.

'We'll see about that in the morning.' Faye closed the bedroom door.

A pearly glow was painting the walls of the corridor and she felt drawn to the window to gaze up at the silvery orb decorating the sky. There was still a faint summer light on the horizon and she leaned her warm forehead against the cool glass, observing a fox prowling in the shadowy garden below.

Peter had gone; there was no sign of his horse tethered by the gate. But it was the image of another man and another stallion that was imprinted on her mind as she stared into the twilight.

The look Ryan Kavanagh had given her as he sat on the grass with the superb steed close by was annoyingly unforgettable. She suspected that if he were to discover how affected she had been by clashing eyes with him just twice, that half-smile of his would turn to laughter.

She pivoted away from the moonlit scene, feeling ashamed for having allowed a stranger to push her fiancé from her mind. And there was something else: the niggling anxiety that her brother had been on the point of disclosing something important about Claire. Faye didn't want to seem to be prying unduly into her younger sister's life…but she was her guardian and the memory of the guilty look on Claire's face earlier that day now seemed to warrant further investigation.

With a sigh Faye resolved to speak to her sister in the morning. Feeling suddenly quite weary, she went downstairs to check the locks, as she always did, before retiring.

The following morning Faye was seated at the parlour table, penning an invitation to Peter to dine with them later, when her housekeeper hurried in to the room.

'You'd best come and take a look at your brother, Miss Shawcross.'

'Why? What is it, Mrs Gideon?'

'I took him up a breakfast tray. Master Michael's still feeling poorly and I'd say there's more to it than scrumping.'

Quickly Faye followed her housekeeper's plump figure up the stairs. Michael had seemed fine when she checked on him before turning in for the night. He'd been sleeping soundly so Faye had blown out the night light she'd left burning at the side of his bed. This morning she'd risen early and gone straight downstairs, not wanting to disturb him.

'He's got a fever and I asked him to show me his chest as it occurred to me that when folk congregate at fairs, infections can spread.'

Nelly Gideon had acted as nurse to both of Mr Shawcross's youngest children and had no hesitation in pulling open the lacings on Michael's nightshirt to display a patch of red skin on his breastbone. 'That rash tells me a doctor needs calling.' Nelly had lowered her voice to an ominous whisper.

A burst of anxiety flipped Faye's heart over. She sat on the edge of her brother's bed and put a hand against his forehead. He felt very hot and clammy and she knew that if he did have scarlatina they should get a doctor to examine him straight away. Faye knew enough about infections to suspect the doctor would tell them to keep themselves to themselves for a week or two to prevent it spreading.

'Would you ask your husband to fetch Dr Reid, please?' Faye turned her blanching face up to her house-keeper's furrowed countenance.

Nelly nodded and hurried from the room. The fact that stoic Mrs Gideon seemed alarmed increased Faye's anxiety and she tried to block from her mind what Bertram Gideon had told her about folk dying of the disease.

Faye got to her feet and smoothed strands of lank fair hair back from Michael's brow. He seemed half-asleep, but his breathing was noisy. He was young and strong, Faye impressed on herself. And there was a possibility that something less serious could be ailing him.

She rushed to the window and gazed out, seeking the doctor's pony and trap although she knew it was far too soon for a sighting of the vehicle. But somebody was coming and she recognised the horse and rider...

Quickly she bolted down the stairs.

'I'm sorry, Peter, but I think it best you don't come in.' Faye stood behind the half-closed door.

'What on earth's the matter?' Peter demanded, taking a stride forward as though he might force entry.

'Michael might have scarlatina. He's very unwell and has a rash on his chest...' Faye's voice tailed off.

Peter immediately stepped off the doorstep. 'I see; have you sent for the doctor?'

'Mr Gideon has gone to fetch him. He should be back soon.'

'I came over to apologise for being grumpy last night.' Peter raked a lock of brown hair back from his forehead.

'Well, if you were, it would be understandable,' Faye said with a strained smile. 'I hope I did not seem unwelcoming. I look forward so much to seeing you. It is just a shame circumstances are what they are.'

'I shall leave earlier than planned for London. I had hoped we might dine together again this evening, but it seems we won't.'

'I had written you a letter inviting you,' Faye said ruefully. 'When will you be home again?'

'In a few months, I hope. I'm off to Malta. But my application for an admiralty position is under review so nothing is certain.'

'That's wonderful!' Faye pulled the door open, but remembered at the last minute not to rush forward and congratulate her fiancé with a hug.

'I am only flesh and blood and I want a wife,' Peter said. 'You are not a children's nanny, my dear, but my fiancée.' He paced to and fro, fingers flexing at his sides. 'As soon as I have the time I am going to Ireland to find that confounded woman. I'll search everywhere for her and make her look after her children.'

'You cannot do that, Peter,' Faye said, stifling her annoyance. 'The children don't want to go to Ireland… and I won't make them—' Faye broke off at the sound of a vehicle rattling along. The hunched figure of Bertram Gideon, pipe clamped in his mouth, hove into view. And he was alone.

Faye immediately pushed open the door and sped to meet him. 'Is the doctor coming soon?' she gasped.

'He's been called out already this morning. Gone to the big house so his servant told me.' Bert climbed down from the cart and lifted up one of his horse's back legs, tenderly prodding it.

'Dr Reid is at Valeside Manor?'

Bert nodded. 'I've left a message with his housekeeper to send him right over when he do get back.'

'Perhaps they have scarlatina at the manor as well.' Faye paced to and fro in agitation. 'Oh, how long will he be, do you think?'

'I was on me way to Valeside to tell the doctor he be wanted here urgent, but Daisy threw a shoe so I turned around. Getting her and the cart down that hill and up again would have crippled her to bits, poor lassie.'

'You mustn't worry too much, my dear.' Peter clasped Faye's hands, giving them a comforting squeeze. 'Your brother was fit as a fiddle just yesterday and eating like a glutton.' He sighed. 'I can't be of much help to you so I'll leave you be.' He gave Faye a lingering look. 'Write to me and we'll speak more about a trip to Ireland when I return next time.'

'I will write…and you must take care, Peter.' Faye smiled weakly. 'Good luck with your promotion.'

Mr Gideon also watched Peter mounting his stallion and waving farewell. He removed the clay pipe from his mouth. 'That horse ain't lame then,' he said sourly.

Faye knew what Mr Gideon was hinting at: Peter could have offered to go to Valeside Manor and give the doctor a message to save time. People were always wary of coming into contact with disease and would avoid it if possible. Nevertheless, Faye felt disappointed that her fiancé hadn't offered his assistance in that small way.

'I'll get the smithy to take a look at Daisy, then I'll set off over to the manor and catch the doctor there if there's still no sign of him.'

'No! You can't walk that distance, Mr Gideon.' Faye frowned at the elderly fellow's bowed legs. He had difficulty climbing up on to his cart at times due to his swollen joints; he'd never manage to walk over three miles. 'I'll go. I can run and perhaps the doctor might turn up in the meantime. I'll be back as soon as I can.'

Chapter Four

Valeside Manor was set at the end of a meandering avenue of lime trees that widened, after about half a mile, on to a circle of gravel with a central fountain and wide flagstone treads leading to the house.

It was an imposing crenelated edifice flanked on either side by heavily timbered wings, extending like arms to embrace manicured lawns and parterres.

Determined not to be spotted dashing up to the front steps like a hoyden, Faye had kept to the shelter of the ancient limes. When so close to the manor's huge oaken doors that she could feel a cool mist on her hot face she came to a standstill, catching her breath.

Leaning her back against the bole of the nearest tree, she watched the fountain droplets glistening with rainbow light as they sprayed high into the air. Her body was trembling with the exertion of running up hills and down dales, her chest rising and falling rapidly. She dried her perspiring hands on her skirts, then attempted smoothing her wild fair hair into the pins at her nape. Her bonnet had long ago loosened to drape down her back on its ribbons. She guessed she looked a fright, but something more important than that was bothering her. There was no sign of the doctor's pony and trap in front of the house; she prayed she'd not had a wasted journey and that he had parked in the stable courtyard at the back of the building. With a deep inhalation she set off to find out because she had no intention of banging on Mr Kavanagh's door for no reason.

'Is it me you're looking for, Miss Shawcross?'

Swinging about with a startled gasp, Faye stared up into a pair of the deepest blue eyes she had ever seen. For a moment she was tongue-tied, overwhelmed by the striking sight of him astride his magnificent horse. He was handsome…breathtakingly so…but it was the awful knowledge that he must have been watching her for some while that made colour flood her complexion. He had come up through the trees as she had and the blood pounding in her ears from running had deafened her to his approach. The idea that he'd seen her haring in and out of the woodland with her skirts lifted high about her knees was mortifying.

'Do you want me?'

His lilting Irish accent was making his rephrased question seem more intimate than it was, Faye imagined as she felt her blush deepen.

'I'm looking for the doctor, sir,' she managed to utter crisply. 'We were told he came here earlier. Is he inside?' She skittered backwards as Mr Kavanagh dismounted and started towards her. 'You should keep your distance, sir; I think my brother might have scarlatina. It spreads quickly, you know.' She glanced at his house, wondering if those inside were under quarantine. 'Has somebody here got scarlatina? Is that why you sent for Dr Reid?'

'The physician was called to treat a groom who'd

tumbled off a nag. There's no infection that I know of.'
He plunged his hands into the pockets of his long leather
coat, continuing to pace her way.

'I see; is Dr Reid still here? I must speak to him urgently.'

'He's gone. I've just passed him on the road to Wilverton.' He jerked his dark head towards the town.

Faye felt her heart sink. 'Thank you, sir, for telling
me.' She gave a farewell nod, but it seemed he had no
intention of letting her go yet and changed direction as
she did.

She avoided him, feeling overpowered by his thrilling
virility, but then swung about, angry at herself for allowing him to fluster her. She was a betrothed woman of
twenty-five years, guardian to two children, not a green
girl acting shy with a boy. 'You should stay back from
me, sir…scarlatina is a nasty illness,' she said firmly.

'I know it is. I had it when a lad and lived to tell the
tale. It holds no fears for me now.'

'You are indeed lucky, then. The idea of one of my
family having the disease terrifies me.' Faye sketched a
little bob. 'I'm sorry to have bothered you, sir.' She set
off again, walking, but intending to break into a run as
soon as she was out of sight.

'Are you going to Wilverton to find Reid?'

'I'm heading home, sir.' Faye sent that over a shoulder, then turned about, pacing backwards. 'The doctor
already has a message to come immediately to Mulberry
House.' Whichever way she stepped either his muscular
body or that of his stallion seemed to be blocking her
path, preventing her marching on.

'I'll give you a ride home on horseback. It'll be
quicker; you look too exhausted to run another step.'

'No! That is, I thank you kindly for the offer, sir, but there is no need.' Faye felt her face prickle in embarrassment; he *had* watched her haring about then.

'Surely there is a need; you must be gravely concerned about your brother to risk visiting this den of iniquity in search of the physician.'

So he was aware the neighbourhood was agog with talk about his domestic arrangement. From the arrogant slant to his mouth Faye gathered he was quite impenitent about it.

'My brother's health is all I care about, sir; nothing else is of any consequence.' Having piously implied uninterest in his affairs she felt a fraud; just a day or so ago she'd avidly listened to Holly describing Valeside Manor's roguish new owner.

'That's settled then; you've no time for gossip and I've the time to get you quickly back to your brother's side.'

His velvety Gaelic drawl made goosebumps prickle on Faye's nape; she couldn't deny that the prospect of the three-mile hike, when she was already weary, was a daunting one.

When he beckoned she hesitated only fractionally before going to him, barely flinching as he touched her forearm and drew her closer. Now she couldn't avoid looking at the expanse of tanned skin exposed by his loose shirt collar, or becoming aware of a pleasing male scent of leather and tobacco. Fleetingly she raised her eyes to the thin white line that crossed his cheek, marvelling that it was less of a disfigurement than an enhancement to his raffish character.

Two large hands abruptly girdled her waist, lifting her atop the stallion with such ease and speed that she gasped. Seconds later he'd swung up behind her and turned the mount's head in the direction of her home.

Had she wanted to speak to him on the cross-country gallop that took them flying over streams and hillocks it would have been difficult with the breeze whipping the breath from her mouth. Her stiffly held torso gradually relaxed and she allowed herself to nestle against his chest with her bonnet brim protecting her face from the elements. She had never ridden on a horse capable of such acceleration and she felt in equal part terrified and exhilarated by the thrill of it. As though guessing her mixed emotions, he put a knuckle beneath her chin and tilted up her face, displaying a flash of white teeth in a smile as he read her expression. One strong arm came in front of her and encircled her shoulders in a way that was oddly possessive as well as protective.

Reining in the horse to a slower pace, he pointed to the east. The doctor's pony and trap was on the skyline, heading in the direction of her home.

'Take me to him, if you will, sir. Dr Reid will let me ride with him and save you the remainder of the journey,' Faye said while constantly pulling strands of fair hair away from her face, whipped there by the wind.

'You're not a bother to me… I'll gladly take you all the way…if you want…' His lips were close to her ear, his breath warm against her skin.

Her hesitation was enough to make him spur the stallion to a trot. A short while later Mulberry House was visible and Faye felt a peculiar pang of sadness to be almost home.

'Thank you for your assistance, sir.'

'My pleasure…'

He reined in the coal-black stallion at the top of the

garden and dismounted. Without warning he lifted her down, keeping his hands fastened on the tops of her arms.

Feeling awkward beneath his brooding stare, Faye managed a little bob, then wriggled free. His long fingers encircled her wrist, stopping her turning away.

'Don't believe all you hear about me, will you now, Miss Shawcross?'

'How do you know my name, sir?'

'I made it my business to find out.'

Faye moistened her lips with a tongue flick. He'd owned up to being inquisitive about her with a boldness born of arrogance, she imagined. It had been good of him to bring her home, saving her legs, but she knew nothing about him other than what two people she trusted had told her. According to Anne Holly and Mrs Gideon, Ryan Kavanagh was rumoured to be a shameless reprobate. And she would do well to remember it, Faye impressed upon herself. Handsome and charming he might be…but she should heed her housekeeper's words and keep a safe distance from him. She certainly couldn't trust Kavanagh. And neither should his young mistress. Fleetingly Faye met his dark blue gaze; the hint of sultriness that she'd heard in his voice was reflected at the backs of his eyes. He didn't know her, yet he desired her, despite having his concubine waiting for him at the manor.

'Thank you for bringing me home, sir,' Faye said huskily then turned and walked quickly towards the house.

'Miss Shawcross…'

Faye pivoted about.

'Is your brother sporting a rash that he scratches?'

'He is, sir…the rash on his chest drives him mad.'

'There was ragwort growing around the fairground by the river.'

'Ragwort?' Faye echoed in confusion.

'It irritates some people.'

Faye frowned and took a few paces towards him. 'You think my brother's ailment might be from a plant rather than from an infection? Why didn't you tell me that earlier?'

He mounted the stallion, a private smile twisting his mouth. 'You know now. If that's what ails your brother, the Romanies will have a cure for it if your doctor doesn't.' He dipped his head and a moment later was galloping away.

Faye hurried into the house to find Mrs Gideon and Claire rushing to meet her.

'Was that who I think it was?' Mrs Gideon hissed in alarm, her hand pressed to her heaving bosom.

Claire's eyes were dancing in merriment. 'Bad Mr Kavanagh gave you a ride home. Why didn't you ask him in? I'd adore meeting him. How wicked is he?' she demanded to know.

'Is Michael any better?' Faye asked, trying to still her racing heart following the excitement of her encounter with Kavanagh. She had vainly hoped that if he let her down at the top of the garden her return might go unnoticed. 'The doctor will be here shortly, we spotted him on his way.'

'Michael isn't as feverish, but the rash still troubles him,' Mrs Gideon informed her before resuming her interrogation. 'Did that brute force you up on to that beast with him?'

'Of course not! I was tired and Mr Kavanagh kindly offered to save me the walk home. By the time I arrived at the manor, Dr Reid had gone from there so it was a fool's errand.'

Faye started quickly up the stairs.

'You'd best hope your fiancé never gets wind of you being so close to that wretch. He'll jilt you for sure.' Mrs Gideon followed her mistress up the treads, shaking her head.

'Mr Kavanagh was simply making sure I didn't fall off during the ride. He was a perfect gentleman and very obliging.'

'I'll bet he was…' Mrs Gideon muttered.

'He's devilishly handsome,' Claire chortled, skipping to keep up with them as they dashed along the landing.

'Handsome is as handsome does,' Nelly interjected with a finger wag.

With a sigh Faye entered Michael's chamber. Her brother indeed appeared brighter. She sat down on his bed, taking his hands in hers and giving them a squeeze. 'You look a bit better now. Did you and your chums go down by the water at the fairground yesterday?'

Michael nodded. 'We were feeling hot so stripped off and went for a swim in the river.'

'Did you lay on the grass afterwards?'

'I had a fight with Edward.' Michael cautiously mentioned Mrs Gideon's nephew, known to be a bully.

'What was the scallywag up to, then? I'll have my brother speak to him. And Peggy's no better. I've a mind to snub the lot of them, kin or no.' Nelly looked grim.

'If you did have a fight, it seems no harm's done,' Faye quickly interjected. Nelly's comment about her niece had brought to mind the moment she'd seen Claire and Peggy creeping out of the copse at the fairground.

'Doctor's here,' Mr Gideon called up the stairs, alerting them to the fellow's arrival.

'What's this about, then?' The physician put down his bag and approached the invalid to examine him.

Dr Reid was a nice gentleman who had taken great care of Faye's father in his final weeks. He'd also done his best, years ago, to save her mother's life, so her papa and Mrs Gideon had told her. Faye couldn't remember that sad time as she'd only been five years old when her mother had died of a winter chill.

'I doubt your brother has got scarlatina; I'd expect to see his tongue looking strawberry red and his cheeks flushed, too.' Dr Reid tapped a finger thoughtfully against his mouth. 'His fever's faded.' He held a hand against Michael's forehead.

'He's been scrumping lately,' Mrs Gideon announced helpfully. 'And fighting.'

'I believe he might have rolled on ragwort after swimming in the river,' Faye added.

'Scrumpy belly and irritation from the ragwort together with a summer chill from going swimming is what I reckon has laid you low, young man.' Dr Reid started packing away his things, turning to Faye. 'If he's not properly back on his feet in a day or two, send for me again.'

Faye and Mrs Gideon exchanged a beam of relief.

'I expect a day of rest and fasting will put your belly right. The apothecary might have something to soothe those spots,' he told Michael, pulling the covers up over him.

'Or the Romanies have a cure, I believe,' Faye said.

Mrs Gideon turned a shocked look on her mistress.

'Mr Kavanagh told me they do,' Faye explained. 'It seems he was right about the rash.'

'Was he now!' Mrs Gideon breathed. 'I'll send Bertram to the apothecary 'cos we don't want anything off the likes of them.'

'It is true that itinerants treat their own ills quite successfully.' The doctor sounded quite unperturbed at the idea of using a gypsy remedy.

'Please come into the parlour before leaving, Dr Reid. Have you time for tea?'

'I must get off straight away and there's no need for me to come into the parlour, Miss Shawcross. I was barely here a few minutes and nothing much wrong, so there'll be no charge.'

The doctor knew about her financial mishap and was offering to waive his payment, Faye realised. 'That's kind of you, sir, but I insist if you've no time to take tea that you do stop long enough to collect your fee.'

Once the doctor had gone with the money she'd pressed on him, Faye opened the parlour window to let in a rose-scented breeze. It was another glorious midsummer day, Faye thought, gazing towards the spot at the bottom of the garden where just a short while ago Ryan Kavanagh had taken her from his horse. The memory of that ride home seemed dream-like now and it was only Mrs Gideon's censorious expression that told Faye she had indeed flown over meadows on a black stallion with the new master of Valeside.

'I promised your father always to do my best by you, miss, so there is something I feel duty bound to say...' Nelly put down the tea tray she'd just brought into the parlour.

'You want to scold me for accepting a lift from Mr

Kavanagh,' Faye pre-empted. 'But he was helpful and I'm grateful. In fact, I should write and thank him, especially for hinting at what ailed Michael.'

'Isn't him you need to thank for that!' Mrs Gideon huffed. 'That hussy of his will be the one knows gypsy lore.'

'What do you mean?' Faye frowned. 'They're gentry from London, aren't they?'

'Maybe they are…but folk are saying she's a Romany and from the look of her I'd say that's true.'

The beautiful young woman certainly looked exotic enough to have foreign blood. It was a depressing thought that the master of Valeside would take a young gypsy girl as a paramour when he was attractive and wealthy enough to choose a woman closer to his own age and station in life. 'Wherever the knowledge about ragwort came from I'm grateful to have it if it helps Michael.' Faye changed the subject. 'Where is Claire?' She looked out of the window to see if her sister had gone into the garden.

'Miss Claire went with Bertram to Wilverton. She said she was bored so she's gone for a ride to the apothecary with him to fetch Michael some lotion.'

Chapter Five

'Tell Miss Claire to hurry inside or her tea will be stewed in the pot.'

Bertram had been pulling off his boots by the kitchen door when his wife called out to him.

'The young miss is stopping in town with Peggy,' he replied, padding to settle wearily on a kitchen stool. Unaware of his wife glowering at him he flexed his toes in his woollen socks and sipped his tea.

'Stopping in town with Peggy?' Nelly barked. 'Who gave her leave to do such a thing? Did you?'

Bertram frowned at her from beneath his bushy brows. ''Course it weren't me, woman. Miss Claire said her sister knew she was to meet up with Peggy this afternoon.'

Bertram pulled from a pocket the bottle of lotion he'd got from the apothecary shop, placing it on the table and trying to ignore his wife's muttering.

'Oh, I was just bringing the tea to the parlour, Miss Shawcross.' Nelly had noticed her mistress on the kitchen threshold.

'Did you say my sister has remained in town with Peggy?' Faye asked, frowning.

'Miss Claire said she had your permission,' Bertram began defensively.

'Well, she did not, but no harm done,' Faye said, with more insouciance than she felt. She didn't want to increase the friction between Mr and Mrs Gideon who, though devoted, she was sure, constantly bickered about their respective families.

Although it was wrong of her sister to tell fibs, Faye understood Claire's restlessness. Sometimes she, too, craved to roam the outdoors in fine weather, or to have a relaxing time with friends free of constraints of family duty. Claire was now sixteen years old and if they were contemplating her come out then she was more adult than child. She deserved a degree of independence and to be allowed to choose her friends. Faye was not a snob, but she realised that some people—Mrs Gideon in particular—might think her sister was becoming too friendly with a girl who might be a similar age but was beneath her class.

'Bertram will go and get her as soon as he gets those boots back on.' Mrs Gideon sent her husband a thunderous look.

'I expect she'll be back home under her own steam for supper,' Faye said lightly. 'She's made the trek before. No need to rush back to Wilverton for her just yet.'

Bertram gulped down his tea, then clattered his empty cup down on its saucer, hoisting himself to his feet with the aid of the table edge. 'No rest for the wicked,' he mumbled, keen to escape his wife's company. 'I'll get that vegetable patch turned over ready for sowing,' he added. 'Rain's on the way and ground could do with a good soaking.'

Faye picked up the lotion and went upstairs to see her brother.

'Yesterday you sounded cross when Claire let on that you'd been scrumping. But by telling us about it she assisted you in quickly getting the powder you needed to soothe your gripes.' Faye began dabbing Michael's rash with a piece of lint soaked with lotion. 'If I asked you to tell me about something important that might help Claire, though she might not want me to know it, you would do so, wouldn't you?' She noticed that her brother avoided her eyes as she tended to him.

'Michael?' Faye grasped her brother's chin, turning him to look at her. 'What is it you know, but don't want to say?'

'Peggy put her up to it,' Michael blurted out. 'Edward told me that it wasn't Claire's fault.'

'What wasn't Claire's fault?' Faye felt a jolt of uneasiness. So something *had* gone on; she hadn't imagined the guilty looks the two girls had been sporting at the fairground.

'Peggy had been making eyes at one of the gypsy boys and Edward said he'd punch him.' Michael chewed his lower lip. 'I said I wasn't getting into a scrap and went off swimming with Samuel Wright. Edward called us cowards, that's why I had a fight with him on the grass and fell on the ragwort.' He fingered the red bumps on his chest.

'How has your sister got involved in any of this?' Faye removed Michael's hand from the rash he was scratching.

'Peggy's scared of Edward so she sent Claire to tell the boy to stay away or else he'd get thumped.'

'I see…' Faye said, standing up. And she did see. Peggy might try to enlist Claire's help again this afternoon, as a go-between. Faye realised that Mrs Gideon would be horrified to know her niece was encouraging a gypsy swain. The lad would soon be gone though, travelling on with his kin in their colourful caravans.

Unwilling to let her brother see her agitation, Faye laced his nightshirt, tucked him up, and went out of the room.

Pacing on the landing, she wondered if the best thing would be to send Mr Gideon to Wilverton to fetch Claire back. Or to keep fuss and questions to a minimum, she could go herself. She knew where Mrs Gideon's brother lived, but didn't want to create a mountain out of a mole-hill. It was likely she might turn up and find the girls doing nothing more exciting than sitting on the grass, making daisy chains for their hair. And then she'd feel a fool for spoiling their innocent fun.

It was at times like this that she wished she had someone to turn to for advice. But, even were her fiancé still in the vicinity, she would try to sort out the matter herself, she realised. Peter would be sure to be critical and intolerant of Claire's behaviour. Peter's parents, impoverished or not, were sticklers for keeping up appearances. They wouldn't like their son's future sister-in-law consorting with riff-raff.

Peering out of the landing window, Faye could just glimpse Mr Gideon, shirtsleeves rolled back, digging over the vegetable patch. It would be an inconvenience for him to have to pack up his tools and harness the pony and trap. But Faye knew that if she didn't seek out her sister and satisfy herself Claire wasn't in trouble, she'd not have a minute's peace.

She pounced on a valid excuse to make the trip to town herself: Anne Holly had sent a note, informing

her that her husband's relations were returning to town
in a day or two. She'd suggested that Claire might like
to get to know Sarah before her niece returned home.
Faye had been on the point of declining because Michael
had suspected scarlatina, but now the doctor had called
and given his verdict, there was no longer a need to shut
themselves away. Faye decided she could pay Anne a
visit to thank her for the invitation and set a date to take
tea at the vicarage. It would be nice for Claire to make
a new friend, especially as they were due to make their
debuts together. More at ease, Faye went downstairs to
tell Mrs Gideon she was going out.

'I'll fetch Bertram to drive you.'

'There's no need, Mrs Gideon. I'm quite capable of
taking the pony and trap out; I've done so on many occasions.'

'But he's only digging over and won't mind.'

Faye pulled on her cotton gloves, giving the woman
a smile. 'I'll not stop long with Anne Holly. Please don't
wait for my return. You and Mr Gideon must get off
home at the usual time. If you'd just leave the stew pot
simmering on the hob, that will do fine. No need to fret
about Michael; he is feeling much better and itching to
be back on his feet.

'If you say so, miss,' Nelly Gideon grumbled. 'Will
you bring your sister back with you?'

'Yes…of course…unless she is already on her way
home and we miss one another.'

Faye hurried out of the kitchen door before her housekeeper could find a reason to stop her. Luckily Bertram
had left Daisy in harness, probably in readiness to collect Claire later that afternoon.

Bertram eased his weary spine by bowing backwards,

hands on hips, as Faye passed him with a wave. Mrs Gideon had come to the kitchen door to watch her leave and Faye noticed that the couple wore matching frowns as she slowly drove herself away from Mulberry House.

They were fine people, loyal and caring, but sometimes their protectiveness seemed stifling. Faye had felt freer when her papa was alive and relying on her assistance. She knew that the Gideons took seriously their vow to Cecil Shawcross to keep a watchful eye on her and her siblings. But she was quite capable of coping on her own and, as kindly as she could, she must make the Gideons see it, too. From a young age she'd had no doting mama to fetch and carry for her, and much as her father loved her, he had allowed her her independence in order to get on with his own business. She had roamed far and wide when not under her governess's care. Edwina Sharp hadn't lived with them, but had driven her little gig from Moreton village every day to tutor her, then returned to care for her elderly parents. They were all gone now. Mr and Mrs Sharp had died within weeks of one another, and as though unsure if her duty were done, their daughter had followed them to the family tomb at Michaelmas the same year.

Once on the rutted road with the balmy breeze at her back Faye felt her tension ease. The pony settled into a trot and she loosened the reins. As she passed the brow of a hill she had a clear view of Valeside Manor nestling in all its glory in the valley below. She turned her gaze from it, concentrating on the road ahead; it seemed the more she learned of the new master of Valeside the less she ought to like him. A gentleman with a young Romany concubine and a careless attitude to what people thought of his morals was surely not somebody she should find charming and attractive. And yet…she did.

Faye urged Daisy to a faster pace, annoyed with herself for allowing such a fellow into her head when her fiancé should have first claim on her thoughts. She pondered on the lack of an opportunity to discuss her financial losses with Peter. He had left unnecessarily early for London; had he known that Michael didn't have scarlatina they would have spent a few more precious hours together.

Approaching Wilverton Faye turned the trap at the turnpike, heading along the dusty main road towards the row of thatched cottages at the far end where Mr Miller lived with his children. Slowing down in front of the last cottage in the row, Faye caught sight of Edward Miller scything the grass and whistling as he worked. Of Claire or Peggy there was no sign. Edward stopped what he was doing to tug at his forelock.

'Miss Shawcross,' he mumbled in greeting, coming to the gate. 'The doctor called on you, didn't he? Is Michael ailing?'

'He is getting better now, thank you, Edward.'

'We heard he'd got spots on him.' Edward took a cautious step back. 'Is it something catching?'

'Luckily it is not. The ragwort he rolled on after swimming gave him a rash.' Faye gave him a stern look. 'You had a fight with him yesterday at the fairground. You should know better. You're a good few years older than my brother.'

'Weren't all my fault,' Edward blustered, glancing about. 'Have you come to speak to my pa about it?'

'Not this time…but if it happens again, I will,' Faye said flatly. She felt sorry for Mr Miller, widowed many years ago and coping alone with his four children. Peggy was the eldest at fifteen and Edward a year younger. 'I've come to take my sister home. Is she inside with Peggy?'

'Ain't seen Peggy or Miss Claire this afternoon.'

Faye gave him an old-fashioned look. 'If you know where my sister is, please tell me.'

Edward shook his head sending his sandy fringe flopping into his eyes. 'Honest…ain't seen 'em, Miss Shawcross. Peggy went out this morning to do chores for Mrs Bullman like she always do every day. Ain't seen her since. And ain't clapped eyes on Miss Claire since the fair. I've been helping Pa indoors 'cos his knees are bad.' He jerked his head towards the wonky open doorway that led into the cottage. A girl of about seven was stationed there, sucking a thumb.

Faye knew that the butcher's wife paid Peggy to help out in the shop in the mornings. But it was possible Peggy had met Claire later on.

'I know about the gypsy boy you were going to punch because he was making eyes at Peggy,' Faye said quietly. She didn't want members of Edward's family overhearing her, but Edward had to tell her more about what had been going on between the Miller children and the gypsies. Since her sister had got embroiled in it, it affected her, too.

Edward blushed and fidgeted. 'His pal was after Miss Claire,' he rattled off. 'I reckon you should thank me for scaring 'em off, Miss Shawcross.'

Faye believed he was telling the truth and in an instant she felt her niggling anxiety over her sister's whereabouts explode. Claire might have a more personal involvement with the gypsy boys than she'd imagined. Quickly Faye banished that awful thought from her head. Claire could be silly, but she'd never play such a dangerous game.

'Do you want me to go and find them?' Edward meekly offered.

'I expect my sister has already gone home. It's supper time soon.' The tone of the youth's voice indicated that he, too, suspected an upset might be brewing. Faye climbed aboard the trap, her heart feeling leaden. From a corner of her eye she saw Edward resume scything. She hoped he had not put too much store on her questions. If a rumour spread about Claire Shawcross and a gypsy boy, her sister's reputation would suffer. With Claire's come out in the offing they couldn't risk a breath of scandal spoiling their plans.

Faye forgot about visiting Anne Holly and turned the trap to head home. She slowed down by the butcher's shop, but the shutters were already closed for the day. It was midsummer and still sunny, but she guessed the time to be gone six o'clock. At the back of her mind whirred a fervent prayer that her worry was unfounded and her sister was already at Mulberry House. Yet…she feared Claire was not.

With a gasp of relief Faye glimpsed the unmistakable sight of Peggy's bushy auburn tresses bobbing along further along the street. Faye pulled Daisy to a halt, then jumped down and hurried towards her.

'Is Claire in the shop?' Faye tilted her head to see past a few customers congregated in the doorway of the confectionery shop. The merchant kept his premises open quite late in the summer months to sell to those playing games on the village green.

'Haven't seen your sister, Miss Shawcross,' Peggy said, edging away.

'Are you sure about that?' Faye lowered her voice to demand, 'Have you and Claire been meeting some gypsy lads on the sly?'

'Don't tell me pa, will you, Miss Shawcross?' Peggy whimpered. 'He'll take the stick to me back.' She dodged past, running towards her home.

Faye was no mean sprinter and quickly caught up with her; grasping her elbow, she whipped the girl around. 'You had better tell me where Claire is, or I'll come home with you now and you can tell your father and me everything that has gone on.'

'We went to the fairground earlier. I came back, but Claire stayed with Donagh because they're packing up to travel on and she wanted to say goodbye.'

'Donagh?' Faye echoed with subdued alarm.

'Donagh Lee is the chief's son. He's keen on Claire…'

'Is she keen on him?' Faye whispered, her mind jumbling with all sorts of imagined disasters.

Peggy nodded. 'I told her to come back with me or she'd get in to trouble. But she said she'd stay just a few more minutes, then head home. They were by the copse where the ponies are tied up.'

'Thank you, Peggy.' Faye could feel the prickle of shocked, angry tears as she hurried back to the trap and climbed on board. At the back of her mind whirred a constant mantra. *How could you be so stupid and selfish, Claire? How could you?*

As she set the trap to a fast trot out of Wilverton her heart was thudding crazily beneath her bodice. She clung to the hope that her sister had gone home and was impatiently waiting for her to return so they could eat supper.

Home or not, Faye knew that she would tear a strip off her sister. She prayed that Peggy and Edward would keep what they knew to themselves in case their father found out they'd also risked trouble with the gypsies.

As the trap bumped and rattled over dry ruts Faye saw that her fiancé and Anne Holly had a point when warning her that the burden of her siblings might prove to be too much for her to cope with. She put up her chin, instilling fresh courage. She must not let this calamity intimidate her, but draw strength from it. Then in the spring when her sister went to London Claire would surely find a husband.

Faye blinked anxious tears from her lashes and flicked the reins, urging the pony on. Too late, her vision cleared and she tried to avoid a pothole just a yard or two from Daisy's front hooves. The animal veered left to avoid it and the trap tilted precariously, then bounced up and down. It landed with a crunch as a wheel buckled and Faye was flung from her seat. She landed on the parched ground on her back with enough force to knock the breath from her body. For a second or two she was lucid enough to be furious at her own carelessness and then the sky above spun and turned black.

Chapter Six

'Miss Shawcross? Can you hear me? What in the name of God's happened here?'

The urgent questions filtered into Faye's mind through the drumming in her forehead. She tried to rise, but every limb seemed under attack from fiery pain and she sank back to the earth with a groan.

'Stay still now…let's see if you've broken anything.'

Faye felt the pressure of long firm fingers investigating her limbs in a swift scientific manner. Her collarbone and shoulders were also subjected to a smoothing massage, then two strong hands slipped beneath her shoulders, easing her upwards.

'Look at me…do you recognise me?'

A strong hand grasped her chin as it started to sway towards her chest.

'Open your eyes and look at me.'

The rough command penetrated her daze and Faye obeyed, blinking until a dark visage ceased shimmering like a mirage and she was staring into a pair of piercing blue eyes. 'Mr Kavanagh…' she murmured, then gasped as a pain shot through her from attempting to get up.

'Be still…let me help you…' He'd been squatting by her side, but now rose, drawing her gently to her feet with him.

'I don't think you've broken anything. But you'll ache like the devil for days.' He touched a finger to a bloody scratch on her ashen cheek. 'I take it you hit that pothole. Your animal is injured. Your rig's in a bad way, too.'

Faye stumbled around to see the trap listing dangerously to one side. But it was the sight of Daisy favouring a front leg that made a sob burst from Faye. The little pony had served them well over many years and she had hurt Daisy. The reason for her reckless speed burst into her mind like a thunderbolt and all else was forgotten.

'I must get home, sir,' Faye implored. 'There is an emergency. She attempted to throw off his restraining hands to stumble on in the direction of Mulberry House. She'd managed only a few steps when her knees buckled.

Ryan caught her sinking form, swinging her up into his arms. 'You little fool. Are you after killing yourself? You've suffered a bad accident and should thank your lucky stars you're not in a worse state. A doctor should take a look at you.'

'I have no time for that. Put me down, I beg of you, sir.' Faye squirmed in his unrelenting hold. 'It is critical that I reach home. It will be the worse for us if I do not.'

Ryan had been carrying her towards his horse, but he came to an abrupt halt, gazing down into her tortured expression.

'What's put you in such a panic that you'd risk your life flying along in that little contraption?'

Faye pushed tangled blonde locks from her brow and squeezed shut her eyes. 'I can't tell you, sir. It is a private matter concerning my family.' Faye felt tears prickle behind her lids. 'Would you take me home, please, so that I may deal with it without delay?'

'If you don't take care of yourself, my dear,' he replied in measured tones, 'you won't be able do anything at all to help your family.' Ryan put her carefully atop his horse, holding her trembling form in position while swinging up behind and anchoring her spine to his chest.

Faye knew he was right; her unwise race to find Claire before she caused an outrage had resulted in a fresh problem. As Kavanagh turned the stallion towards the meadow she was aware that he wasn't allowing the horse its head as he had on their last ride together; a jolting gallop would be agony for her bruised bones.

Mulberry House hove into view and never had Faye felt more relieved to see that Mr and Mrs Gideon had not obeyed her and gone to their own home situated along the lane. The couple were stationed in the kitchen doorway.

The sight of her mistress being returned home on horseback by Kavanagh for the second time caused Nelly to rush forward to confront him over it. The scolding died on her lips as she noticed her mistress's pallor and the smear of blood on her cut cheek.

'What in heaven's name have you done to her?' she whispered, aghast. 'Bertram! Come here this instant,' she yelled for her husband's protection.

Mr Gideon shuffled up on his arthritic legs, shovel in hand.

'Your mistress has had an accident on the road,' Ryan explained, dismounting and helping Faye down. Undaunted by Bertram shaking the shovel at him, Ryan strengthened his grip on Faye as a wave of giddiness made her totter.

Nelly crossed herself, elbowing Ryan aside to embrace her mistress. 'Oh, what next! Is Miss Claire hurt, too? Where is she?'

'Is my sister not home?' Faye gasped in dismay, disentangling herself from her housekeeper's hug.

'Why…no…we thought you were bringing her back with you.' Nelly turned to her husband. 'Peggy's to blame. It's not like Miss Claire to stop out so long. Fetch the dog cart; I'm going to speak to my brother.'

Faye turned her head aside so her servants wouldn't see how upset she was. If the Gideons stormed off to Wilverton to have it out with the Millers, then there was scant hope of keeping secret her sister's infatuation with a gypsy boy. She needed some time to order her thoughts and decide how to contain the matter.

'Is your sister's whereabouts the problem you spoke of?' Ryan asked quietly while Mr and Mrs Gideon bickered.

Faye barely hesitated before giving a single nod. 'Please don't ask more,' she whispered. 'Should the details get out…' She gestured in a way that was more eloquent than any words might have been.

'Your sister was with you at the fairground the other day,' Ryan stated.

'Yes…'

'I saw her there…with her friend…'

There was a significance in his tone that made Faye raise her head and her soulful green gaze was captured by a pair of steady blue eyes.

'I know where your sister might be.'

Faye moistened her lips, remembering what Mrs Gideon had told her: Ryan Kavanagh was acquainted with the Romanies from his mistress's association with them. 'Would you take me to her immediately, please, sir?' Faye caught the edges of his sleeves, unconsciously giving them an urgent shake to make him agree.

'You must go inside and rest.' Ryan tipped his head at her house. 'You're in no fit state to go anywhere. I'll bring your sister home.'

'I must come with you. Claire will be wary of going anywhere alone with you, sir.'

'As were you,' he returned mordantly. 'But you've conquered your fear and let me bring you home on two occasions.'

'I'm not afraid of you, Mr Kavanagh.' Faye put up her chin. 'I'm able to take care of myself. But Claire is only sixteen; I am considerably older.'

'Considerably?' he echoed. 'You look no more than twenty.'

Faye wasn't sure whether he was flattering her or being serious. Either way she wasn't about to disclose her age to him. She was thankful for the distraction when Mrs Gideon hurried up, pointing at the dog cart creaking closer.

'I'll go into town with Bertram and fetch her back.' Nelly untied her apron, about to remove it.

'Claire's not in Wilverton with Peggy,' Faye admitted. 'I've already looked for her there.' She inwardly winced as Nelly staggered back a pace on hearing that.

'Where is she then?' Mr Gideon growled. He'd alighted from the cart and was limping closer.

'Take your mistress inside,' Ryan addressed the couple. 'Miss Shawcross has taken a nasty tumble and needs to rest.'

'I knew Bertram should have driven you,' Mrs Gideon quavered, wringing her hands. She caught hold of Faye's elbow, tugging her towards the garden gate.

'I am feeling better now and don't need to recuperate. I must help put things right. The trap is still blocking the road and poor Daisy is lame.' Faye bit her lip, gazing earnestly at her rescuer.

'I'll have the trap removed and as for the pony…' He hesitated, knowing that the animal's injury might be too bad to cure.

'Daisy will be fine, won't she?' Faye asked tremulously.

'I know a fellow who will take a look at her,' Ryan said kindly. 'And I'll investigate the other business for you.'

Before she could again protest that she must accompany him, Ryan started striding towards his stallion.

'Thank you, sir,' Faye called out, her heartfelt gratitude causing her voice to wobble. 'Whatever the outcome, might I trouble you to come back later and put our minds at ease over it?'

'It's no trouble.' Ryan swiftly swung into the saddle and, with a final polite nod, spurred the stallion into action.

'What in the Lord's name has gone on this afternoon?' Nelly cried as she helped her mistress be seated at the kitchen table.

Bertram helpfully fetched Faye a glass of reviving lemonade from the jug, but his wife snapped, 'She needs something stronger than that. The port's in the parlour.'

'Did Kavanagh cause your accident?' Nelly demanded when Bertram had left the kitchen. 'Did he come up on you unawares and try to force his company on you, startling Daisy?'

'He's done nothing but good and, if he had not made me accept a ride on his horse, I'd probably have stumbled about in a daze until I landed in a ditch.'

Mrs Gideon crossed her arms over her middle. 'You indeed are suffering from a bang on the head! You're defending that rogue *and* you've asked him to come back later.'

'If he is a rogue, then he is the most mannerly and obliging one of my acquaintance. I do not know what I would have done without his help.'

Mrs Gideon pursed her lips. 'Let me see if you've broken a bone.' She made to pull back Faye's sleeve.

'Mr Kavanagh has checked me over and says I have not,' Faye blurted with a lack of due consideration.

'Has he now?' Nelly trumpeted. 'You'd best hope nobody saw him doing it. Especially that spitfire he keeps at the manor. Jealous minx she is, by the looks of her.'

Faye could believe that to be true; she recalled the way the young woman had possessively clutched at Kavanagh's arm the first time she'd observed them by the drapery shop.

Upending the kettle, Nelly filled a basin with warm water, then tore a strip of clean rag off a towel. She began dabbing at Faye's complexion to clean away the grime. 'Best tell me about it; you'll need help to sort it out,' she coaxed. Bertram returned with the decanter and Nelly put down the cloth to pour Faye a tot.

Uncomplainingly, Faye did as she was bade, taking a fortifying sip even though she didn't like the taste of strong wine. After a short silence during which she weighed up whether or not to disclose her sister's shameful behaviour, she eventually concluded that her housekeeper was right; she couldn't sort this out herself. Whether or not Mr Kavanagh was successful in finding her sister, Faye couldn't lie to her loyal servants and destroy their trust in her.

Following another sip of port, she gave the bare bones of Peggy's confession about the meetings she and Claire had had with the gypsy boys.

Having listened, mouth agape, Mrs Gideon sank into a chair, her eyes popping in disbelief. Her husband muttered a curse beneath his breath and started shaking his head.

'This is Peggy's fault!' Nelly warbled. 'She's led Miss Claire astray…my brother shall hear of it…'

'No!' Faye pushed unsteadily to her feet. 'You mustn't say anything, however angry you feel. Rumours will spread and damage Claire's future.'

'I don't suppose Mr Collins would be happy to know what's gone on today either.' Mrs Gideon's warning was accompanied by a significant nod at the small sapphire adorning her mistress's finger.

Faye frowned. She had completely overlooked the fact that her fiancé was bound to be angered by the incident, should he ever find out about it. Neither would Peter like the idea of a disreputable stranger manhandling his betrothed even if it were simply to check her for broken bones.

'Mr Kavanagh is going to try to find her.'

'You've told such delicate business to *him*?' Nelly squeaked in disbelief.

Who else had she to turn to, Faye thought, now she felt weak as a kitten in body and mind following the carriage accident? 'I had no choice but to accept his aid.' She sighed. 'It has been a very bad day for us…'

'Why is it a bad day?' Michael had appeared in the kitchen doorway in his nightshirt. 'What's happened? Have we lost more money and become even poorer?'

'Not at all,' Faye quickly reassured him. 'I just had

an accident on the road, but I'm feeling better now. And so are you feeling better by the look of you.'

'I'm in fine fettle.' Michael pulled his nightshirt open to expose his clear pale skin. 'The rash has gone.' He grinned. 'I saw Mr Kavanagh outside helping you off his horse. Is he not a rogue after all? Did he fetch you home after the accident?'

'Never you mind about him,' Nelly rumbled. 'I expect you're hungry, Master Michael.'

'I'm ravenous, but I'm going to the fair to see my friends now I'm well again. I'll buy a pie there…'

'The fair has finished, Michael. The camp has packed up to leave,' Faye interjected quickly.

Michael grimaced disappointment. 'I'll walk to Wilverton and see Edward instead.'

'You can go tomorrow,' Faye said. 'The sun will be going down soon.'

Michael was ready to fire more questions, but Mrs Gideon interrupted him. 'Go and sit yourself down in the parlour and I'll bring you in some tea and ginger cake.'

When Michael was safely out of the way, Faye closed the kitchen door, closeting herself with Mr and Mrs Gideon. She could tell that her housekeeper had more she wished to say on the subject of Claire's disappearance.

'What if your sister's been kidnapped and ravished?' Mrs Gideon dabbed her eyes. 'Your father will be spinning in his grave.'

Faye felt bile rise in her throat. She'd not allowed herself to ponder on the possibility that her sister was being held against her will…perhaps having been assaulted by a boy she thought she could trust as a friend. But now her housekeeper had forced her to confront her worst fears.

'I can't just sit and wait. I must go and search for her,

too.' She surged to her feet. She made it outside as far as the gate before a wave of dizziness forced her to a halt.

Faye turned about, leaning her spine against the timber rails as her servants hurried towards her. She sighed in defeat. 'We have to put our trust in Mr Kavanagh this evening for I shall only hinder rather than help if I collapse again.'

'A bad day indeed it is when the Shawcrosses need rely on a reprobate to safeguard their family and their reputations.' Nelly shook her head.

Wearily, Faye walked back to the house, thinking that there could be some unpalatable truth in her housekeeper's grumble.

Chapter Seven

The scent of wood smoke drew Ryan deeper into the cool dark forest, but even without that lure natural instinct would have led him to the campsite. He heard a clatter of cooking pots and a rich savoury aroma of game stew seasoned with herbs and wild garlic wafted on the air.

He dismounted, leading the stallion closer and calling a greeting. A tall man with black hair winged with silver rose from squatting by the fire. He held himself regally as he approached Ryan, holding out his hand.

'You're travelling alone then, Bill.' Ryan glanced at the single caravan and the brace of ponies close by.

'Maybe we'll catch the others up tomorrow. Maybe we won't. Maybe we'll go our own way. I've hung back on purpose because I had a feeling you'd come.'

A pause ensued in which the two men locked stares.

'And why did *you* come?' Ryan asked quietly. 'I thought I'd seen the last of you for a while when we parted company in Dublin. Why have you followed me here to Wilverton?'

'There's rich pickings from the gorjas at these country fairs and we're in business to make money.' Bill used a thumb and forefinger to stroke his bristly chin. 'But you're right—I headed this way knowing I'd bump into you now you've set yourself up as an English country squire in this neighbourhood. We've unfinished business, you and I, and I want it settled before heading back home when the nights draw in,' Bill said.

'I offered to settle with you in Dublin.' Ryan's voice was low and even, but his blue eyes had narrowed and with little cause from aromatic wood smoke drifting from the campfire.

'Ah…but then we couldn't agree terms, could we now?' Bill shrugged, looking foxy. 'Of course, those conditions that I wanted might not be so important now things have changed. It could be that I'll just take the payment you offered. Donagh's the fly in the ointment, isn't he now? At times I don't know myself what my son will do next, or where his eye will land.' He elevated his chin proudly. 'He's a lusty lad and I remember so were you and I at that age…getting ourselves into all sorts of trouble with willing colleens.' He grinned, then bawled out, 'Donagh! Come out here. You've a visitor.'

Ryan grunted a mirthless noise. 'You know why I'm here?'

'Of course. I told him somebody would come after her. I wasn't sure that it would be you. But now you're respectable I guessed it might be the lord of the manor hunting us down.'

'Respectable?' Ryan echoed drily. 'Not many think that of me.'

'Ruby does…she told me so. She's beguiled with her new life and doesn't talk much of Ireland, does she now.

Perhaps some of her ideas have rubbed off on my son. He's keen to put down roots hereabouts.'

'We'll see about that…' Ryan growled, hunkering down by the fire. He nodded at the quiet old woman sitting opposite, smoking a clay pipe. She gave him a brown-toothed grin and carried on stirring the pot of stew.

'Donagh!' Bill bellowed for his son a second time.

A handsome youth of about seventeen emerged from behind the canvas covering the caravan doorway. His head was tilted belligerently. 'She wants to stay with me. We'll be married.' He sounded confident, but his shifting dark eyes told another story.

'That's not possible,' Ryan said calmly. 'It's not how things are done with her people. You come from different worlds.'

'You're a fine one to talk,' Donagh scoffed. 'You know it's how things are done with *our* people,' he said. 'I've chosen her and she's given her consent.'

'Where is she?' Ryan asked. He drew a cheroot from a pocket and lit it with a glowing twig pulled from the fire. He offered Bill a cheroot and the man took it.

'You'll stay and eat with us?' Bill asked affably, lighting up.

'I can't… I have to get back. But thank you for the offer.'

'I want to stay here, Mr Kavanagh.' Claire had joined Donagh and put her hand trustingly on his arm. She looked warily at the man she had heard called a villain. 'Did my sister send you to get me?' Claire hadn't expected to be pursued by this fellow. He looked even taller and stronger than she remembered. And that mark on his face that had looked insignificant at a distance now made him seem the embodiment of the black-hearted rogue Nelly Gideon had named him.

'Your sister wanted to come herself.' Ryan smiled thinly. 'She would have done so, if well enough. She's had an accident and is recuperating at home.'

Claire flew down the few caravan steps to join Ryan at the fire. 'What sort of accident?' she gasped in consternation. 'Are you tricking me to make me go back?'

Ryan slowly stood up, directing smoke from the corner of his mouth. 'Indeed, I am not making up stories, Miss Shawcross,' he said with a stony inflection. 'Your sister turned over the trap she was driving too fast while out searching for you.'

Claire clapped a hand to her mouth. 'Oh, why did she do that? I wrote her a note saying I would be all right with Donagh and she needn't worry about me.'

'And even had she received such a message, do you think your sister would have allowed you to just go off with a stranger?' Ryan asked. Even now with the delicate negotiations to release the girl barely underway he couldn't put Faye Shawcross from his mind. She was spoken for, yet he couldn't stop her from burrowing into his mind and beneath his skin. And he didn't want that…he didn't need complications in his life. Ruby was all the trouble he could handle right now.

'In the spring when I go to town I'll be expected to go off with a stranger and get married,' Claire burst out sourly. 'I've met somebody sooner and can save my sister the cost of my come out. We can't afford the expense of it now anyway.'

'I'll not argue with you, Claire Shawcross…you'll do as you're told.' Ryan ground out the half-smoked cheroot beneath a boot. 'I'll not argue with you either.' His narrowed gaze swung between father and son. 'She comes with me.' He grasped Claire's elbow and though she fought with kicks and punches she couldn't loosen his grip.

Donagh leapt down the steps of the caravan and made to attack Ryan, but his father held him back with surprising ease.

'If you take his intended wife, then you steal my daughter-in-law, too,' Bill shouted over his son's shoulder. 'This is the second time you've taken his woman. You know we need one in the family since my Marie passed on.' Bill looked at his elderly mother as she continued stirring the pot. Gertie Lee was showing little more than mild interest in the prospect of a fight erupting.

Ryan pulled a roll of banknotes from his pocket. 'I'll compensate you for her loss.'

'And what about Ruby?'

'We'll speak about that matter another time,' Ryan growled angrily.

Bill gave a nod of acceptance.

The protocol of the exchange observed, he tossed the wad of cash and Bill Lee snatched it from the air, single-handed. Having given the notes a cursory examination, he pocketed them.

'What's going on? Who is *she?*'

A pony was approaching at a trot and the young woman seated astride urged the piebald to a faster pace. Before the animal was properly reined in she jumped down and ran to confront Donagh. She swung a dark, jealous glance between the chief's son and Claire.

'What in damnation do you think you're doing here, Ruby?' Ryan growled. Dragging Claire with him, he strode over to fasten a possessive hand on the newcomer's arm.

'My Donagh attracts them like bees to a honeypot,' Bill said proudly, then gave a guffaw. 'Did you not know now, my lord,' he mocked, 'that your little minx still likes my son almost as well as she likes you?'

'Like him or not, she's going home with me now.' Ryan drew his lips flat against his gritting teeth. 'And if you try and stop me on that, or ever lay one finger on her, you'll not get a settlement, but a bullet between the eyes.' His warning was directed at both Bill and his son.

'Take her then, but Claire stays here with me,' Donagh snarled, legs and arms flailing as he attempted to free himself from his father's bear hug. 'We'll be married; she'll be respectable.'

'The gorja's been released to her family with this.' Bill Lee calmly waved the banknotes. 'If it's a fair-skinned girl you fancy, you'll soon attract another; you'll make us rich, my boy, by selling the lasses back to their kin.' He chuckled, then his manner changed. 'Get back in the caravan; I'll deal with this now.'

His scowling son obeyed without so much as a backward glance at the young woman he'd said he hoped to marry.

Ryan plonked Claire atop his horse, giving her such a threatening stare that she froze into stillness on the stallion. She'd believed that Donagh would protect her, but could see that he was his father's puppet. And Bill Lee was only interested in Kavanagh's money.

Ryan gave Ruby a similarly icy look and the sulky young woman allowed herself to be deposited back on her mount.

Once in the saddle Ryan took the reins of Ruby's pony and the two horses set off at a walk towards the road.

'Luck go with you…' Bill called, pocketing the cash.

Ryan raised a hand in acknowledgement, but didn't turn around.

'Oh! At last!' Faye's voice held exasperation and thankfulness as her sister slunk in through the kitchen door. 'Why on earth did you go off like that?'

Claire squirmed from her sister's fierce embrace. 'You've spoiled it now, sending Kavanagh to get me. I would have been married tomorrow and you would have been saved the cost of my come out.'

That bombshell caused Faye's complexion to whiten in shock and she clutched the table edge with knuckles that showed bone. Then dizzying relief overtook her; it seemed that her sister had been apprehended in the very nick of time. Equally appalling to Faye was the knowledge that Claire was lacking in remorse for frightening them all half to death. Aware that she might get a fuller report of what had gone on from Mr Kavanagh, she sped to the door with the intention of quizzing him. Through the gathering dusk she glimpsed him on the lane. The stallion was stationary as though he'd waited to see her sister safely indoors. But he made no move to dismount and come to speak to her. All she received was a nod before he turned the animal towards Wilverton. Within seconds the horse and rider were fast moving shadows in the distance.

Faye wished she'd at least had a chance to thank him for the great service he'd done them. But it seemed that would have to wait till another day. Besides, there were more important matters to be addressed now Claire was home. Not least of those was making her sister admit to how many people were aware of what she'd been up to. And what exactly *had* she been up to? Faye closed the kitchen door and momentarily leant against it, bucking herself up.

Mr and Mrs Gideon were seated at the table, but neither had said a word to Claire. Their pinched expressions made it plain they were sorely disappointed with the younger Miss Shawcross for what she had put them all through.

'You must get home now to your beds,' Faye urged the couple. 'Thank you for being such a help.'

'Don't you want your suppers? Michael ate his meal hours ago and has retired for the night.' Nelly went to stir the pot of stew.

'It's rather late and I'm not hungry now, thank you, Mrs Gideon.' Faye looked at Claire for her answer.

'I was going to have supper with the Lees. They had game stew with venison and hare and…'

'This is prime beef,' Nelly barked in an affronted voice. 'And properly prepared and cooked by decent folk.'

'Donagh praises his gran's dinners…'

'A cup of tea will do,' Faye said quickly, defusing matters.

Mrs Gideon shook the kettle vigorously, mumbling beneath her breath.

'I can manage to make a pot of tea.' Faye removed the utensil from her housekeeper's quivering fingers. She realised then just how badly affected the servants were by Claire's misbehaviour. When they were alone she intended giving her sister a severe scolding.

'You'd best lock that one in her room,' Mr Gideon said

without rancour as he picked up the lantern to light their way home, then closed the kitchen door behind them.

'You've no need to lock me in,' Claire said bitterly, slumping down at the table. 'Donagh won't take me back now you've paid his father a ransom for me.'

Faye sat down, too, opposite her sister. 'What payment are you talking of?' she demanded, confused.

Instead of answering, Claire cried, 'Why did you not heed the note I wrote you telling you I'd be fine? I love Donagh and wanted to be his wife. I don't want a town fop who cares nothing for me.'

Faye gestured astonishment. 'How can you possibly have fallen in love with somebody you met just a few days ago?'

'I met him a week or more ago in Wilverton when I was with Peggy, if you must know. It was before the fair had set up. He was with his friend that Peggy likes, getting a sack of flour from the grocer. We got talking even though I knew that you'd get cross about me spending time with a gypsy boy.' Claire snorted. 'Oh, it is all right! Nobody saw us, I made sure of it. We were all hidden away behind the stables at the White Hart.' Claire flushed as she saw her sister's horrified expression on hearing that. 'Donagh said he'd come back with the fair and that he wanted to see me again because I was special,' Claire hastened on. 'He's the right one for me, Faye! He's handsome and strong and all the girls want him. Even Ruby.'

Faye had sensed the blood draining from her cheeks the moment Claire admitted to having acted so secretively. The reason for her sister's recent lack of interest in her debut, and her eagerness to visit the fair, made sense now. She blamed herself for not being vigilant enough;

she'd not had an inkling that Claire had been meeting any boys…let alone an itinerant youth, when she was meant to be in Wilverton having innocent fun with a friend. As her guardian and her sister she *should* have known that Claire was ripe for a clandestine love affair.

'I've not had your note.' Faye pounced on one of the facts dancing chaotically in her head. 'Did you leave it hidden in your room for me to find?'

'Of course not!' Claire scorned. 'That would have been daft!'

'Letting a stranger compromise you is even more stupid!' Faye retorted, done with patience. 'Don't you realise what you've done, you little fool! How could you be so selfish and risk our good name?'

'I gave the letter to Peggy; she promised to give it to you,' Claire explained meekly.

Faye sighed in frustration. 'I saw Peggy earlier, but she didn't hand anything over. It doesn't matter anyway. Whether I'd received it or not I'd have been frantic with worry.'

'I guessed Peggy might get me into trouble. She was jealous of me and Donagh.'

'Peggy might be a bad friend, but you've got yourself into trouble,' Faye said flatly. 'Heaven only knows how we're going to hush this up when already people know of it.'

'I expect you'll ask Mr Kavanagh to help, won't you?' Claire said sulkily. 'You seem very friendly with a man known as a rogue.'

'And I am thanking my lucky stars that he has been obliging!' Faye returned.

'He said you had an accident in the trap.' Claire frowned at her sister while looking her over. 'Were you badly hurt? You appear quite well apart from a mark on your face.'

'I'm sore, that's all. Mr Kavanagh was good enough to help me get back on my feet.' Faye touched the graze on her cheek.

'Well, I'm sorry that you went out looking for me and got into trouble, but there was no need. I was safe enough with the Lees—'

'You said you were allowed home after a payment was made,' Faye interrupted, pouncing on something else she recalled Claire had uttered.

'Mr Kavanagh gave Donagh's father some money. It was from you, I suppose,' Claire accused.

'It wouldn't have occurred to me to send a ransom for you.' Faye raked some tangled blonde locks off her forehead. 'And who is Ruby?'

'She's the young lady you called Mr Kavanagh's friend. Peggy said she's his harlot.' Claire's cheeks turned rosy. 'Kavanagh was furious when Ruby came looking for Donagh.'

'Did she stay at the camp with the Lees when Mr Kavanagh brought you back?' Faye asked, astonished.

'No! Donagh wanted me, not her,' Claire said proudly. 'Anyway, Mr Kavanagh wouldn't have allowed it. He threatened to shoot Donagh if he laid a finger on Ruby. He must be very jealous.' Claire paused. 'He took Ruby home first on her little pony and shouted for his servants to take her inside, then he galloped straight around the fountain and brought me back here on horseback.'

Suddenly it became clear to Faye why Kavanagh had not stopped long enough to speak to her about the evening's events: he'd been in a rush to get back to his fickle mistress at Valeside Manor.

'I'm going to bed.' Claire sounded quite timid.

'Not yet, you're not, miss!' Faye said sternly. 'You've another vital question to answer.'

Claire hesitated by the door she'd been about to open, a guilty flush on her cheeks as though she'd guessed what was coming next.

'Were you and Donagh ever completely alone together?' Faye unconsciously held her breath while waiting for her sister's answer.

'I suppose we were, but his father and granny were just outside the caravan and all Donagh did was kiss me a few times.' Claire chewed her lower lip. 'I swear that's all.'

'And if it gets out, it'll be more than enough…' Faye said in a resigned murmur.

'I'm not sorry… I love him,' Claire mumbled.

'I'll bring you up some tea.' Faye addressed her sister's back as Claire fled from the room to avoid further interrogation.

Having put the kettle on the hob, Faye sank down into the chair. Claire was safely back home, she impressed on herself. That was the most important thing. Mr Kavanagh's business with Ruby was his own. Yet it seemed strange to her that a woman—even one as young as Ruby appeared to be—would risk her relationship with a handsome, landed gentleman to favour an itinerant youth.

She massaged her aching temples, suddenly too exhausted to carry on any further inner debate.

The kettle whistled and Faye made a pot of tea, stirring the leaves and watching the whirling specks until she felt pleasantly entranced. Her lids fell over her eyes and she undulated her aching shoulders. Mr Kavanagh had warned her that she'd ache like the devil tomorrow and indeed it was so even though the clock on the wall had only just struck half an hour after midnight. She poured two cups of tea, then put the crockery on a tray and carried it upstairs.

The wavering light from a single candle and her sister's muted snuffles gave Claire's bedchamber an eerie air. For a moment Faye was tempted to carry on to her own room without giving Claire her tea. Her sister needed to reflect on what she'd done, but Faye guessed those tears were prompted by feelings of self-pity rather than shame. She placed the cup and saucer on the dressing table, then went out again without saying a word.

It wouldn't hurt Claire to dwell, uninterrupted, on the consequences of her behaviour, Faye thought as she quietly closed her sister's bedroom door.

Chapter Eight

A few settled days passed by during which a strained calm returned to Mulberry House and the Shawcross family. Michael had received a sketchy explanation for his sister's disappearance a few nights' ago and seemed uninterested in hearing more. Now properly recovered, he was getting itchy feet and was keen to lark about with his friends. Faye thought it best to keep him apart from Edward until recent dramas had faded in everybody's minds.

As for Claire, the more she dwelled on the way Donagh had bowed down to his father, the clearer it became that she would have been as firmly under Bill Lee's thumb as was his son, had she stayed with them. She felt despondent about her lost love and about the damage she'd done to the people she cared about. Peter Collins was the sort of character who'd avoid having a wife with a sullied sister and Claire knew she'd never forgive herself if Faye was jilted.

Now a semblance of normality had returned, Faye had decided that making contact with Mr Kavanagh was long overdue. He would be entitled to believe her the veriest ingrate if she didn't soon thank him. She didn't want him to think ill of her because she thought well of him. Whatever others said about his character she would judge as she found and she found him to be a very generous and helpful neighbour.

Committing to paper the details of her sister's mischief wasn't an option and an equivocal note of thanks would serve no purpose. She needed to talk to him privately to discover more about the Lees and what money he'd paid them on her behalf. Claire might deem a few kisses bestowed by her gypsy lover as nothing much, but just that news circulating would be enough to ruin her. Nevertheless, Faye hoped it was the truth. Her sister had seemed besotted by Donagh Lee and heaven only knew what liberties she might have allowed him had Mr Kavanagh not dragged her home when he did. The caravans had moved on, yet Faye fretted that the youth might sneak back to try to persuade Claire to elope with him again.

Pulling paper and pen from the drawer in the bureau, Faye sat down at the table, mulling over how to phrase a request for Mr Kavanagh to call. Or she could pluck up the courage to go and see him. Faye knew she harboured a vulgar wish to meet Ruby. Of course, they couldn't be introduced, but she might bump into Kavanagh's fascinating young mistress by accident if she visited Valeside Manor.

Barely had she written his name in elegant script when the rattle of an approaching vehicle could be heard through the open window. She put down her pen and hurried to peer along the lane.

Faye recognised her small trap and at the reins was

the tiger who had attended Mr Kavanagh's curricle in Wilverton. Quickly she went outside.

Her slender fingers were shielding her eyes from bright sunlight as she gave the lad a smile. 'Thank you for bringing my vehicle back.' Faye noticed straight away that the damage had been repaired and a new wheel fitted to replace that splintered by the pothole. She glanced at the sturdy pony in harness.

'The master says you can keep this one till your own pony's healed. I'll ride back on Star.' He indicated the larger animal tethered to the back of the trap.

Faye gazed earnestly at the lad as he climbed down. 'I feared the worst for poor Daisy. Is she recovering, then?'

'She was in a bad state, but Old Willie's worked his magic on her. She'll need a good resting, but will be fully back on her feet in time.' He grinned. 'That's if she's not too fat to move. That little mare loves her nosebag.'

Faye gave a relieved laugh on hearing that Daisy was fit enough to enjoy her hay. 'Oh, yes, she does tuck in and she likes carrots and an apple, too.'

'I'll spoil her with a carrot when I get back.'

'Thank you,' Faye said huskily, blinking back tears. She realised that with all the commotion she had forgotten about little Daisy's plight. But it seemed Mr Kavanagh had not. He'd got his man to tend her pony and nurse her back to health. Not only that, he'd loaned her one of his own animals so she had transport.

'I'll see to that,' Mr Gideon growled, indicating to the lad that he'd uncouple the placid pony and lead it away to Mulberry House's stable. He'd hurried from the kitchen with his wife on hearing voices; they were both regarding with suspicion the master of Valeside's gift.

The boy took no offence, preparing to mount his ride

home, then he hesitated. 'Oh...I forgot...the Viscount asked me to give you this.' He pulled a letter from his pocket.

'The Viscount?' Faye queried in surprise.

'Mr Kavanagh—he goes by different names depending where he is and who he's with. Some folk know him as Major Kavanagh.' The boy seemed proud of his master's many guises.

'I see,' Faye said faintly, taking the parchment; she regretted that she'd not sent her letter first. It was bad manners on her part that she'd delayed for too long and he'd had to write to her, possibly with a note of what she owed him.

'Well...too good to be true is *the Viscount*, if you ask me,' Mrs Gideon opined sourly, watching the tiger riding away. 'Good turn after good turn *Major Kavanagh* does you.' She jerked a nod at the parchment in Faye's hand. 'Now, I wonder what *that* says?'

'I expect he enquires after my health after that tumble I took. Or quite rightly he might expect to be reimbursed for what it cost him to liberate my sister.'

'That's more like it,' Nelly said flatly. 'And I reckon he might have a proposition for you about paying the debt off,' she added drily. 'Especially if he's heard about your business with that charlatan Westwood. And who hasn't round here?'

Faye darted her housekeeper a sharp glance. She knew Nelly wasn't criticising her, but issuing a blunt warning. Mrs Gideon cared about her and didn't want to see her at the mercy of a lecherous rogue. But Faye didn't think Ryan Kavanagh was a rogue...

'I've seen the way he looks at you. Hungry eyes.' Nelly nodded portentously. 'A man like that does a pretty

woman favours because he wants favours in return.' She
stood, hands on hips, staring at the note in Faye's hand
as though expecting her mistress to open it and read it
to her. 'It's a crying shame that Mr Collins went back to
his ship and isn't here to protect you.'

'Mr Collins will always have his ship to return to,
Mrs Gideon. But it doesn't matter; I am used to his absences and can look after myself,' Faye said stoutly. 'I'll
have a pot of tea in the front parlour, please.' She had
noticed her housekeeper's eyes were still on the letter
so slipped it out of sight into her pocket. 'I've the house-
hold accounts to go through; please let me know what
we are short of and I'll put in an order for it.' She started
walking back towards the house, aware of the couple's
mumbles as they followed her.

Once the tea tray had been put down and the door
had closed on her housekeeper's stiff back, Faye let fall
to the blotter the pen with which she'd been writing in
the ledger. Slowly she drew forth Kavanagh's note from
her skirt, but momentarily was too timid to open it. Exasperated with herself, she broke the seal with a quick
snap of her fingers.

Unfolding it, her emerald gaze flew over the few lines
of bold black script. She read it once more, slowly. As
she'd anticipated the note expressed his hope that she
was recovering from her accident and confirmed what
the tiger had told her: her pony wasn't yet well enough
to be returned, but she was welcome to borrow his animal until Daisy was able to walk home. Of the drama
with the gypsies, or the debt she owed him, there was
no mention.

Faye felt strangely disappointed, without knowing

why. She felt restless, too, without knowing why. She needed to speak to him, she decided, and stood up and paced to and fro. She was sure that Mrs Gideon was wrong about Kavanagh wanting to coerce her into bed. He had looked at her with desire in his eyes, but he wasn't the first stranger to do that. She'd been told by her father at her debut that she was fortunate to have such lovely looks and that her fair hair and green eyes would snare her any husband she wanted. She'd already set her heart on her childhood sweetheart, but she was woman enough to secretly appreciate a gentleman's smouldering glance confirming her allure.

The master of Valeside had a beautiful young mistress to satisfy his needs and he had seen Peter accompanying her home from the fair. Kavanagh had told her he'd made it his business to find out about her. It was no secret in Wilverton that she was betrothed to Peter Collins, just as it was no secret that she'd suffered a financial setback. He knew all of that.

None the less, she wished that her losses *had* escaped his notice. She didn't want him feeling sorry for her. If he had omitted a request for reimbursement because he felt that way…

Faye dropped his letter into a drawer and locked it. Turning for the door, she marched up the stairs and into her chamber to tidy her appearance. She perched on the stool in front of her dressing-table mirror and studied her reflection. Her clear ivory complexion had just a hint of indignant colour heightening her cheekbones. Yet she had no proof that Ryan Kavanagh thought pityingly of her…or that he ever thought about her much at all… whereas she found it hard to put him from her mind for any length of time. And she knew that was wrong. Peter should occupy her thoughts yet, lately, he rarely did.

Abruptly dropping the hairbrush with which she'd been teasing her fair curls into place, she found the cash she kept at home in a safety box in her wardrobe. If she owed more than the three sovereigns she had, then she'd have to visit the bank. Collecting her bonnet and light silk cape from her clothes press, she knocked on her sister's door. Claire was lying on her bed's coverlet, flicking over pages of a journal.

'I'm going out, but you must stay in. Don't go calling on Peggy.'

'I don't want to see her!' Claire glanced up sheepishly. 'Will we still be able to go to town in the spring and stay with Auntie Aggie?'

'I don't know… I expect so…' Faye forced a smile for her sister; she'd no idea what the future held any more. But hiding away hoping for the best wouldn't help; she had to do something to limit any scandal brewing. Tackling Kavanagh over what had gone on seemed as good a way as any to start.

Mr Kavanagh's pony was a biddable creature, but a gelding and more sprightly than Daisy. Faye kept him to a slow trot even when she felt the little animal straining to increase the pace. It was an intelligent beast, too, turning homewards at the bend in the road before she'd needed to steer the trap towards Valeside Manor.

This time when travelling up the long drive beneath a canopy of whispering lime leaves, Faye made no attempt to conceal her arrival and, heart in mouth, went boldly right up to the front entrance.

The house remained quiet even after she'd clattered

the bell for the second time. Faye strained to listen, wondering if she could hear a servant approaching within or whether the beat of blood in her ears was mimicking the pad of feet.

Feeling deflated, she waited a few more seconds, then slowly descended the long flight of stone steps with her skirts in her fists. It seemed her intrepid mission to beard the lion in his den had been a squandered effort.

'How did you find him?'

'What?' Faye had spun about at the first syllable uttered by that velvety baritone voice, primed as she'd been to hear it.

'The pony...was he easy to handle?'

'Yes...thank you...' she gasped out automatically.

He had approached, unseen and unheard, along the terrace that led to the east wing and now stood high above her close to the oaken doors she'd moments ago rapped on. He was stripped to the waist and the skin of his slick, muscled torso resembled cloth-of-bronze satin. His long black hair was wind-whipped, giving him a youthful and wickedly mischievous air.

'I...I seem to have interrupted you in...something...' Faye stuttered in acute confusion. She was unsure what he had been doing that necessitated him being wet with sweat and half-naked. But in the ensuing silence she could hear a faint sound of male shouts issuing from the stable yard behind the house. 'I'm sorry... I should have sent word of my visit.'

Ryan raised the towel in his hand, drying his damp face and nape in a single cursory rub. 'Then you'd have sent another cancelling it.' He impaled her with a blue stare of subtle mockery. 'Too impulsive, aren't you now,

Miss Shawcross…like me.' He draped the towel about his strong brown neck and gave her a crooked smile.

Faye quickly descended the rest of the steps, her heart hammering crazily. If he was telling her she'd acted inappropriately, he had no need to. She knew it already. But when one's sister had already risked dragging the family name through the dirt, observing etiquette seemed *de trop*—containing the scandal was vital. 'I'll come back another time as you are busy. But I must speak to you urgently, sir,' she called breathlessly from the safety of the gravelled drive. She gathered the reins in her hands and held fast to them.

'Why run away, then, if it's urgent? You can speak to me now.'

His lazy challenge made Faye throw down the reins and pivot on a heel to gaze up at him with sparking green eyes. About to remind him that she'd told him before that she wasn't afraid of him, she swallowed the untruth. He might have been a boon to her and quite unlike the man he was painted to be…but something about him made her feel wary. And she knew what it was: the likelihood of Mrs Gideon's warning about him expecting payment in kind coming to pass.

He approached the balustrade that spanned the width of the mellow red-brick building, propping his sinewy forearms nonchalantly on mossy stonework, and watched her with quiet intensity, as a tomcat might assess its prey before leaping…devouring.

Hungry eyes… Mrs Gideon's rough description filled Faye's mind and she felt certain that he could pounce even from that height and catch her, if he wanted to. Like a creature that accepts it has been cornered she remained still and silent, her eyes locked with his.

He broke the spell. 'Go and wait inside…' He drew from his breeches' pocket a key and unlocked one of a pair of blackened oak doors, shoving it open. 'I'll join you in a few minutes.'

He walked back the way he'd come, not once looking around. Faye watched as his noiseless cat-like stride took him around the side of the building towards the stables. She realised she'd not heard him approach because he was barefoot. Either he didn't care now if she bolted or he was confident enough of his hold over her, and the choice she'd make, to leave her be.

Chapter Nine

The hallway of the house was blissfully cool and it took some moments for Faye's vision to adjust to the dim interior after the bright sunlight outside.

Blinking, she glanced to and fro, spying a pair of chunky high-backed chairs against a wall a few feet away. She approached one and sat down, concentrating on the list of things she must say to the master of Valeside. The jumble of words in her head resisted marshalling; her mind was filled with the image of Ryan Kavanagh's majestically brutal appearance while her eyes strayed to study her surroundings. The furniture wasn't opulent, rather it had a strong earthy grandeur. Heavy ebony trestles and carved chairs were set against the walls and the vast centre space was covered by a huge, many-hued Eastern rug. Then her roaming gaze settled on a portrait on the wall. As though in a trance Faye rose and walked to stand before it, gazing up into a face of exquisite beauty. Ruby's delicate features were framed by lustrous jet-black hair that draped in soft ringlets to her slender shoulders.

'Come into the library and sit down.'

'She's very beautiful,' Faye spontaneously blurted out the thought in her head, on whirling about. Quickly she stepped away from the picture, wishing she had returned to her chair just moments sooner rather than be caught gawping at it.

And now she was staring at him. The half-dressed savage of minutes ago had been replaced by a sophisticated gentleman, resplendent in buff breeches and a crisp linen shirt. He had a tailcoat pegged on a finger and as she watched he shrugged into the charcoal-grey garment, straightening his pristine cuffs.

Having opened the door to the library, he indicated that he was waiting for her to pass over the threshold. Faye bit her lip; so it seemed he was not going to acknowledge her comment about his mistress's loveliness. Perhaps he deemed Ruby too precious to be discussed. Either that or he saw her comment as another lack of manners; a young lady never acknowledged the existence of a gentleman's mistress. But then she didn't officially know the nature of their relationship.

'Here will do very well, sir, thank you,' Faye said stiffly. 'It seems private enough as your servants are absent. I cannot tarry, but there are things that I must say to you.' She perched again on the hallway chair and folded her hands neatly in her lap.

With a mutter that she couldn't decipher, but that she guessed was Irish blasphemy, he pulled the ornate chair by her side away from the wall and sat facing her. 'My apologies; I'd offer you tea but the servants have the afternoon off. The housekeeper and the maids are out shopping. The men are in the stable yard. We don't receive many visitors…' he added in a rueful tone.

Faye refrained from remarking that if his alleged debauchery didn't keep callers away a lack of a response to bangs on the door was sure to put people off returning. From the indolent way he lounged back in the chair she guessed that he was his own man and cared little about visitors or what anybody thought of him.

Faye took off her bonnet, but resisted waving the brim at her pink cheeks to cool them even though a burning blue gaze was increasing the warmth in her complexion.

'The mark on your cheek is almost gone; you look remarkably well after your accident.'

'I am well, sir, thank you, and you also look well now.' Faye wished that she'd considered her reply more carefully before uttering it and making that look appear in his eyes. She glanced away, blushing.

Ryan dipped his head in acceptance of her compliment, subduing his smile. She was aware of the nature of his interest in her. He'd hoped to see her, but now she was here he wasn't sure how to proceed and that in itself was unusual. Without conceit he knew that the women he desired were usually more than happy to know he wanted them and respond to his overtures. He was generous in bed and out of it. Apart from with his time and his affection. That he reserved for Ruby. But something about Miss Shawcross made him feel that could change…if she'd just give him a sign that her absent fiancé wasn't a stumbling block to them getting closer. He noticed she was fidgeting as though she might get up. He didn't want her leaving too soon.

'I was breaking in a stallion.' He broke the silence and settled a foot encased in highly polished leather on his knee, resting his fist upon the boot. 'Handsome creature, spirited as the devil, though, and strong as a lion. We had quite a tussle.'

'I see,' Faye said, pondering on his explanation for his dishevelment earlier. As a child of about eight she'd watched her father and a groom training a wild horse. It had been a fascinating battle between man and beast. She didn't recall either man having been shirtless and shoeless, but it had been a long time ago and it probably hadn't been in high summer. 'And who won the fight?'

'Neither of us yet…but I think he'll let me ride him tomorrow.'

So he was confident of victory. She wondered if he'd deliberately praised the stallion in terms easily applicable to himself. He didn't seem vain, but he obviously knew he was very good looking. Even Mrs Gideon had set aside her prejudice long enough to grudgingly admit he was a fine figure of a fellow.

'I'm sorry to call unannounced…thank you for helping us.' Having rattled that off, she took a deep breath, determined to express the rest of what she had to say more slowly and eloquently. 'I expect you can guess why I am here, Mr Kavanagh.'

The foot propped on his knee was returned to the floor. 'So, Miss Shawcross, if we are done with small talk, let's indeed get down to business. I take it your sister has told you that she put up a fight to stay with her gypsy.'

'I do know she was cross to be brought back,' Faye replied. 'Did she…hit you, sir?' She hoped that wasn't the case. Claire had enough black marks against her character as it was without adding to the list an assault on the master of Valeside.

'My shins took the worst of it,' he said with a glimmer of humour. 'What I meant by my remark was that you should know your sister went with him of her own free will. She wasn't forced.'

Faye nodded and a flush spread on her cheeks. Whatever the truth of what had gone on between her sister and Donagh Lee, she knew it had not been a callous seduction. 'Claire gave her friend a note to deliver, telling me not to worry about her going off with the Lees.' She gestured the futility of such reassurance being of benefit.

'I take it you didn't get the letter.'

'Claire believes Peggy kept it because she was jealous and wanted to get her into trouble. She said all the girls want Donagh.' Before she could stop herself her eyes flitted to the portrait on the wall.

'Are you wanting me to tell you who she is?'

The question was coolly blatant and Faye jerked her wide green eyes to his. She'd made her interest in his concubine far too evident. 'There's no need for you to do so, sir,' she managed to say levelly. 'Claire told me that you also brought a young woman called Ruby back from the gypsy camp.' Faye looked deliberately at the painting. 'Any more than that is none of my business.'

'Is it not?' he enquired drily. 'I thought as we are getting to know one another we might commiserate on relatives being a bother to us.'

'Relatives?' Faye murmured after a shocked silence in which she digested what he'd said.

'Who did you think she was?' The blue of his eyes was barely visible between close black lashes as he waited for her answer.

Faye blushed at the implication she'd too easily believed ill of him. 'If you wish me to confirm that I have heard the talk about you, sir, then I will do so. And if you know the rumours for slander, then I urge you to broadcast the truth or stop flaunting your relative.' Her eyes again returned to the portrait. 'If she is your sister, it is very bad of you to allow gossips to harm her by speculating otherwise.'

There was indeed a resemblance, Faye realised, gazing at the girl's raven's-wing hair, but her eyes were the colour of amber, not sapphires. If they *were* siblings, then she imagined Ruby to be a great deal younger than her brother. It seemed he wasn't about to confirm or deny her guess at their relationship. He stood up abruptly and strode away from her. Unsure whether he'd dismissed her, Faye stood up, too, and with rapid steps headed for the exit.

'I don't flaunt her; she nags to go out.' He swung about. 'You believed Ruby was my paramour, young as she is.' He gave a humourless grunt. 'You don't like me, do you, Miss Shawcross?'

'I don't know you, sir,' Faye objected, halting a few feet away from him. He stood between her and the door and she wished he did not. 'We've only met a few times. I've no true idea of your character or...habits.'

He smiled sardonically at the ceiling rather than at her. 'My habits run to women considerably older than Ruby or your sister.'

Faye knew they were both thinking of the time she'd told him she was considerably older than Claire.

'I'd say you're about twenty-five,' he said softly, a sideways glance leisurely travelling from the top of her glossy blonde head to her sturdily shod small feet.

'You said before you believed me twenty.' Faye was unable to stop that escaping, feeling as she did oddly irked that he'd discovered her true age.

'Looks can be deceiving. You're no green girl, that's

for sure.' His lips quirked cynically. 'Rest assured, Miss Shawcross, my wicked desire for diversion is well served elsewhere, far from Wilverton.'

'I'm sure the locals will be relieved to know it, sir… if they don't already,' Faye retorted, her cheeks scarlet. How dare he bring his paramours to her attention!

'Do you count yourself amongst them?'

'I was born and bred in the area,' she answered stilt-edly, noting his amusement at her evasiveness. She quickly changed the subject. 'And now I must return home.' She'd ceded the verbal duel, accepting Kavanagh was far more adept at the game. 'My sister seems to be coming to her senses now, but if Donagh came back the silly girl might be persuaded to go with him again,' she added solemnly. 'I need to keep a close eye on her.' She donned her bonnet, emphasising her intention to leave.

'The Lees won't bother you.'

'How can you be so sure? Claire told me that Donagh wanted to marry her.'

'He said that he did…'

'You believe him fickle?' Faye had picked up the hint of derision in his voice.

'I believe he is a young man of seventeen with a rov-ing eye…so he is probably no better or worse than any youth of that age.'

'Even a youth of that age should know not to lead on an impressionable girl,' Faye snapped.

'Indeed…but we're only human and sometimes we don't always act as we should.'

Was he talking about the male sex in general or was there something more personal in his comment? Faye wondered. If he was trying to excuse his own reputed rakish behaviour, carrying on with two paramours at the same time, it was a poor attempt to justify himself. But Faye dithered too long trying to think of a way of following up his comment.

'On the whole the Romanies are honourable people,' Ryan continued. 'Bill Lee has accepted the marriage won't be. If Donagh should ever turn up and make a nuisance of himself, you've only to mention my name.'

'Which name do they know you by?' Faye asked quite seriously, recalling the tiger telling her that Kavanagh used different titles depending on who he was with.

She saw that he hadn't expected her to know that about him. It was unclear from his abruptly shuttered expression whether the fact that she did annoyed him.

'I wasn't prying, it's just that your servant said…' Her voice tailed off; she hoped she'd not got the young tiger into trouble. 'I hope you are right and the episode is far behind us. It might be possible to hush such a thing up just the once, doing so again would be very doubtful. Thank you very much for bringing Claire back.'

Faye produced from her pocket her sovereigns, thrusting them his way. 'Claire told me about the ransom. I hope that will cover the cost of her release. I must pass on her apology and add it to mine; we deeply regret putting you to such trouble, Mr Kavanagh.'

'There's no need for that.' He barely glanced at her money. 'I would have paid them to go whether or not your sister had become involved.' He paused as though debating whether to continue. 'Claire might have regained her senses, but Ruby seems still infatuated with Donagh. I want him away from her until we return to Ireland.'

'You're going away so soon?' The idea that the wicked master of Valeside was off abroad might please Mr and

Mrs Gideon, but for Faye the news both surprised and saddened her.

'I have family to see and business to attend to.' He moved closer, angling his head to read her lowered expression. 'You sounded as though you might miss me, Miss Shawcross.'

Faye's small teeth sank into her bottom lip and she allowed the brim of her bonnet to shield her eyes from his astute gaze.

He tilted up her chin with a firm finger. 'You will miss me, I see...' A hint of satisfaction strengthened his mockery. So, fiancé or no, she was swayed to like him rather than just feel grateful.

Jerking her face free, Faye stepped back. 'I can't deny you have been a help to me, sir, in time of great need.'

'But you'd like to, is that what you mean? Honesty and manners are all that brought you here today?'

'I'd like to think I possess those traits, Mr Kavanagh,' Faye said, meeting his eyes squarely.

'I'd say there's more to it than that,' he drawled, his gaze caressing her face before leisurely travelling over her rigidly held petite figure.

Faye burned beneath those sultry blue eyes, as though she might have been naked instead of sensibly dressed in outdoor clothes. 'It is good of you to say you will bear the cost of sending the Lees on their way. Still, I should like to make a contribution as we have both benefited from what you did.' Quickly she again offered him her cash.

'Put your money away,' he said gently. 'I'm better positioned to bear the cost.'

So he did know of her losses! She gave the sovereigns in her hand a little shake to make him take them, tilting her head defiantly. But he'd started pacing to and fro, hands thrust into his pockets while frowning into middle distance.

'Are you not worried of being lonely at Mulberry House on your own?'

His query prompted Faye to whip around close to the front door. 'I'm not on my own, sir, far from it. I have my brother and sister and my servants with me.'

'Your brother will return to school, your servants will retire and your sister will find a husband.'

'And so will I marry,' Faye said sharply. 'As you have made it your business to find out so much about me, I'm sure you know I'm betrothed to Mr Collins.'

'And have been for many years,' Ryan said drily. 'Your Mr Collins is a foolish man…or perhaps it suits you to keep things the way they are.'

'What do you mean by that?' Faye demanded.

'Does he willingly tolerate the situation? If I were Mr Collins, I would have wanted my wife by now.'

'But you are not he, are you, Mr Kavanagh?' Faye retorted hoarsely. The tension in the atmosphere was unbearable. Faye wanted to burst outside to breathe. She had only to take a few more paces towards the half-open door and she would feel the soft summer air on her skin.

Yet the thrill fizzing in her veins had a strangely narcotic effect on her, keeping her subdued. She was betraying Peter staying a moment longer with the master of Valeside when what occupied her mind was whether Kavanagh's sarcastic mouth softened when he kissed a woman…

Ryan stalked her with predatory steps, leaning across her to shove the door shut with two flat palms, entrapping her between his arms.

The door reverberated into the frame and when the tremors had faded away he spoke.

'I lied to you earlier.'

'What?' Faye glanced over a shoulder at him before facing him very slowly. No more than a few inches separated their bodies.

'I fear my wicked desire may not be as well served elsewhere as I thought.'

Faye remained quite still, mesmerised, as she had been when outside and an Adonis-like ruffian had snared her with his deep blue stare. He raised a finger touching the graze on her face. 'It's healing well. It won't mar your beauty.'

'You have also had an accident, sir.' As though she was powerless to stop it, a trembling finger touched then quickly withdrew from the scar on his cheek.

'It's not a duelling injury,' he said abruptly. 'Whatever you've heard about a fight over a woman is false.'

'Whatever caused it…it must have been a nasty accident…'

'The Battle of Waterloo was a tragedy rather than an accident.'

'But we won…' Faye said.

'Five thousand English and allied corpses at Quatre Bras never knew that,' he returned with quiet bitterness before his mouth swooped. He kissed her with a savage passion that would have made her stumble had he not pinned her between his torso and the door. He raised his head.

'Do you want to slap me? Do it… I'll let you go.'

Faye's eyes were locked with his as she struggled to liberate herself. True to his word the pressure of his hard body eased away from hers, but she saw that some inner conflict and frustration were making him grit his teeth. Whatever he'd said, he hadn't wanted to release her and was tempted to kiss her again.

And she wanted it, too. A tiny guttural sob rasped in her throat as her need for him fought with her shame. Just moments ago she'd contemplated how hurt her fiancé would be should he discover she'd fantasised about the dangerous master of Valeside's cruel lips on hers... Indeed his mouth had been hard and bruising...the pulse in her lips still beat...but she yearned for him to do it again.

She was falling under Ryan Kavanagh's spell and were he to ask her to be his mistress because he lacked female company in Wilverton...she might succumb.

It was the sobering thought of his pampered women in London that drove the intoxicating sensuality from Faye's mind. He had a mistress either end of town, so Anne Holly had told her, and both had been treated to jewels and carriages.

Faye knew she never wanted to join their number. She put the back of a trembling hand against her scarlet mouth. 'If you please, I should like to leave now, sir.'

He shoved himself away from her so he no longer barred her escape.

'My apologies, Miss Shawcross, for behaving like an uncouth lout.' He jerked open the door and bowed low in a way that might have been mocking. But she guessed it was not. Not to her anyway. As she watched him stride away into the bowels of the house without once looking back she guessed that, of the two of them, he mocked himself.

Chapter Ten

Anne Holly and her husband had been admitted to Mulberry House by Mrs Gideon. Notwithstanding the housekeeper's gruff reassurances that her mistress was right as rain, Anne had rushed into the parlour and immediately grasped Faye's hands to her bosom.

'We heard that you had an accident in your trap, my dear, and have come to see how you do.' Having examined her friend from sleek blonde head to slippered toe, Anne added, 'Thank the lord you seem so well…but is that a bruise on your cheek?' She wiped a tear from the corner of her eye and hugged Faye. 'If it is all that you have suffered, you are lucky indeed.' Anne had lost her elderly parents in a winter coaching accident some years ago so her agitation was understandable.

'I wasn't going to tell you because I knew you'd be upset.' Gently Faye disentangled herself from her friend's clutch. She felt quite a fraud. It wasn't just that she wanted to save her friend's feelings; the fewer people who knew about it the better. Questions would surely be asked and one thing would lead to another. Before long it could be common knowledge that she'd turned over her trap, racing to find her errant sister.

'I ached dreadfully for a few days, but the bruises are fading already.' She indicated that her guests should sit down. 'It's so nice to see you. I'll ask Mrs Gideon to bring some tea.'

Anne settled comfortably into the sofa and removed her hat and gloves. 'You're very good at driving, too; far better than I. The idea of steering Derek's gig, all alone, terrifies me half to death.' She gave her husband a fond smile and he patted her hand solicitously.

'You'd be surprised at what one can do with little option but to do it,' Faye said wryly.

'Was Daisy spooked? How is your little pony?' The Reverend Holly joined the conversation as Faye was about to ring the bell to summon her housekeeper. 'Is your trap still in one piece, Miss Shawcross?' Derek was a mild-mannered fellow who took his calling seriously, but was never too uppish to get his hands dirty. 'I'll bring over some tools if bolts need tightening.'

'Mr Kavanagh has already had it mended for us and now it's good as new. He's given us a pony, too,' Michael piped up from his seat at the table by the window. Having dropped that into the conversation, he continued building a tower from dominoes.

Anne's pop-eyed stare swerved to her friend. 'Mr Kavanagh?' she snorted, sounding scandalised.

'What good fortune, for you,' Derek Holly remarked. 'That gentleman might be a bit of a puzzle, but I'm sure he's not the rogue he's painted.'

'Indeed, it was lucky that he was riding in the vicinity when the trap hit a pothole. He kindly helped me home and has said we can have his pony while Daisy's leg mends.' Faye kept her explanation succinct, then put a question of her own. 'How did you find out about my accident?'

'I overheard Peggy Miller speaking to Mr Bullman about it in the butcher's shop.' Anne frowned. 'Once I knew of the calamity I wanted to come immediately to find out for myself how you were.'

'I expect you discovered that Michael didn't have scarlatina and it was a false alarm.'

'Indeed, everybody knows he is quite well. We had no fears on that score.'

Faye slanted a suspicious glance at her brother. He avoided meeting her eyes and slipped from his seat.

'Shall I ask Mrs Gideon to bring you some tea?'

'Yes…thank you, Michael.' Faye hadn't banned her brother from going out; she guessed that he had used her absence earlier to slip away to town to see Edward. But she would have hoped he'd be sensible enough not to discuss their family crises.

In a backwater like Wilverton where little of note happened often, a woman overturning her vehicle would keep people speculating for days. One poor soul who had landed in a ditch had been branded a drunk simply for losing her footing while carrying ginger beer.

Faye knew she had no right to carp at Michael about sensible behaviour after the way she'd acted! She had convinced herself she'd gone to see Kavanagh from rectitude, but she'd not persuaded him that was the case. He'd suspected there had been more to it. And so did she…now. Duty, once served, should have put the master of Valeside from her mind. But she couldn't forget him, even for a minute. Even now she wasn't fully concentrating on her friends' visit though usually she'd be delighted to have their company.

A seductive Irish voice whispered constantly in her mind and the words wouldn't be blotted out... *'I fear my wicked desire may not be as well served elsewhere as I thought.'*

Faye was tempted to go back and tell him she was glad he wanted a local woman, such was her yearning to again have his kiss burn her mouth. She abruptly stood up, exasperated with herself for allowing such daft thoughts to drive her mad when she was betrothed.

'Are you all right, Faye?' Anne asked in concern.

'A slight twinge of pain...the bruises remind me of their presence.'

Anne smiled sympathetically. 'Your fiancé will be relieved to know you've suffered no broken bones.'

Immediately Faye sensed Kavanagh's firm dark fingers smoothing the length of her limbs, checking for injuries. 'There is no need for Peter to be informed.' She pushed up the sash to allow in a breath of air to cool her complexion. 'He has a lot on his mind with his promotion in the offing.'

'We know he left Wilverton earlier than expected. A promotion, you say?' Anne nudged her husband's arm. 'Isn't that excellent news for a man soon to be married?'

Mrs Gideon appeared with the tea tray, relieving Faye of the need to find an answer.

'Where is your sister?' Anne asked, selecting a treacle oatcake from the plate of biscuits.

'Oh, Claire's probably browsing a fashion journal in her room.'

'Preparing for her debut is an exciting time for a girl. It's a shame my niece didn't get to know Claire. Sarah has returned to town with her mama, but I have her address. I scribbled it down to give to you.'

Faye took the piece of paper that her friend proffered and pocketed it.

'Sarah said she'd love to have a letter from Claire before they meet up in the spring. Lady Jersey has promised to get Almack's vouchers for Sarah. It might be possible to get some for Claire as well.'

Faye was sure that her friend's tone wasn't patronising. She was the one at fault, becoming too prickly and defensive due to recent trying events.

After the Hollys had left Faye went in search of Michael. She was determined not to be cross with him because she felt optimistic that fate would be kind to them in future. It was clear that Anne hadn't heard about Donagh Lee which meant that the story hadn't leaked out in Wilverton. Peggy might have gossiped about the carriage accident, but thankfully it seemed she'd kept quiet on the other business.

Her brother was gazing morosely out of the window when Faye entered his chamber. 'You'll be glad to get back to school, won't you?'

Michael grimaced an affirmative.

'Would you like to take up Mr and Mrs Scott's offer to stay with them?'

Michael nodded. 'I know I can't because of the cost of it.'

'Oh…I think we might manage to scrape up the funds for your holiday.' Faye had made a snap decision. Her brother had been denied his chance to enjoy the summer with his friend because of her financial losses. But it would have been better if Michael *had* been out of the way during the recent turmoil.

'Shall I write and see if I can arrange it for you after all?'

'Yes please.' Michael gave his big sister a spontaneous hug.

Faye left her brother with a grin on his face and trod lightly to Claire's door. As she'd suspected Claire was lying on her stomach on her bed coverlet, reading.

'Sorry...did I make you jump? I should have knocked.'

'What do you want?' Claire demanded over a shoulder, snapping shut the journal. She abruptly sat up, a startled look on her face.

'Well, nothing really. I just came to tell you that Michael is going to spend the rest of the summer with his friend's family.'

Claire felt with her toes for her slippers and jumped to her feet, brushing down her dress. 'Lucky him. I'd like to get away from here, too.'

'Don't be like that, Claire,' Faye said softly. 'I know you are growing up and are impatient for more excitement than is to be found in Wilverton. It will come soon enough, I promise, when we go to town next year.'

'I doubt that we'll go after all the trouble,' Claire mumbled grumpily. 'What did the Hollys say?' She glanced at the window. 'I saw them leave. I didn't come down in case I got questions thrown at me.'

'They only visited because they'd heard I'd had an accident. It seems things in town are as they should be.'

'You mean nobody's yet found out about me falling in love.'

Faye's gesture hinted at impatience. 'You are very young to be talking of love and marriage, Claire.'

'You won't say that in six months' time,' Claire riposted.

'*Touché...*' Faye gave a faint smile. 'Very well... I admit that I think you are almost ready for a husband, but if you'd married your gypsy I think you would have regretted it,' she gently explained. She thought of what Ryan Kavanagh had said about the youth's inconstancy, but kept it to herself. She didn't want Claire any more upset than she already was. Besides, there were other reasons why the match was unsuitable. 'I imagine a Romany's wife has a spartan life...no feather beds or fireside chairs in winter, you know. You would be cold and miserable—'

'I could have come home if I found life was unbearable,' Claire interrupted.

'No...you could not,' Faye quietly yet firmly differed. 'Marriage is a serious business, not something to turn one's back on. Besides, I will be a wife myself soon and have my husband to think of. Things are changing for us all. When Peter comes back next time we will set a date for the wedding in the spring. It is long overdue.' Faye had again made a quick decision about the future, but she knew she must stick to it. She was engaged to a decent man and she should have listened to him. He'd told her time and again that the children would be a responsibility she'd be unequal to handling. And so it had proved. Things now seemed under control, but she'd not want to cope with another such drama. Besides, she was no different to any woman in that she'd like to have a wonderful wedding day and, God willing, children of her own before she got too much older.

The master of Valeside perhaps understood her better than he should. '*Are you not worried of being lonely...?*'

His words filtered back into her mind. At the time she'd been indignant that he should think she lacked company. But now, she could see that on a certain level she *was* bereft.

'If you're setting the day, I shall *have* to go and find Donagh. Lieutenant Collins won't want me under his roof; neither do *I* like the idea of it,' Claire said flatly. 'We shall do well enough with a horse and caravan of our own… I couldn't abide living with his bossy father.'

'You know I wouldn't see you homeless, Claire. Before I marry you'll find your perfect match.'

'Perhaps I have already done so,' Claire returned petulantly.

Faye rolled her eyes in exasperation. 'I'm not a snob, so don't think that. I know it seems romantic having a handsome gypsy husband and the open roads in front of you.' Picking up the journal, she added wryly, 'But there would be no fashion plates to pore over for a start…' Her voice tailed off as a paper fluttered out from between the pages.

Quickly her sister pounced on it and thrust it into her pocket, but not before Faye had a glimpse of some pencilled scrawl.

'Is that a letter from Donagh?' Faye felt a coldness wash over her.

'No, it isn't.' Claire clammed up, but then relented on seeing her sister's fierce frown. 'If you must know, it's from Peggy. She gave it to Michael to give to me.'

'Let me see it, please.' Faye held out a hand.

'It's nothing.' Claire pulled the note from her pocket and crumpled it up, but her guilty expression wasn't so easily concealed. 'Peggy won't do anything, she's bluffing because she is still jealous of me.'

Faye felt the knot of anxiety tighten in her stomach. If she'd not been certain before she now definitely knew that the intention behind Peggy's note was to cause trouble. Prising the paper from her sister's fingers, she smoothed it out and read the ill-spelt message in which Peggy warned she'd tell about Donagh Lee unless Claire gave her the new bonnet with blue ribbon.

Faye momentarily closed her eyes in consternation as her mind was bombarded with awful consequences should that childishly written threat become reality.

Of the two pieces of paper she now had in her pocket Faye knew the greatest danger came from that written in elegant script, given to her by Anne Holly and bearing the address of Lady Jersey's friend.

Peggy might break the scandal in Wilverton, but eventually it would leak through to London's *beau monde*. Once the tabbies got their claws out Claire's chances of attracting an eligible man would lie in ruins.

Faye knew Anne wouldn't deliberately pass on gossip, but she'd tell her husband and an overheard word in the wrong ear was like a pebble hitting a pond, ripples would spread far and wide. Besides, Faye didn't want to discuss an intensely private matter even with her best friend.

'Shall I give her the bonnet?' Claire offered in a small voice, having watched her sister's pale brow gathering furrows.

'There's no point; Peggy might still tell tales or want more from you.' Faye bit her lip.

'What will we do, then?' Claire sank to the edge of the bed with her face cupped in her palms, the enormity of the problem she'd created having finally sunk in.

'I'm not sure I know at the moment,' Faye said. 'But what I must do is write that letter to Mr and Mrs Scott before supper time. I want to post it tomorrow. I won't let Michael down.'

Chapter Eleven

Her letter to Scotland posted, Faye set off along Wilverton's High Street, to the butcher's shop. She was tempted to go in and confront her sister's tormentor. But giving in to her anger would only inflame matters. She stood slightly to one side of the entrance, out of sight; by leaning a little to the left and peering from beneath her bonnet's straw brim, she could see Peggy's frizz of auburn hair. Faye walked on aimlessly, frustrated by her inability to decide what to do.

To allow a brainwave time to happen she entered the drapery to browse the wares. It was quite a wide, deep shop and the proprietor had a good stock of silks and satins to choose from as well as cheaper calicos. The finest rolls of cloth crammed the space close to the door, doubtless positioned to catch the eye and draw customers in. They were piled up thick and high like a jewel-hued shimmering forest. Faye took off her linen gloves and smoothed her fingers over emerald velvet. She'd had a gown made for her debut of an identical luxurious material…to match her green eyes, her dear papa had said when choosing it with her in Pall Mall.

A sense of calm drifted over Faye as she wandered further into the cool dim environment. Even the starchy scent of plain cotton was pleasant. Across the top of a swathe of blue silk Faye spied Anne Holly by the counter with her neighbour. Stepping around the obstacles, she started forward to say hello when snippets of their conversation reached her ears, making her proceed cautiously.

'I wouldn't believe a word that girl uttered,' Anne's elderly neighbour was saying, inspecting a gossamer glove the draper had placed in front of her. 'Mrs Bullman complains she's a daydreamer. Fanciful nonsense is what it is.'

'I'd call it downright lies,' Anne Holly returned pithily. 'I know Claire is a decent girl, whereas Peggy Miller...' A snort stood in for her opinion.

'Miss Shawcross will not want this coming hot on the heels of her bad business with Westwood and her accident. The poor lamb's nerves must be shredded. What a shame Mr Collins is not here to take matters in hand...'

'My friend copes marvellously and needs no man to deal for her!'

Anne's voice held such a strength of pride that Faye felt a smile tilt her lips despite the horror of knowing Peggy Miller had carried out her threat. She hoped she could live up to Anne's praise, but feared that things were running out of her control. With her fiancé far away and limited resources to call on since Westwood had decimated her inheritance, the problem of protecting her siblings and her family's good name was an ever more daunting task.

'When Derek is back from his meeting with the

bishop I shall have him drive me to Mulberry House. I want the family to know that we do not believe a word of that little minx's lies…'

Faye didn't wait to hear more. Quietly, with bolts of cloth and laden shelves giving cover, she slipped from the shop.

This time when Faye employed the huge brass knocker on Valeside Manor's heavily ironed door her summons was speedily answered by a smartly uniformed manservant. Politely he asked her business.

Before Faye could answer a lilting Irish voice addressed her.

'I know why you are here, Miss Shawcross.' Ruby had materialised from the shadows and now stood peering about the butler's solid frame. Her petite figure was clad in pastel muslin and she looked enviably cool, Faye thought, as she made use of the shade cast by the porch.

'The Viscount is out; you may come in and talk to me, though.' Without waiting for an answer Ruby turned away, throwing her next words over her shoulder. 'I expect you would like some tea…or perhaps something cool, like lemonade, might be more to your taste.' She pivoted about in a swish of skirts and started pacing backwards. Silken ringlets draped her shoulder as she cocked her head to one side, assessing her guest's hot and bothered countenance.

'Tea would be very nice, thank you.' Faye strove to keep her voice level. She would not allow a child to unsettle her. Now she had been face to face with Ruby she could tell that Kavanagh's relative—if indeed she was such—was about the same age as Claire.

'Come in then and sit in the parlour with me. Graveson will arrange for tea, won't you, Graveson?' Ruby skipped ahead.

The butler murmured an assent to his young mistress's order as he led Faye past the grand old furniture in the hallway. Turning into a panelled corridor, he showed Faye into a sitting room that was at least ten times the size of her own cosy parlour.

Faye stepped over the threshold, already regretting having allowed her natural inquisitiveness about Ruby to get the better of her. She should have returned home on discovering that the master was out. This young lady would be of no help to her; Faye wasn't sure that Ryan Kavanagh would be either. But she was hoping he'd agree to listen to her outrageous request. If he caught her quizzing Ruby behind his back, he'd suspect her of prying. In truth, Faye knew she'd like to discover more about his relationship to Ruby. She was also intrigued to know how the master of Valeside could be an aristocrat, a soldier and just a plain mister.

'Will Mr Kavanagh...that is...the Viscount, as you named him...be away from home for some time?' Faye asked. She perched on the sofa, obeying her young hostess's patting hand insisting she settle beside her.

'Oh, goodness only knows when my guardian will return,' Ruby said with pronounced ennui. 'He is always busy with this and that and I'm lonely and long to see him.'

'He is your guardian?'

'I'm an orphan.' Ruby sighed theatrically and gazed at her visitor with dark, dewy eyes. 'The Viscount is very good to me.'

'Should *I* address him as Viscount Kavanagh?' Faye asked quite seriously.

'Only if you want to annoy him. I just do it to tease him and he lets me because he is fond of me. Neither does he like to be called Major, yet he should be proud of that title as he is a great hero and was decorated after Waterloo. He can fight with pistols and swords, you know.'

'I see.' Faye didn't really see at all why he preferred to be addressed plainly, but she hadn't forgotten his bitter remark about the battlefield carnage at Quatre Bras.

Her late father had had friends in the military and he'd relayed to her stories, passed down, of returning soldiers, outwardly brave faced, who'd privately regretted having taken the King's shilling. So many, he'd said, had resented the glorification of the Peninsular Wars that had stolen their youth and their limbs, leaving them scarred in mind and body, and poorer than church mice.

Faye became aware that Ruby was studying her minutely so removed her bonnet and gloves in a show of ease, then placed those things by her side on the sofa. As Kavanagh had said they were related Faye guessed Ruby might be his niece as well as his ward. Were they brother and sister the young woman surely would have said so.

'I know why you want to see him.' Ruby twirled an ebony curl about a finger. 'It is to do with your sister running off to Donagh Lee, isn't it?'

'If your guardian is going to be away for some hours, I should return another time.' Thoughts of a pleasant chat had been dashed. The last thing Faye wanted was to be drawn into an argument with Claire's rival for Donagh's affections.

'I expect your sister has told you that I fell in love with Donagh and I know she did, too. She can have him, though, if she wants. He doesn't want to marry me any more and even if he did my guardian said he'd shoot him if he comes after me again.' Ruby pulled a little face. 'The Viscount was very angry with me for going out late to the gypsy camp even though the Lees are my kin.'

'You are related to the Lees?' Faye remembered the whispers about Kavanagh's mistress being related to the gypsies. Sudden enlightenment hit her like a thunderbolt. If Kavanagh had told the truth about Ruby being his relation, then he also had Romany blood.

'You and your sister are very pretty. But Claire seems much younger. Oh, tea has arrived…' Ruby rattled off as the door opened.

'It was kind of you to offer me refreshment, but as Mr Kavanagh might be some time, I really can't stay, Miss…' Faye floundered, unsure how to formally address her ingénue of a hostess.

'Her name is Ruby Adair. I'm sorry I wasn't at home to properly introduce you to her earlier.'

Faye leapt to her feet, her heart vaulting to her throat. She swung about to see Ryan Kavanagh standing on the threshold of the room, looking as disturbingly handsome as ever. His clothes and hair looked dusty from riding and Faye immediately recalled the last time she'd seen him unkempt…stripped to the waist on that occasion. It suited him to be dishevelled, she realised; it gave him a buccaneering air that sat well with his swarthy good looks.

A maid bearing a tea tray bustled past him to deposit the crockery on the sideboard. When her master politely gave her leave to quit the room the servant immediately did so.

Ruby rushed to slip her arm through her guardian's. 'Miss Shawcross came to speak to you, but she is just about to have a drink and a chat with me.'

'So I see...' Ryan drawled.

Faye flinched beneath his sardonic regard; he believed that she'd come to snoop in his absence. Tempted though she was to turn tail, she knew if she did his suspicions about her motive would appear justified.

She had come to see *him* and only him. It was not her fault that Ruby Adair had ambushed her, then divulged information that perhaps she should have kept to herself.

'I apologise for this intrusion, but would beg a few moments of your time, Mr Kavanagh.' Faye quickly regained composure.

'You remembered not to address him as a viscount, so that's a good start,' Ruby said saucily. Her clutch on his arm seemed possessive and her narrowed eyes held a glint of rivalry as they watched Faye.

'Go and find something to do while I'm busy, Minx.' Ryan brushed the back of a finger over the girl's cheek, then turned her towards the door.

'But I should like some tea,' Ruby protested, wriggling free of his hands.

'Ask Mrs Bateman to make you some more. Take it into the garden and enjoy the last of the sunshine. Clouds are blowing in...' His mild tone held an edge of authority, causing Ruby to pout but dutifully leave.

'I'm very sorry to turn up again and bother you, sir,' Faye blurted as soon as the door had closed.

He strolled to the table and poured two cups of tea. Having splashed milk into the brew, he held out her drink to her. His own he left on the tray. He propped himself against the furniture on two straight arms, his head lowered, concealing his expression.

Faye watched him, her cup and saucer unsteady in her

hand. Viscount or no, it seemed he was not too high and mighty to serve himself and his guests from the teapot.

'I made it obvious when you were last here that I like being bothered by you, Miss Shawcross.' Slowly he straightened and turned to face her. 'In fact, I'm hoping you've saved me the journey to Mulberry House to speak to you. If you're back to tell me you feel the same way about me, I can suggest what we can do about it.'

The irony in his voice couldn't quite disguise the fact that he meant every word. And heaven only knew she did crave having his strong arms about her again. She knew if he bruised her mouth with his own as he had before, his fiery passion could eradicate every worry from her head as easily as sunlight dissolved snow.

'I deduce from your silence that you're in two minds on it. Perhaps I should help you decide.' He plunged his hands into his pockets and pinned her down with a dangerously challenging stare.

Faye put down her untasted tea in a rattle of crockery. 'I bid you to be serious, sir, if you will.'

'I've never been more serious in my life,' he returned.

His vivid, unsmiling eyes tangled with hers before travelling over her body in a way that caused iced heat to streak through her veins.

'And neither was I more serious than when I told you I will soon be married.' Slashes of bright colour accented Faye's cheekbones. 'You shouldn't have kissed me, Mr Kavanagh, and I shouldn't have...' Unable to explain herself, she snatched up her hat and gloves from the sofa.

'You shouldn't have betrayed your fiancé by liking it?' he suggested. 'Perhaps your feelings for Mr Collins aren't as strong as you thought they were.'

'You are the most arrogant and conceited man!' Faye

breathed, furiously aware that he was too incisive in his taunts. 'And my feelings for my fiancé are unchanged. I love him.' She marched towards the exit.

He didn't attempt to block her way this time as he had on the last occasion she'd felt an unbearable tension building between them, prompting her to flee. By the door she twisted about; she would make some explanation for her visit even if it had been fruitless. 'I have learned about another problem threatening my family following the debacle with the Lees. Impetuously I came straight here to speak to you about it.' She gave a small mirthless laugh. 'I can see now that was not wise; I also regret that I intended to take advantage of your good nature.'

'Good nature?'

He echoed her words in an amused way that made Faye sorry she'd not kept her praise to herself. But she added stiltedly, 'You have been helpful and generous to me and my family... I believe that shows you to be a decent man.'

'It's sweet of you to say so,' he drawled. 'But my generosity comes at a price, Faye Shawcross, and you know it. So what's your answer?'

He approached her in slow strides, but halted when there remained a distance between them. She knew she could turn about and leave if she wanted to. But still she stood where she was, aching for him to touch her—even just a little would do. She'd felt jealous of Ruby when he'd stroked her cheek.

'Whatever it is you want of me, you know I'll give it, don't you? I'll keep you and your family safe, if that's what you've come to ask.'

'And in return?' Faye whispered.

'Come, we're adults, there's no need to act coy. Your fiancé is away...the date of your marriage...should it ever come...is uncertain. We are two people in need of one another. So, if you wish it spelled out, in return for my help I want you as my mistress. I desire you and want to sleep with you...as you know.'

So there it was. Out in the open. In an odd way she respected him for being so blatant and honest. No beating about the bush, no mealy-mouthed words of false affection. Yet she hated him, too, for treating her as though she were just another of the women pandering to his *wicked desire for diversion,* as he'd termed his lust.

She *had* expected his proposition, he'd been correct in that as well. Mrs Gideon had warned her about the master of Valeside's *hungry eyes,* but by then Faye had already felt the weight of them on her. And she had been fooling herself as to why he had often put himself at her disposal. It wasn't out of neighbourly concern, it was so that she would feel obliged to put herself at his disposal.

From the very first time their gazes had collided on Wilverton High Street she'd sensed he found her attractive. Instinctively she had hurried home that day, avoiding coming face to face with the rakish new master of Valeside and his paramour as she'd then believed Ruby to be.

'I came to beg for your assistance in helping me stifle a scandal. In return, you say you would like to damage us even more.' She gave him an icy stare. 'Yet you have the nerve to talk of keeping me and my family safe.'

'And so I will. Naturally the affair would be conducted discreetly.'

'Oh, would it!' Faye emitted in a suffocated gasp. 'How good of you, sir. And what, pray, should I tell my fiancé about your disgusting offer?' She spat, 'Peter might kill you if he ever discovers what you have done.'

'I doubt he'll manage to put a scratch on me, but if he wants to meet me in a misty glade at dawn, I'll oblige.' Ryan's tone was oddly diffident rather than boastful. 'It would be better if you keep the matter to yourself if you love him as you say. You might be a fire in my blood, my dear, but I'll not intentionally take a bullet, even for you, so the best I can offer is to wing him.'

Faye's wide green gaze flitted over his heartbreakingly impassive face. Before today she had thought she was coming to know and like Ryan Kavanagh; but he remained a stranger and she'd been a fool to ever think otherwise.

'I hoped we might become friends, sir, but I see now all you want is a business partner. From what you've said I believe you have enough of those already.' She ignored his amusement at her reference to his paramours, battling to keep her composure. She would not scuttle away, but leave in a dignified manner. 'Please thank Miss Adair for her hospitality.' Faye haughtily tilted her chin. 'I will have Mr Gideon return your horse in the morning and will reimburse you for every penny you have paid out on my behalf the moment I have your account. Good day to you, sir.'

Ryan shrugged and extended his hand as though in acceptance and farewell. The moment her small digits touched his he jerked her against him with a muttered oath. His long bronzed fingers looked stark against her pale cheek as he cupped her face, keeping her still while kissing her with seductive leisure. Faye writhed against him, but as heat surged through her blood and a heaviness stirred in the pit of her stomach the fists she had

rammed against his chest relaxed, then crept to curl over
his shoulders. His mouth worked its wooing magic and
a subtle movement of his hand parted her jaw, allowing
his tongue to caress the silky contour of her lower lip. It
was nothing like the last time he'd bombarded her with
sensual delight; yet whether his kiss was savage or sweet
she couldn't resist it or push him away. His hands slipped
from her face to her throat to her breasts, tormenting the
tingling flesh through her bodice. The hard pressure of
his palms and butterfly brushes from his fingertips drew
a moan of pleasure from Faye and he lifted his mouth
from hers. Her lashes drifted up and her drowsy vision
met a pair of sapphire eyes that were watching her sci-
entifically…just a hint of mockery present.

She stumbled back from him, her cheeks burning.
No words were needed by either of them, she realised,
dragging her eyes away; he'd proved in the most basic
way that he could seduce her if he chose to and make her
beg him to touch her again and again. Most cruel of all,
he'd shown her how easily he could make her forget her
fiancé while she was luxuriating in his sensuality. Faye
gave a guttural cry of shame and her open palm flew
up at his face, striking the thin white scar on his cheek.

'You are a selfish and callous man. I can see that now.
You don't care who you hurt, do you?' Faye's bodice
rose and fell in erratic rhythm as she struggled to control herself. 'You would take another man's happiness
and crush it beneath your foot as though it were nothing, simply to feed your ego.'

Ryan realigned his jaw and shook his head with a resigned grunt at having got what he deserved.

'And what of your happiness?' he asked coolly.

'I am happy with Peter…very happy…' Faye avowed.

'Are you indeed? Why approach a stranger for help, then?'

Faye moistened her pulsing lips with a tongue tip.

'God in heaven! Don't do that!' he growled, throwing his head back with a strangled laugh.

'Do what?' Faye asked warily.

'That…' He ran his thumb over her pillowy scarlet lips, collecting the warm dew.

'Let's talk of your Mr Collins then.' He turned abruptly from her, walking away. 'I imagine he is not aware you've been seeking my protection instead of his.'

It was a direct and pertinent enquiry that made Faye go white and stutter, 'I…I would naturally prefer to seek his assistance rather than yours if I could, sir. Unfortunately Mr Collins is at present far away in Portsmouth… or he might already have set sail for the Continent. I have no other kin to call on other than an elderly aunt and a stepmother who abandoned us all. But I understand your reluctance to risk upsetting my fiancé by taking on his role.'

'I've already said I'll gladly upset your fiancé, my dear.' Ryan turned to her. 'The question is, why are you risking upsetting him? Or perhaps you're intending to keep all this bad business from him, are you?'

'Of course, I would not want to hurt him! And I would not want to keep secrets either,' Faye said hoarsely. 'My fiancé will understand why I accepted the help you offered once he knows the circumstances.' Faye felt her heart flutter and jump. She'd just lied. Peter might well be furious that she was obliged to the local rogue for her own safety and that of her sister. But she had no intention of telling him about Claire's disgrace unless there was no option but to do so. He had demanded time and again that she discover Deborah Shawcross's whereabouts in Ireland and send her brother and sister there. Faye had intended to let Peter believe that she had taken his advice. 'My fiancé cannot give me any practical help as he is many hundreds of miles away.' Faye pulled on her gloves. 'Good day to you, sir...'

'He's closer than that.'

'What do you mean?' Faye paused with her hand on the doorknob. Suspicion was needling her skin as she slanted a glance at him and recognised savage satisfaction darkening the sapphire of his eyes.

'Your fiancé is in London...close enough for you to call him home should you want him rather than me to assist you.'

She tutted disbelief and would have opened the door, but his cool scorn stopped her.

'You don't believe me?'

'I am afraid I do not, sir. Mr Collins was going to London, but only for a short while. By now he would have travelled on to Portsmouth.' She frowned. 'Has somebody reported seeing him?'

'*I've* seen him. I returned from town this afternoon. I had business in Cheapside yesterday and observed him with another man, entering a tavern.' He watched the disbelief in her beautiful green eyes transform to wariness. She didn't want Collins to know anything about this debacle with the Lees. She didn't believe her fiancé would help in the way she needed him to so wanted it all kept secret...and that gave Ryan hope that, despite her declarations to the contrary, she didn't love the man in the way she said she did.

'You must be mistaken, sir,' Faye finally ejected in a shocked voice.

'I think not; I know him and I know Westwood.'

'Peter was with Mr Westwood?' Faye's mind was immediately racing ahead, wondering if Peter had somehow found out about her losses, then tracked the lawyer to his London office to have it out with him. Westwood deserved to be taken to task, but she didn't want a public scene made over her.

'My fiancé has used Mr Westwood's services in the past; perhaps an urgent appointment delayed him in London.'

'You also employed Westwood.'

Faye shot him a sharp glance. 'Please don't *you* be coy now, sir. You may speak plainly. I know my situation is common knowledge in Wilverton.'

That caused him to smile and pace to the window. 'You've told Collins about your financial situation, I take it?' Again satisfaction curved his mouth as he stared out, waiting for her to reply. Perhaps they had been engaged for a ridiculously long time, but it seemed she still didn't trust him enough to confide in him about much at all.

'I've not had a chance to speak to him on the subject, but if you are correct in seeing them together then I imagine word has reached him from another source,' Faye rattled off. 'My fiancé has probably delayed returning to Portsmouth to have it out with Westwood. He will make him apologise at least.'

'Perhaps he should apologise to you for allowing you to put your faith and money in his friend's hands.'

'You seem to know a lot about a matter that is none of your concern. Besides, they are not *friends*, but business acquaintances.'

'Rather like us, then...' Ryan said drily. 'Or we would be if we could but agree on terms.'

'Indeed…but as we never shall it only remains for me to thank you for what you have done so far and tell you I need nothing more from you.'

'Unfortunately, I don't feel that way about you.'

'I'm sure you will, sir,' Faye said sweetly. 'Once you have had your desire for diversion met elsewhere.' She couldn't look at him; she knew if she did he'd be laughing at her. None of it was serious to him. Whereas for her, every look, every touch he gave her was of such importance that it was a brand on her memory and she hated him for it.

She banged shut the door and hurried along the corridor towards the vestibule.

The butler showed her out and she descended the steps speedily with her skirts held away from her flying feet. But she had no need to fear he might prevent her escape.

As she flicked the reins over the back of his horse she took a glance at the house. All was quiet, nothing stirred. All Faye could hear was her heart in her ears. All she could feel was the trickle of hot salt water on her cheeks. When out of sight around the bend in the drive, she dashed away her tears, then let the light patter of rain wash clean her complexion. He had been right on that, too…the clouds had rolled in to blot out the sun.

She set her shoulders as she turned on the uphill road to Mulberry House. She knew she had a grave task in front of her now, trying to keep Peggy's spite contained until she could get Claire safely away somewhere to let the matter die down. She had hoped to ask Kavanagh to make some enquiries about her stepmother's whereabouts as he'd said he and Ruby were off on a visit to Ireland soon. If he'd agreed, she'd then have spoken to her sister about writing to Deborah Shawcross. The least

Claire could do after causing such trouble was try to tolerate a short sojourn in Ireland with her mother. Whether the woman would have agreed to have her on a visit, of course, was another matter. But now, following her confrontation with Kavanagh, it seemed that the idea would wither without being tested. Without him helping her find Deborah, she'd have no address to write to.

Faye could see some sense in what she'd impetuously chosen as a solution. Deborah Shawcross, whether the woman liked it or not, had a responsibility to Claire and, that apart, it would be good if old family rifts could be put behind them. It was doubtful that they would ever all be friends, Faye knew that, but lifelong enmity with her stepmother wasn't what she wanted either. And she doubted that Claire and Michael did either, in their hearts.

Chapter Twelve

A few days later Faye had just finished breakfast when the postman arrived bearing two letters.

One she opened immediately, guessing it was from Mr and Mrs Scott. She scanned it, sighing in gladness. Finally some good news! The Scotts would be delighted to have Michael to stay and had generously sent a carriage to collect him, due on the morrow.

The other note she slipped into her pocket, recognising it as bearing Peter's handwriting. She wanted to wait for some peace and quiet later to savour his news.

'Michael!' Faye waited at the bottom of the stairs for her brother to respond to her summons. As soon as he appeared on the top step she flapped the parchment.

Michael needed no further encouragement to hurtle down the treads, hollering, 'I may go to Scotland?'

'Indeed you may, young man and very soon.' Faye struggled from her brother's bear hug. 'Your friend's parents have sent a coach for you. It will be here tomorrow.' Faye ruffled her brother's fair hair, realising that he was quite overcome with gratitude. 'You'd best get packing.'

'Thank you,' Michael mumbled gruffly. Then with

a whoop of joy he bounded back up the stairs, unintentionally barging Claire out of the way as she met him on the landing.

'He's going on holiday, then.' Claire sounded envious. 'I wish I was. I'm hungry...' she added and headed off towards the kitchen.

There was an appetising aroma of freshly baked biscuits and usually Faye would have followed her sister and also gone to sample one. Instead, she returned to the parlour and sat down to read her other letter. As she unfolded it she was mulling over what Claire had just said about wanting to get away from the area. A tap on the door interrupted her and she folded Peter's letter as Claire entered with a plate of biscuits for them to share. Aware that her sister was bearing a peace offering, Faye smiled and took one.

'I've been thinking...' Claire said, in between chews. 'It might be best if I went away for a while. Peggy can't blackmail me for my new hat if I'm not around. And I doubt she'll bother blabbing either if she knows I won't be here to be upset over the gossip.'

'She already has blabbed. I overheard talk in the draper's...' Faye briefly explained.

'The minx!' Claire cried. She looked agitated. 'So everybody will know about me and Donagh?'

'Not everybody will believe what Peggy says,' Faye said calmly before her sister became overwrought. 'What had you in mind when you say "get away"?' She wanted to quickly follow up Claire's earlier comment as it tied in closely with her own thoughts.

Claire sighed. 'Well, I haven't many options. It is either a case of throwing myself on Aunt Aggie's mercy or...on my mother's.' She shrugged. 'And of the two, my mother owes me her support far more than does my aunt.'

'Indeed she does; if we could find out where Deborah is, you would like to go to Ireland?' Faye felt pleased that her sister had come up with the same solution to the problem.

'I'm not sure I'd *like* to go...' Claire sighed. 'But I *should* go. I know I've caused bad trouble and I deserve to suffer to put it right,' she said in a rather martyred tone.

'Well, I can't deny the truth in that,' Faye replied bluntly.

She knew they wouldn't be able to hide away in Mulberry House for ever, avoiding questions. When she had returned home after her emotional battle with Ryan Kavanagh, Mrs Gideon had told her that the vicar and his wife had called in her absence. Faye knew what they wanted to talk about and had been grateful for the reprieve. She had still been feeling jittery, not least because she understood there were benefits—both personal and practical—to be had from Kavanagh's proposition.

It was not fancy clothes and jewels or the security he provided occupying her imagination and putting a tingle in her blood, but the memory of his passion...and then she hated herself for being so weak. She had known her future husband since she was a child and couldn't understand how a stranger had, in a short while, made her feel confused about her future with Peter. She enjoyed her fiancé's company; she liked having his kisses. But Ryan Kavanagh could make her chill with excitement simply by looking at her. A single touch from one of his long fingers could cause a fiery sensation to melt her bones, the like of which she'd never before experienced.

And it frightened her to feel that way, as though she'd no will of her own.

But it wasn't just about the wonderful way he made her feel...she knew that he wasn't judging her for having been negligent with Claire. He understood her dilemma because he'd faced a similar problem with Ruby. He knew what it was to have the task of guarding a girl burgeoning into womanhood. Yet sympathy and understanding was something that she doubted she would have got from the man who wanted her as his wife. With a quiet sigh Faye realised that she wished she'd not parted company so frostily with Ryan Kavanagh because she'd appreciated his advice and support. Her mind was snapped back to the present by a pertinent question from her sister.

'How can we find out where my mama is? You won't send me overseas on my own, will you?'

'I shall accompany you there, of course, and eventually bring you home again,' Faye answered.

Claire looked reassured. 'So how will we find her?'

'I shall have to put some thought into that. I'd rather not make the journey and hope for the best,' Faye replied.

Claire approached the door as they heard their brother dragging his trunk across the floorboards overhead. 'I suppose I should go and give Michael a hand as I won't see him for a while.'

Faye felt some relief that progress was being made on a way to minimise the scandal that was brewing. She picked up Peter's letter and quickly scanned the few paragraphs of news. His promotion was imminent, he wrote, and he also reminded her that he had not forgotten his vow to travel to Ireland when next on shore leave. He had underscored a sentence expressing his desire to be her husband without further delay because he loved her dearly. At one time reading of Peter's devotion would have caused little butterflies to circle her stomach and perhaps a poignant tear to sting her eyes. From the age of fourteen she had been sweet on Peter Collins. At five years her senior he had shown little interest in her until he came down from university. The Shawcross family, being friends and neighbours, had been invited to the Collins's to celebrate Peter's graduation. Faye recalled swelling with feminine pride that the man she'd secretly wanted for two years couldn't take his eyes off her that evening. He had strolled with her in the garden after dinner and beneath a starry sky she had received her first ever kiss when just sixteen. From that moment she had decided she wanted to marry Peter Collins.

By that time Peter's elder sister had married and moved away and shortly after Peter also left the family home to embark on his naval career. But he'd liked returning to his childhood home in Hertfordshire and had boasted that one day the house and acreage would be his. Much to Peter's disgust, his father had sold the estate and moved away to the coast.

But since Kavanagh's arrival in the neighbourhood everything had changed. When Faye lay in bed in the blissful state between sleep and wakefulness, it was no longer her fiancé that she fantasised about. Neither were the male features that floated across her mind fair and pleasantly attractive; they were dark and starkly beautiful with eyes of deepest blue that seemed to bore into her soul from between lengthy black lashes.

Faye abruptly stood up, a small frustrated cry rasping in her throat as she attempted to shake off her obsession with the master of Valeside. No matter what he had done for her so far, he had blatantly revealed himself to be a lecherous opportunist, she reminded herself. He had masqueraded as a friend while using her various misfortunes against her. And he had lied to her about seeing Peter with Westwood. If her fiancé were in London, he would surely have mentioned it in the note he'd sent her. If Kavanagh thought to undermine her trust in her fiancé to get her into bed, the ploy would not work.

The soft sounds and scents of summer smoothed the frown from Faye's brow as she stepped closer to the window. The blowsy roses were batting against the glass in a gentle breeze and a few bees were whirring industriously to collect nectar from the lemony blooms. The good weather would be gone far too soon, she realised. Once Michael had set off she knew she would need to turn her full attention to her sister's predicament. She knew nothing of Ireland or its language, but somehow must discover where Deborah Shawcross had set up home. It could not be so difficult! Faye exhorted herself, pushing up the sash to pluck an unfurling rosebud. Holding it by the stem, she breathed in its perfume.

'Mr and Mrs Holly are on their way. I've just spotted them from the landing window, driving over the brow of the hill.' Mrs Gideon had come into the parlour to deliver her warning. 'Shall I say you're indisposed, Miss Shawcross?'

Mrs Gideon, in common with everybody else in Wilverton had heard of her niece's spite towards Claire. Outwardly the woman contained her anger to a permanent pursing of her lips. But Faye had heard her housekeeper muttering to herself that she'd *'swing for the girl, and gladly...'*

'I'll receive them, Nelly.' Faye placed the rose stem on

her desk and gave her housekeeper a wry smile. 'Best get it over with,' she murmured to herself. Before Nelly quit the room she asked, 'Has your husband brought Daisy home yet?' Every day, Faye had sent Mr Gideon to the manor to return Kavanagh's horse and collect Daisy, and on each occasion her servant had returned with the sprightly gelding, plus the news that her pony was still recuperating.

'Bertram brought the gelding back again. Mr Kavanagh's groom said he'd get in trouble with his master if he let Daisy go before she was fit and ready, and he wasn't to take back the gelding till then.'

The rat-a-tat on the door made Mrs Gideon raise her eyebrows. 'Still time to tell them you're under the weather, if you want.'

Faye gave a rueful smile. The vicar's wife was her good friend and had staunchly championed her in the drapery. Nevertheless Faye intended to keep the meeting as brief as possible without being impolite. They were preparing for Michael's trip to Scotland so had a valid reason to do so.

Mrs Gideon had cooked and cleared away supper then departed to her own home with her husband over an hour since when Faye heard the sound of an approaching rider. She'd been seated at her writing desk for quite some time, but had penned just a few sentences in reply to Peter's letter; her usual flowing prose when telling him her news and enquiring after his seemed to have deserted her. She pushed the parchment away and got up to investigate. Having discerned two sets of hooves hitting ground, she supposed that two horsemen were approaching along the lane.

She was the only one still up. Having decided he must rise at the crack of dawn in readiness for his trip to Scotland, Michael had jumped into bed as soon as he'd eaten. Claire had also sought her own room and her fashion journals, taking two candles with her to read by, as cloud had brought dusk down early.

Pulling back the parlour curtain, Faye held aloft the lamp and squinted into twilight; her flitting gaze steadied, then whipped back to a dark silhouette. She froze. By the front gate was Ryan Kavanagh seated on his stallion. The animal moved restlessly and she glimpsed her little mare in its lee. Kavanagh had seen her and rather than pretend ignorance of his presence, she opened the window to speak to him.

'Thank you, sir, for bringing Daisy back,' she said a trifle breathlessly. 'I'd be grateful if you would put her in the coach house. Please take your pony home with you. Goodnight…'

Ryan raised a booted foot over the stallion's neck, then leapt agilely to the ground.

'Are you going to invite me in?'

His voice was as quiet as hers had been, but she heard it very well, straining as she was to catch every smooth syllable.

'I'm afraid not, sir. It is late and my family have retired. I'm about to go to bed, too…' That last remark was a mistake, she realised. She might not be able to clearly see his face, but she knew he was smiling sarcastically.

'Come out here then.' He opened the gate and walked closer, stopping halfway down the path.

For what seemed like an age their eyes merged and strained and no sound broke the stillness other than the hoot of an owl. Then the eerie bark of a vixen calling her mate startled Faye into reaching to close the sash.

'You said you weren't frightened of me, Faye,' he provoked her softly. 'Neither do you need to be. I was stupid to say what I did.'

'If that is your way of apologising for having insulted me—' Faye broke off and pressed together her lips, conscious of her brother and sister upstairs. She didn't want them to know he was here let alone be privy to this conversation.

'Offering you anything you desire and my protection is an insult?' He thrust his hands into his pockets and glanced along the lane. 'What is it you want, then? Tell me.'

'I want you to leave me alone.'

'No, you don't.' He swung his face back in her direction and his dark eyes captured hers.

I do... The words keened in her mind, but she couldn't utter the lie and she saw that her silence was enough for him.

'Come out here... I need to talk to you about something.'

'I can't...we might be spotted together on the lane.' Faye whispered in a hiss of frustration. Already there was that heaviness in her belly and breasts that she was coming to associate with him; it made a bittersweet restlessness bedevil her. She knew not what she wanted, but feared that he did, and could make her beg him for it. So he must go.

'I'll take you for a ride...away from here...nobody will see us.'

Faye's eyes widened in shock. Surely he was joking.

But it seemed he was not. He raised a hand and beckoned lazily.

Faye quickly dropped the sash and the curtain into place. She backed away, a hand pressed to the pulse bobbing crazily in her throat.

Instinctively she made to extinguish the lamp, as though intending to hide in the dark. She snatched her hands from it and tilted back her head, her eyes squeezing shut. She was not a timid mouse! She was an independent woman with responsibilities. And he…he was a scoundrel who should leave decent women alone!

Before her yearning body could argue against that opinion on his character, she lit her speedy way up to her chamber. She glanced from behind an edge of curtain. She could see nobody out there now. But she'd not heard him go. Sitting down on the edge of her bed, Faye dropped her face into her cupped palms as a spasm of excitement shook her to her core. She gripped the mattress to prevent herself jumping up and racing down the dark stairs and out into the night to find him.

After sitting still for what seemed like an hour, but was probably not even half that time, Faye got up and peeped out. All was quiet; the moon was veiled in fleecy nimbus and just a few stars twinkled at the edges of the heavens. She imagined he had done as she asked and stabled her pony before leaving. There was no sign of Daisy tethered by the gate.

Impetuously Faye turned and sped noiselessly down the stairs, then eased back the bolts on the door. She hesitated on the step, listening, before dashing towards the coach house, the lamp swinging in her hand. The large planked door whined open and she went in with the light held up high.

Indeed he had put her pony in the stall his gelding had occupied. Daisy whinnied softly to welcome her. Faye hurried closer and put the lamp on the brick floor. Gently she ran a hand over a velvety flank, then spontaneously put her arms around Daisy's neck, laying her cheek against soft warm flesh. 'He has mended you well and I must thank him for that...if nothing else. I have missed you, little Daisy. Show me your poor leg... I'm sorry I hurt you.' Faye crouched down to test the animal's bony shins, glad that Daisy had no tender places that made her protest on being touched. 'You are quite fit again, aren't you, little one?' She stroked the docile mare's nose.

It was the scent of tobacco that brought Faye upright and made her whip around. She glimpsed a red glow and although she couldn't see the smoke in the dark she could smell it as he exhaled. 'What are you doing?' she demanded shakily, feeling embarrassed that he'd overheard her murmuring to Daisy.

'I'm wishing I was that horse,' he said drily.

In a fluid movement he rose from the upended crate he'd been seated on and ground underfoot on cobbles the half-smoked cheroot.

'You knew I'd come out here, didn't you? You waited for me!' Faye accused. She was filled with tumultuous emotion, torn between bolting for the house and striking him for having almost startled the life out of her.

'Of course I waited for you...you knew I would.'

'I did not! Where are your horses?'

'Tethered outside.'

'You think you're so clever, don't you? You're so arrogant you think you can have anything you want...'

He'd come close enough now for her to properly distinguish his tall broad shape, but his features remained indistinct. He stopped a few yards from her. 'Tell me what you want, Faye.'

'I want you to go away and leave me be,' she whispered. 'I...I am frightened of you.'

'You're frightened of yourself, not of me. I won't force you to do anything you don't want to do.'

'Go, then...'

'I can't...'

'Why not?'

'You'd be forcing me to do something I don't want to do,' he said solemnly.

Faye bit her lip to quell a hysterical giggle. 'I don't care about your feelings,' she retorted. 'You're a stranger and you're trespassing on my property.'

'I'm no stranger to you. A few days ago you spoke of us being friends. Besides, you've trespassed on my property.'

'I have not!' Faye snapped indignantly. 'I went to the manor with good reason and Ruby invited me in.'

He'd come closer and was now a mere arm span away. 'I've come here with good reason.'

'I'm grateful for what you did.' Faye glanced at her well-groomed and nourished pony.

'My pleasure...' he drawled. 'But there's more to it than that, isn't there?'

Faye's wide glossy eyes darted to him. 'What do you mean?'

'You want me to take you to Ireland to find Deborah Shawcross, don't you?'

'No!' Faye was astonished that he'd worked that out. 'It's true I must discover my stepmother's whereabouts. When you said you were going there with Ruby I wondered if you might make enquiries to help me locate her. Claire has said she wants to go and visit her mother and I think it is wise…given the circumstances here at home.' Faye paused. 'But that was before. Now you need not fear I will ever impose on you again.'

'Why will you not?'

'You know the answer to that, sir.'

'And if I tell you my generosity no longer comes at a price?'

'I would answer…why is that?' Faye's voice was husky with doubt and suspicion.

'And I'd say…damned if I know…' he drawled. 'Nevertheless it's the truth. And there's something else you should know.'

'Yes?' Faye angled her head to try to read his expression. In the gloom all she could see of his eyes was a shadow of long lashes on his lean cheeks.

'There's no need to search for her; I know where your stepmother is.'

Chapter Thirteen

Faye was momentarily too stunned to speak and he didn't interrupt her spinning thoughts with a comment for a full minute.

'Are you sending your sister away because of Donagh Lee?'

Faye murmured confirmation. 'I've no choice now. Her friend has started talk in town. Had you not been away in London I expect you would have heard it, too. Everybody in Wilverton knows about Claire and a gypsy boy.' Faye paused. 'Thankfully few believe it because Claire's friend is a known troublemaker. But we can no longer brazen it out and hope to get away with it.'

'Send Claire away and it'll be assumed she's guilty.'

'She is guilty!' Faye cried in a suffocated voice. 'The stupid girl has brought herself close to ruin. She is due to make her debut next year.' Faye wasn't sure why she was telling him, of all people, about it. But now she'd started it seemed hard to stop unburdening herself. 'I don't like implying Peggy Miller is a liar. The Reverend Holly and his wife came this afternoon to show us support and tell us they don't believe a word the girl has said.' Faye made an anguished little sound. 'Do you know how hard it is to constantly pick a path between truth and lie when conversing with friends about such a delicate matter?'

'I suspect my conscience is not as troubled as yours by such things,' he said ruefully. 'But it is troubled by something else,' he added after a pause. 'And telling you about it was one of the reasons that brought me here this evening.'

'What have you done?' Faye immediately asked.

'It's my fault that your sister came into contact with Donagh Lee in the first place. Let me do what I can to help put things right. I might be a mere man, but I understand what lies in wait for a genteel young lady when her reputation is compromised. One of the reasons I left Ireland was to put distance between Ruby and Donagh before she fell completely under his spell.'

'She said he wanted to marry her.'

'He wasn't as keen on the match as his father. Nevertheless Ruby was easily flattered when he started to romance her and quickly thought herself in love. She is sixteen and far too young and immature to be talking of being anybody's wife. So I brought her to the English countryside out of their reach...or so I thought.'

Faye marvelled anew at how similar the master of Valeside's predicament was to her own. Then comprehension dawned as their eyes merged in the dusk. 'Are you saying that the Lees followed you here from Ireland?' She sounded incredulous.

'Yes...they followed us here. In attempting to solve my problem I have created one for you. And for that I am truly sorry. Had I not come to Wilverton, then your sister would never have met Donagh Lee.'

'You weren't to know that this would happen,' Faye said graciously but nevertheless she gave a deep sigh. 'Bill Lee must have taken the matter of his son's marriage very seriously to pursue you like that.'

'Marriage is a serious business,' Ryan said. 'And nobody but a fool would enter into it without due consideration.'

'Indeed…' Faye sensed the barb in the comment and felt the weight of his eyes preying on her. 'And the other reason?' she blurted. 'You said that your conscience wasn't the only thing that brought you here this evening.'

'In truth, it wasn't even the most pressing… I wanted to see you, Miss Shawcross, and well you know it. You have me twined quite firmly about your finger…as I'm sure you're aware.'

'I know nothing of the sort! And neither do I want you twined about my finger.'

'Do you not?' he asked suggestively. 'Why not?'

'If I needed a man at my beck and call, then I would want it to be my future husband.'

'I doubt you would get your wish; he seems to do without you quite well.' Ryan moved a step closer. 'Whereas I can't sleep for thinking about you.'

Faye felt too aware of the soft darkness enclosing them and the narcotic pull of his powerful presence just beyond her fingertips. 'Might I have Deborah's direction so I can take my sister to her without delay?' she blurted.

'No…'

'Why say you know where she is, then, if you intend keeping your knowledge to yourself?' she said in frustration. 'Or perhaps you are lying again…'

'Again?'

The single word was uttered in a perilously silken

tone. Faye rubbed goose pimples from her arms, backing away until her spine was against the wooden rail of Daisy's stall.

'When have I lied to you?'

'I've received a letter from Peter; he made no mention of having seen Westwood in London, or even of being in London.'

'Perhaps he doesn't want you to know they met, or where he is.'

'What are you implying, Mr Kavanagh?' Faye sharply demanded.

'I'm implying nothing; I'll plainly say that your fiancé was in town with the man you unwisely entrusted with your inheritance.'

'If you are trying to drive us apart by making me think badly of Peter, it will not work.' She choked an acrid laugh. 'Westwood is obviously too cowardly to own up to my fiancé about his dreadful incompetence. And Peter was obviously unaware he was in the company of a fellow who has let us both down. If he has recently been in London I expect he has been granted some extra days' leave and I hope he enjoyed himself,' she ended defiantly.

'He did…take it from me,' Ryan said sardonically, remembering the two tavern whores the men had been with. 'And you, my dear, will make the perfect consort if you never require a plausible explanation for a man's absences.'

'I will make Peter Collins a good wife; *he* is the only man I want.'

'Is that so?'

'Yes…' Faye whispered, shrinking back as he moved a step closer. She threw back her head, meeting his black diamond eyes through the flickering lamplight. 'Why won't you give me my stepmother's address?' she whispered. After seconds of pulsating silence she answered her own question. 'I think you were lying about not wanting your assistance rewarded. Mr Gideon could have brought Daisy back earlier. And assuaging your conscience could have waited until another time. But you didn't want that, did you? You came here at dusk to see me because you wanted to tantalise me with information about my stepmother, hoping to force me to ride with you to the woods to learn more, and once there you could do what you want to me...'

'Go on...' Ryan growled, dragging her against his tense body. 'You're firing yourself up...and me, too. What is it I want to do to you, Faye? What is it *you* want me to do to you?' he coarsely provoked her.

'Nothing... I want nothing from you,' she cried raggedly, making to dodge past him. But she was wedged between the wooden stall and his immovable frame and the heat of his torso in the cool dewy air was enticing her to rub against him. The darkness was conspiratorial, too, covering her blushes, and she tilted up her face, arching her back to tempt his hands and mouth to plunder her lips and body.

Ryan's mouth descended so fast and hard that she would have buckled at the knees with the force of it but for his pelvis rammed against hers. His hands deftly unhooked her bodice buttons with a speed she would have found difficult to achieve. His long fingers splayed over her warm throbbing breasts, teasing the little nubs with thumb strokes before easing the silken mounds free of her chemise. He lowered his head, suckling one then the other with tender savagery that drove Faye wild and made her grasp the back of his head to imprison him.

He lifted her against the stall, seating her on its lip while working up her skirts with practised skill. Then his fingers were under the hem of her drawers and he was teasing the core of her femininity with artful movements of a knuckle. His mouth stroked and played back and forth between the sensitive breasts he held cupped in one large, possessive hand, the nipples made long and rigid by his cleverly attentive tongue. So sensitive was her bare bosom that just a slick of his warm breath as his mouth descended was enough to make her whimper and writhe in ecstasy.

'Does he make you feel this way when he touches you?' Ryan mouthed harshly against her cheek.

'No…' The word was gasped out, but she could say no more although the words spun in her head. Peter would never do this to her because he loved and respected her too much. But Faye was caught in a web of carnal desire and neither her dignity nor her reason could pull her free.

With a feral growl Ryan lifted her down, taking her to the straw on the ground with him. He'd pushed back her knees and plunged his hips between them before Faye had drawn breath to protest even had she wanted to. And she didn't want to.

'Shall I stop, Faye?' he asked, his forehead resting on a cushion of her tangled blonde locks. 'Tell me. I swear I'll go now if you want me to.' A tormented laugh followed as though he regretted having said that.

She shook her head and he felt the movement against his face. 'Tell me!' he demanded roughly.

But she could not. She simply swung her face, feeling enervated, and allowed her pulsating lips to sweep over the scar on the cheek presented to her.

'Faye! Oh, where are you?'

With a groaned curse Ryan was on his feet and adjusting his clothes before Faye had properly assimilated the awful news that her sister was just outside the barn, calling to her.

He lifted her up on to her wobbly feet, jerking her forward to fasten the buttons he'd undone. With a swift thorough kiss he turned her about and gave her a gentle push towards the exit. 'Saved in the nick of time...' he muttered with savage frustration. 'I'll come and talk to you tomorrow.' Without another word he turned and disappeared behind stacked straw, heading towards the back door that led to the garden.

Faye felt her heart racing so fast she thought she might faint. She clung to the wooden rail of the stall, finding the sense to shake out her crushed skirts just as the lamplight glowed in the doorway of the barn.

'Oh...there you are!' Claire sounded very relieved. 'I thought I heard voices a little while ago, but couldn't find you. Did Mr Gideon come back?'

'No...' Faye said weakly as her sister hurried closer.

'Oh...Daisy is home! Did somebody from the big house bring her over?' Claire rushed forward to pet the pony.

'Yes... I was just making sure she is comfortable.' Faye was slowly managing to compose herself and curb the peculiar ache low down in her belly.

'She looks very well; Mr Kavanagh is kind to help us like that.'

'Come...we must get to bed,' Faye said. 'Michael's

transport to Scotland will be here before noon so we must be up early.'

Claire linked arms with her sister. 'I hope he has a nice time. I'm not absolutely sure I like the idea of staying with Mama, but if she'll have me I promise I will go. Then in the spring I can go to London and have a nicer time. I've seen some wonderful new fashions in my magazines. I'd love a gown in the Parisienne style that is all the rage.'

Faye turned to close the barn door, barely aware of her sister's chatter. She knew that she was still in shock; tomorrow it would sink in just how close she'd brought herself to ruin. Yet, she'd had the nerve to speak to Kavanagh of Claire being stupid and risking her reputation! She was a dreadful hypocrite! And so was he! Having said he understood the consequences faced by a young woman who'd been compromised, he'd gone on to seduce her. Or perhaps he thought that her betrothal gave her some protection against disgrace. Or perhaps he didn't care either way as long as he got what he wanted from her. Yet…she believed that he sincerely regretted having brought the Lees into the neighbourhood. Faye took a deep calming breath as she followed her sister into the house.

'Are you coming up to bed?' Claire frowned. 'You have checked all of that already.' She was watching her sister making sure the locks and bolts were secure and that the windows were firmly closed.

Faye sat down at the writing desk, placing her oil lamp close by so that it illuminated her letter. 'I shall just finish this for Peter before I go up. You get yourself tucked in. Sleep tight…'

Claire left her alone and for a long while Faye stared

sightlessly at the parchment. Then the guilt and shame battering at her conscience grew too much and tears that hovered on her lashes flowed silently down her cheeks, dropping on to the ink and blurring it. When her eyes were dry she smeared the wet from her face with her fingers. Crushing the spoiled paper in her hand, she put it in her pocket and lifted the lamp to light her way to bed.

'It seems quiet now Master Michael's gone on his travels.' Mrs Gideon made that comment while pushing the flat iron back and forth on a laundered pillowcase.

'It does indeed,' Faye concurred. Her brother had left at eleven o'clock that morning, in a sturdy coach with his trunks stowed on top. They had all been there to wish him a safe journey, Mr and Mrs Gideon and Claire, and even a few of the neighbours who'd heard he was going away had waved from their open casements. As soon as he could Michael had escaped his sisters' tearful hugs and exhortations to be good and had clambered aboard, clutching the huge food parcel Mrs Gideon had prepared for him to eat en route. Then as the driver had cracked the whip he had hung out of the window to salute them until he was lost from sight behind the bend in the road.

After his departure Faye had managed to write a very nice note to her fiancé and she intended to post it to the naval base in Portsmouth. If Peter had tarried a few extra days in London he would be at the port by now, she was sure.

Faye had banished any thought of Ryan Kavanagh from her mind. And in time she would conquer her guilt and shame, too…she must if she were ever to find any peace and happiness with Peter. For the whole of a restless night she had thanked the lord that Claire's arrival outside the barn had shocked her to her senses yesterday. She had behaved with disgraceful wantonness and despicable disloyalty to her future husband.

Just a few minutes more pinned beneath him on the ground and she would have been a fraud walking down the aisle wearing a white wedding dress.

'Mr Kavanagh brought Daisy home yesterday evening,' Faye informed neutrally, then she rushed on to say something that she knew would take her housekeeper's mind off finding questions about that visit.

'I'm hoping to take Claire to Ireland to find her mother. After recent events my sister thinks it would be best if she stayed there until her debut in the spring and so do I.' Faye saw the other woman's look of relief.

Nelly replied flatly, 'It's as well to get her away from here and no mistake.'

'And I hope to be married as soon as possible,' Faye continued lightly. 'After all this time I don't want a lavish affair and I doubt my fiancé does either. A simple country celebration in Wilverton will be quite acceptable.'

'If it is what you really want, then good luck to you both, I say,' Mrs Gideon said stoutly.

Faye smiled, yet she felt rather disconcerted by Nelly's lukewarm response to her news. 'A wedding breakfast at the White Hart for just a few friends will do.' Faye paused. 'And now I'm off to town to post my letter to Peter telling him to come back as soon as he is able so we can make plans.'

Faye hadn't been to Wilverton for a while, not wanting to run the gauntlet of stares and whispers. But the townsfolk seemed at pains to act normally when they spotted her. She was ruefully aware that she probably had the Hollys and the Gideons to thank for that.

Mrs Bullman had come out of her shop and patted Faye on the arm before bustling back inside without a word. Faye noticed that Peggy was inside the butcher's, looking sulky; she was glad the girl hadn't lost her job over it all. Peggy deserved punishment for being malicious, but Faye didn't want her family to suffer the loss of her wages. She was coming to know what it was to penny pinch and felt sorry for Mr Miller rearing his brood. He was in a far worse position than she was.

Having posted her letter to Peter, she strolled on towards the perimeter of town where she'd left Daisy in harness in the shade of a large oak tree. As she reached the White Hart Faye hesitated. A mail coach had just pulled in and harassed people were noisily disembarking. It reminded her of the journey she and Claire must soon make. On impulse she followed the passengers inside, intending to pick the landlord's brains about travelling to Liverpool to catch the boat to Ireland. She imagined she might need to change coaches many times on such a lengthy journey.

The interior of the tavern was dim and smoky and as she hesitated by an open doorway, several fellows in coarse clothing turned her way, their clay pipes gripped in stained teeth. Faye pressed on in her search for Mr Rowntree, turning right and left in the maze of narrow corridors, hoping to find the landlord. She hadn't stepped foot in this place since her father was alive.

Once in a while Mr Shawcross had frequented this hostelry to take a drink with neighbours. On one occasion he'd been from home on a day when his son, playing hide and seek with Claire, had taken a tumble on the stairs. Fearing Michael had broken his leg, Mrs Gideon had sent Faye to fetch her father from the White

Hart and tell him he must return immediately, bringing the doctor.

Faye reflected on that accident, judging it to have been about seven years ago. She could clearly recall running as fast as she could to Wilverton on a balmy, light evening, feeling fearful for her little brother. Michael had suffered no more than bruises; the doctor had patched him up with arnica and lint, and her father hadn't taken another trip to the pub for many months thereafter.

She stopped by a door that was ajar and peered around it into a room that looked to be reserved for a more refined clientele than she'd previously chanced upon. Hot and bothered lady passengers were fanning themselves, seated at blackened oak tables. Several young serving girls were whizzing to and fro, carrying laden trays. But of the landlord there was no sign.

'Why...Miss Shawcross...how can I assist you?' Charlie Rowntree had emerged from a door opposite. He held a tray aloft, piled with plates of succulent-looking sliced meats and a crusty loaf. The aroma of the freshly baked bread made Faye's mouth water. On rising she'd had no appetite following a sleepless night, but she realised she felt hungry now.

'I...I wanted to speak to you, sir, about coaching times. But perhaps another day would be better. I can see you are dreadfully busy.' Faye had noted that she'd lost the fellow's attention already.

'Oh...just coming, sir...right away...' Charlie had dipped his head obsequiously to somebody.

'Take it into the room, if you will...'

Faye recognised the accented baritone instantly, but managed to stop herself swinging around. She gave Mr

Rowntree a nod and even restricted herself to walking, rather than dashing away.

Unsure of which corridor to take, she chose left and came to a dead end. She turned, her bosom rising and falling with her rapid breaths. He had followed her, as she'd known he would, and had propped himself against the wall some yards away.

'Did you go to the manor, then come here looking for me?'

Faye choked a sour laugh. 'No, I did not, sir. But I can understand why your conceit might make you think such a thing.'

'You're angry with me?' It was a toneless enquiry.

'Angry with you?' Faye repeated in a suffocated whisper. She gestured disbelief. 'You are so unbearably arrogant!' she fumed as quietly as she could. 'You think you can do as you please…take what you want…' Faye pressed together her lips. She was not about to air any more Shawcross dirty linen in public. 'Please remove yourself so I can pass,' she said distantly.

'I take it you require an apology for my wicked ways yesterday evening. Be fair…there was little time for fond farewells.'

'I expected nothing from you, sir, least of all that,' Faye said acidly.

'I expected more from you…' His deep blue gaze had turned as sultry as his voice. 'And almost got it…'

Faye swallowed the block of humiliation in her throat, but she refused to reply or even glance at him.

'So…if you didn't enter this place looking for me… what are you doing here?'

'I'm investigating the times of the mail coaches, not that it is any of your concern,' Faye replied stiltedly.

'It is my concern if you're intent on travelling abroad with your sister, unaccompanied, and with no idea of what lies in front of you.'

The authority in his tone put a spark of green fire in Faye's eyes. 'Show your concern then, Mr Kavanagh, by making things easier for me and telling me where to find my stepmother.'

'I said last night I'd come to talk to you about this. I'd planned to call on you later.'

'Well, please do not for I shall not receive you!'

'Why not?'

'Because I do not want to!' Faye answered, feeling frustrated by his calm. She wished she could find some of that composure he had mastered, but her insides felt as though a nest of vipers writhed in the pit of her stomach. For two pins she would slap him. But she dared not. She knew what happened when she touched him…even in anger. 'You may think you can bend me to your will, sir, but you will find you are mistaken.'

'You have a way with words, Faye, that greatly disturbs my equilibrium.' He smiled at the hand he'd splayed on the wall. 'Rephrase your complaint about me so I can concentrate on something else and make amends for whatever it is I've done wrong. I want to help you.'

'No, you don't. Your only concern is feeding your conceit and quenching your lust. You should go back to London; your two doxies will appreciate your attention more than I.'

'I doubt that,' he said quietly, slanting her a glance. 'If my memory serves…'

Faye felt the blush start in her cheeks, then spread to burn her throat. Oh, she knew what he meant by that! Just as he intended she should. Neither of them had forgotten her arms tightly imprisoning him or her animalistic mewls of delight as he lavished her body with kisses and caresses. But he'd not denied the existence of his pair of pampered mistresses who were capable of greater self-control than she.

'I have done you no harm,' Faye murmured, gazing through a tiny bullion window at distorted figures in the courtyard. 'When you first arrived in Wilverton I spoke up for you...asked others to give you the benefit of the doubt rather than believing gossip and condemning too soon. And in return you would destroy me.'

'I would destroy a fantasy you have in your head about Collins. But I'd never harm you...you know me better than that.'

'I don't know you at all.' Faye's fierce emerald eyes veered to him. 'You're a stranger; I don't even know how to address you. Major Kavanagh... Viscount Kavanagh... Gypsy Kavanagh...who are you really?'

'All of them,' he answered without hesitation.

'How can you be?' she said, desperately wanting an explanation.

'By an accident of birth.'

'The Lees are your kin?' Faye knew that they'd have little time to talk privately in such a public place and from his concise answers it seemed he was also aware of eavesdroppers.

'The Lees are cousins.'

'And Ruby...how is she related to you?'

'Oh...there you are, Ryan. I thought you had abandoned me.' A woman appeared behind him. 'Are you not hungry, my dear? The food looks most appetising.'

Faye watched with thundering heart as a brunette slipped her arm through his. Moments ago she had flung at him that he should go back to London to be fawned over by his mistresses; it seemed he had no need to for one had joined him. And she was very beautiful.

'Oh…I see you have company.' The lady cocked her head to get a clear view of Faye. 'Are you not going to introduce us, Ryan?'

'We are barely acquainted,' Faye blurted, jerking her weak legs into action. 'Mr Kavanagh might not recall my name.' She felt dreadfully frustrated that their conversation had been curtailed at such a crucial point. 'I am Miss Shawcross.' She held out her hand to give the lady's expensively gloved fingers a brief shake. 'Please excuse me; I must dash off now.' She'd taken a few paces away before she remembered her manners. 'Good day to you both…' she sent quietly over a shoulder.

Chapter Fourteen

'Mr Kavanagh still wants to speak to you. He said he'll wait outside rather than come in, if you prefer.'

'I shan't receive him, Mrs Gideon. I have a headache. He can leave a message with you, if he wishes.'

Mrs Gideon blew a sigh. 'Don't reckon he believes you've got a headache any more than I do. He's the look of a man sticking to his guns because he knows he'll get what he wants in the end.'

'Indeed…that sums him up,' Faye muttered acerbically. 'But today he's to be disappointed and, actually, I do have a headache,' she added, rubbing her throbbing brow.

Mrs Gideon sat down opposite Faye at the table, enclosing her mistress's white fingers in her chapped hands. 'You've had nobody to talk to about those things that confuse young women, have you, you poor lamb?'

'I had my papa's counsel till I was twenty-one,' Faye pointed out with a wan smile.

'It's not the same as having your mother to guide you. I could see that governess of yours wouldn't instruct you in anything that didn't have a fraction or a verb attached to it.'

'What are you trying to say, Mrs Gideon?' Faye gently withdrew her hands from Nelly's.

'I know I was wrong about the Irish fellow. He's been a boon to you. From the start you saw the good in him. But now something's changed and I shan't pry into what it is. I don't suppose he's perfect; none of us are, but he's done things for you and your family that no other man has since your papa died.'

'He has a motive, I assure you; you were right to warn me of that. Don't think him a saint.' Faye felt her cheeks growing warm. She stood up and went to the kitchen window, peeking out from behind the curtain. He was leaning on the front gate, gazing out over the fields as though he didn't have a care in the world.

Yet her heart was breaking. She'd fallen in love with him. She wanted him, not her fiancé, and that was why she must avoid seeing him again. She'd been in love with Peter when still a child; she was now a woman and she loved Ryan Kavanagh. But for him it was different. He'd spoken of wanting her, but lust wasn't love and wouldn't last. She yearned to be with him, but she wouldn't loiter in shadows waiting for the crumbs of his time and affection to be tossed her way.

He'd asked if she feared being lonely in the future… she would be if she agreed to his terms: sharing his bed and perhaps bearing his bastards until his eye landed on somebody else. Peter might not be rich and charismatic, but he was steadfast. And she would never reward his loyalty by choosing a philanderer over him.

'A motive, has he?' Mrs Gideon gave a wise nod. 'Perhaps you ought to let him know that you've one, too, concerning a ring and a vicar.' She stood up and comfortingly rubbed Faye's shoulder. 'You're not the first woman to outgrow her childhood sweetheart.'

Faye turned away from the window and started to clear away the teacups into the tin bowl. Mrs Gideon's comfort mirrored the hopes she had. But she knew they'd never come to fruition. Kavanagh would only give material comforts and sensual pleasure. And when she dwelled on the blissful way he made her feel, the ignominy of being a kept woman almost seemed worth bearing.

Offering you anything you desire and my protection is an insult? he'd mocked when she'd asked if he was apologising to her for treating her like a harlot. What more could a country spinster of straitened circumstances expect, he might have added had courtesy not held him back.

'We could make him a cup of tea, at least,' Mrs Gideon said. 'I doubt it'll satisfy him, but at least we'll have been hospitable.'

'Yes, we should be hospitable,' Faye said wryly. 'And as for satisfying him... Mr Kavanagh is probably not too bothered about that; he tells me he is well served elsewhere.' Faye felt slightly uneasy talking so to her housekeeper, yet it was nice to have a confidant. Mrs Gideon had been her closest, and most trustworthy, female companion for the last twenty years.

'I know he's not a saint; it must be hard for such a good looker not to be tempted when women throw themselves at him. Go and speak to him.'

Faye nibbled her lower lip, feeling swayed to follow the housekeeper's instruction.

'If he tries any funny business, I'll put a shovel over his head myself as Bertram's out.'

'You would, too, wouldn't you?' Faye said with a soft chuckle.

'I'll try to keep Miss Claire out of your way if she comes in from the garden.' Mrs Gideon wrinkled her nose. 'Your sister's brewing up rose petals for scent. It smells poisonous.'

With a deep intake of breath, Faye tucked a few loose tendrils of fair hair into their pins, then opened the door and stepped outside. If he'd heard her, he didn't turn about until she was almost within arm's reach.

'I take it asking you to come for a ride is out of the question.' He sent a crooked smile skywards before looking at her.

'My acceptance certainly would be.' Faye kept her eyes on the horizon rather than on him. Whenever they were close she was always struck anew by how handsome he was. Even that first sighting of him in Wilverton had stirred something in her that was too strong to be forgotten. She had thought about him every day since. She became aware of her hands quivering and clasped them together behind her back. 'You wanted to speak to me, Mr Kavanagh?' Her voice was firm and clear.

'Where to start...' he drawled.

'Perhaps you might like to explain why you have tempted me with knowing where Deborah Shawcross is in Ireland, but have refused to disclose more.'

'You wouldn't want to know more. And travelling to Ireland simply to take your sister to her would be a waste of time. You'd not leave a dog in that place.'

After a shocked silence Faye whispered, 'What do you mean by that, sir?' But she was intelligent enough to have already concluded that what he meant was that Deborah had fallen into the gutter.

'She's living in a brothel,' he confirmed quietly. On hearing Faye's spontaneous gasp he drew her closer, discreetly comforting her with a caress. 'I'm sorry to have to tell you such news.'

'Are you *sure* it is her?' Faye gazed up into his dark features. 'Could it be a case of mistaken identity?'

'I wish it were. But as soon as I knew you were interested in finding her I sent investigators to seek her whereabouts. I recalled an English woman living under the protection of a decent fellow. He was a judge…not of advanced years, but he became ill. He died a year or so ago now.' Ryan shrugged. 'His wife and family were provided for, but your stepmother was not. It is a common enough tale for a woman of middle years and poor connections. I believe she had nobody else in Ireland to call on.'

'My father had passed on as well by then. If she did seek to contact him through his lawyer it would have been too late for him to help, even had he felt so inclined.' Faye inwardly shuddered, imagining her glamorous stepmother reduced to such squalor. But Kavanagh had called such a fall from grace *a common enough tale*; indeed it was and one that she too might have known at some time in the future had she accepted his proposition. How did any mistress fare if she had no independent means and her provider succumbed to an accident or illness and left no lasting provision for her?

She at least had some of her father's bequest left, but it would not see her through many decades. There was no need to fret about it, she impressed on herself. She was marrying a decent man and in time her infatuation with Ryan Kavanagh would fade. Her affection for Peter might reignite into the exciting passion she'd felt for him when he'd kissed her for the first time. If they could spend more time together, things might be different, she thought wistfully. But Peter seemed to enjoy his work so it was unlikely he'd retire when they married, or even, God willing, when he became a father.

It was a great blow that her sister couldn't go to Ireland to allow gossip to die down. Instead, they would have to batten down the hatches and pray that the tale of Claire Shawcross and a gypsy boy stayed in Hertfordshire. Then in the spring her sister *must* find a suitable husband in London.

Ryan had allowed her to digest the distressing news about her stepmother without interruption before saying gently, 'There is a solution that might suit, if you still want your sister to go away for a while.'

'I can't send her to my relative in London before the spring, if that is what you are about to say, sir.' She paused. 'Mrs Banks isn't well off and she wouldn't want to cope with Claire for that amount of time.' She gave a tiny half-smile. 'Neither would my sister agree to being cooped up with her widowed aunt; she is a lovely lady but she rarely goes out. Claire would be bored stiff.'

'I wasn't thinking of London. Ruby is going to Dublin to stay with family and she would like your sister to go with her. She wants them to be friends.' Ryan smiled. 'I imagine Donagh will be in for some fierce criticism from the two of them, but that apart there will be plenty of other things for them to do…outings and so on that young ladies seem to enjoy.'

'I…I don't know what to say, Mr Kavanagh…' Faye felt a surge of optimism, but knew she couldn't make a snap decision on something of such importance.

'Are you trying to find a polite way of saying that

you're not sure you trust me enough to put yourself, let alone your sister, into my hands?'

'Given what I know of you that's hardly surprising, is it?' Faye returned crisply.

'I thought you knew nothing of me. I'm a stranger, you said.'

'And so you are!' Faye was aware of his amusement at having had a chance to remind her of that. She glanced to the right; a neighbour along the lane had just thrown open a window and was craning her neck to get a better look at them.

'Shall we go inside and finish this?' Ryan suggested.

Faye hesitated despite the sense in what he'd said.

'I meant Mulberry House…not its barn…' he muttered drily and, gripping her wrist, he strode to the kitchen door, making Faye skip to keep up with him.

'Mr Kavanagh would like some tea, Mrs Gideon,' Faye burst out breathlessly as he shut the door behind them.

'Then some tea he shall have.' Mrs Gideon began filling the kettle. 'Why not sit in the parlour and I'll bring it along.' She added darkly, 'You should know, sir, that my husband will be back from town very soon.'

If Ryan deemed a fellow with a limp, approaching sixty-five years of age, of no significant threat to a man half his age, who'd dragged himself from battlefields with a burning gun and a bloodied sword, he graciously didn't show it.

'I have taken note of it, ma'am,' he said in his soft Irish burr.

'Hmmm…' Mrs Gideon said, turning away so he couldn't see her subduing a smile.

'You shouldn't joke with her like that.' Faye uttered the first thing that entered her head as he closed the door.

He leaned back against it, regarding her steadily. 'I wasn't joking. I swear I'm on my best behaviour. Have you told her about us?'

'There is no…us,' Faye said quickly. 'She knows… that…' She found she could go no further.

'What does she know?'

'Mrs Gideon knows that trouble is brewing because of many things,' Faye said shortly. 'And she will be horrified to hear the Shawcrosses have suffered more bad news. I will not pretend that in the end Deborah was liked by any of us, but neither would we have wished on her such dreadful luck.' Faye felt desperately sad for her father's sake. Mr Shawcross had grown cold towards the woman who'd abandoned him, but he would not have wanted to see the mother of his two youngest children suffer such degradation. She wondered if he would have helped her, had he been alive to do so. Faye hoped that he would have shown pity. Instead of the woeful tale increasing Faye's dislike for her stepmother she felt more charitable towards her. Deborah had married Cecil Shawcross, but her love for him had withered…as sometimes was the case between a man and a woman, as she now knew herself. Deborah had had the courage to risk all and follow the man she loved…and she had paid the price. Faye wondered if her stepmother thought the sacrifice had been worth it.

'Please sit down if you will.' Faye perched on the edge of the armchair opposite the seat she indicated he should take.

'We were speaking of your sister travelling to Ireland

as Ruby's companion.' Ryan sat back, clasping his hands between his knees.

'It is good of you to make the offer but I hadn't yet agreed to the proposal,' Faye pointed out with a steady emerald stare.

'I think you will if you let me tell you more about it.' A ghost of a smile moved his mouth as he considered introducing a prickly subject into the conversation. 'Why haven't you asked me who I was with at the White Hart?'

'Why haven't you told me?' Faye shot back. She flicked a hand. 'It is none of my concern who you spend time with.'

'So you don't want to know who she was.'

'No...I do not...' Faye immediately gained her feet. 'Mrs Gideon is a long time making tea.' He had got up as she did and was now gazing into the garden with his hands planted against the casement frame. 'Who were you with?' Faye demanded, unable to maintain insouciance.

'My sister,' he answered, still staring into sunlight.

'Your sister?' Faye echoed tartly. 'How odd that you entertained her at a tavern rather than at your beautiful home.'

'You like the manor?' He turned from the window to look at her.

Faye hadn't been expecting that. 'Of course...who would not like such a wonderful house?'

'Had you been inside before I took it on?'

Faye shook her head. 'My parents were invited to dine on a few occasions when I was a child. But then old Squire Benford died and his heir used it very rarely. Mostly it was empty but for servants. We didn't even know it had been sold until you turned up.'

'Do you wish I hadn't turned up, Faye?'

'No…the house deserves a new lease of life.'

A rueful smile met her evasiveness.

The door opened and Mrs Gideon backed in ,carrying the tea tray. She poured while sneaking glances at the couple, then exited the room with a polite bob.

'So let us return to the matter of my sister,' Ryan said immediately the door had closed. 'Valerie was at the White Hart because one of her horses went lame close to the end of her journey; she was waiting while the blacksmith shod him. She is now at the manor and will be staying about a week before escorting Ruby to Dublin. Claire can go, too, if she wants. She will be perfectly safe in my sister's care. Valerie has children of her own and has a very comfortable house.'

'I greatly appreciate your offer to help us, sir,' Faye said. 'But I cannot agree or decline without first mulling things over. And I should speak to Claire, of course. She is of an age and character to be troublesome if sent away against her will. I would not inflict more of her temper on you than you have already borne.'

A sympathetic smile twitched Ryan's lips; he knew very well what it was to deal with a petulant young lady.

'We didn't get a chance to talk properly at the inn,' he said, crossing his arms over his chest and looking unusually diffident. 'There's a great deal I need to tell you…about myself and about Ruby. I hope that when I do explain you'll understand why I've not said anything before.' He was watching her face closely for her reaction.

'What can be so bad that it needs to be kept a secret?' Faye made a small gesture. 'I know you have gypsy kin and one of them is Ruby Adair. It seems odd that an aristocrat might be so related, but it is not dreadfully shocking to me, if that puts your mind at ease.'

He dipped his head in gracious thanks and said, 'It does. I hope you take the rest of what I have to say so sweetly.' He seemed about to carry on, but suddenly looked over her shoulder. 'Valerie would like to meet you and your family. Will you come over later and dine with us?'

'Are we invited out to the manor?' Claire had slipped in through the French doors and was beaming at the idea of an outing to the big house. 'I should like to see Ruby again. Do let's go.' She turned a plaintive look on Faye.

'Very well…thank you, Mr Kavanagh.' Faye kept her frustration hidden that their conversation had been interrupted. She was sure she'd been on the point of learning more about him. 'Our brother has gone on holiday to Scotland, so it will be just the two of us.'

'I'll send a carriage for you at seven.' Ryan dipped his head, ready to depart.

'I didn't say sorry for the trouble I caused you, did I, Mr Kavanagh?' Claire rattled off. She'd rather get her apologies out of the way privately than do it later in Ruby's hearing. 'I shouldn't have acted so daft and I'm very sorry that I did.'

Ryan held out a hand for her to shake. 'Ruby tells me she feels the same way about misbehaving for Donagh Lee's sake. She'd like to be friends; I think you two young ladies should get along in future.'

Claire gave a shy smile on hearing that.

'Will you accompany me to the gate, Miss Shawcross?'

'Yes…of course… Come out this way, Mr Kavanagh, through the garden.' Faye opened the French doors. 'It is very pleasant in the sun.' Faye wanted to avoid running the gauntlet of Mrs Gideon's knowing looks.

They stopped by the gate and gazed at one another in a way that Faye realised held a new and profound intensity. The pull of desire between them still simmered, but a quiet understanding seemed to have cemented the base of a friendship during their short meeting.

'When you come over later we must finish our talk in private,' Ryan said softly. 'The more I think about it, the more I wish I'd opened up to you sooner.' He rubbed a hand about the nape of his neck. 'But…you seemed withdrawn at times as though you didn't want me to get too close to you…in body or mind.' He raised a hand as though he would touch her, but instead stepped away from her. 'We must also talk about my recent trip to London…and your fiancé.'

'If I've seemed distant it is because you have been unwilling to reveal much about yourself,' Faye said in a quiet intense voice. She glanced about, exasperated that they were out in the open and couldn't continue to talk for long. She wasn't sure she had the patience to wait until later to resume this heart to heart. 'I admit to being confused about your relationship to Ruby and if I have seemed suspicious or guarded at times that is why.'

'But there are things about you that confuse me,' Ryan said smoothly. 'I'm not the only one wary of revealing more about a close relationship. You have just avoided speaking of a certain person, haven't you?'

'What do you mean?' Faye asked indignantly.

'Your fiancé. I don't understand why Peter Collins has your trust. You're not a fool, are you?'

Faye glanced sharply at him. But there was no malice in his eyes, just a look of concern and, yes, a glint of jealousy. 'I do not avoid speaking of him.' She knew that wasn't completely true and felt a guilty flush spreading on her cheeks, so hastened on, 'We are betrothed...of course I trust Peter.' She scanned his dark features and bit her lip. 'Do you really think he was up to no good in London when you saw him there?'

Ryan plunged his hands into his pockets. 'I don't know...' he said honestly. 'I have no proof, but I could easily find out.' He trailed a finger along the curve of her sharp little jaw, quickly and discreetly. 'I've no wish for us to quarrel and I can see that we might if I say more on the subject.'

A twinge of uneasiness tightened her stomach. 'If you have something specific on your mind, I'd sooner hear it, sir.'

'I believed I was coming close to hearing you call me Ryan and now we are back to "sir" because of that confounded fiancé of yours.'

'I'd sooner you didn't speak of my future husband in that tone,' Faye retorted; indeed, harmony between them was dispersing now that Peter Collins had been introduced into the conversation.

'We'll talk about it later.' Ryan sounded equally firm as he swung into the saddle of his stallion. Soon he was galloping away, leaving Faye feeling exasperated yet staring longingly after him.

Chapter Fifteen

Following Ryan's departure that afternoon Faye had immediately brought up the subject of Claire going to Ireland as Ruby's guest. Her sister's reaction to the offer had been to jig excitedly. It had taken Faye's best efforts to persuade Claire that it wasn't necessary to start packing straight away. The matter had yet to be confirmed with Mr Kavanagh, she'd explained. But Faye had been glad to see Claire in a light-hearted mood after the recent upsets. Her sister had then spent hours sorting through her clothes for a pretty outfit to wear to dine at the manor. It was good to see that Claire was still in high spirits, but the glass of sweet wine she'd been allowed with her dinner seemed to have gone to her head, making her a little too gregarious.

'Are you feeling rather outnumbered by us ladies, Mr Kavanagh?' Claire had asked cheekily, just moments ago.

'My brother likes being surrounded by pretty females,' Valerie Mornington teased him. 'Don't you, Ryan?'

Their host smiled, but said nothing, turning over the

music on the piano at which Ruby was seated and playing 'Greensleeves' with a modest accomplishment.

'Do play something else,' Claire urged as Ruby's fingers stilled on the keys. 'You sing remarkably well, too.'

'Do you think so?' Ruby beamed. 'My music teacher
judged my voice shrill.'

'My governess thought I ought to concentrate on
painting as I was tone deaf and couldn't sing or play.'
Claire giggled. 'But she praised my dancing. Other than
that Miss Bates gave up on me the day I turned fifteen,
didn't she, Faye?'

'Dancing gracefully and painting well are worthy
achievements,' Faye said wryly.

Claire had always preferred to read Gothic novels to
set texts and though she could easily calculate how much
of her allowance would remain after she'd purchased
ribbons and combs, applying herself to her sums for her
governess was another matter. From a young age Claire
had spoken dreamily of romantic love, even though her
own parents had provided little experience of a blissful
wedded state. Faye had believed Claire would get her
heart's content: a marriage to a fine gentleman who'd
idolise his vivacious bride and take good care of her and
their children.

But now things had changed; Claire might have to
lower her expectations and rely on reserves of inner
strength she'd not yet built. No matter how gay they
were this evening, and how much assistance Ryan Kavanagh provided them with, they couldn't fool themselves
that there would be no calamity resulting from Claire's
risky dalliance with a gypsy boy.

'I love to dance.' Ruby trotted over to her new friend

so they could clasp hands and whirl about together on the carpet.

Faye sipped her wine, watching the lively scene, wondering how she could have ever imagined such an ingénue as Ruby Adair was Ryan Kavanagh's mistress. Had the idea of it not been introduced by others, she inwardly argued, it wouldn't have crossed her mind to think so. She took a peep at him as he closed the music book and seated himself on the stool that Ruby had vacated. He began picking out a slow melody with the long supple fingers of one hand. She imagined his mistresses to be charming sophisticates who were well versed in pleasing him, be it by singing or dancing or lovemaking...skills in which she lacked experience. She wondered now... whereas before she never had...if Peter liked the way she responded to him. He'd always wanted more physical passion from her than was possible to give with the children around—even had she felt comfortable with such intimacy. It hadn't occurred to her before that he might be disappointed with her as a lover, but now the question hovered in her mind.

And she knew why that was; the things that Ryan had done to her, that she'd adored and craved to have again, were what all men wanted to do with women they desired. Peter was to be her husband, yet she only wanted Ryan Kavanagh touching her body in that exquisitely special way...so how *could* she respond in the way Peter wanted?

'Have you lived long in the area, Miss Shawcross?'

Ryan's sister broke into Faye's torrid reflections with a polite enquiry.

'I have been in Wilverton all of my life.' Faye hoped her cheeks were not too flushed as she turned, smiling, to Valerie beside her on the sofa. 'I was born in the house where I now live.'

'My brother tells me that your parents have passed on.'

'My mother died a very long while ago, my father more recently. I miss them both,' Faye said simply.

Valerie gave an empathetic sigh. 'Our parents went early, too. Ryan was just twenty-two when he took his birthright. He is a viscount, you know.'

'I had heard as much,' Faye replied quietly, glancing from beneath her lashes at his chiselled profile.

On arrival at Valeside Manor she had been made to feel very welcome by their hostess. They had exchanged pleasantries at the dining table, but this was the first chance they'd had for a proper conversation. Faye believed she could come to like Ryan's sister, given an opportunity to get to know her better. Valerie had thankfully made no mention of their meeting at the White Hart. Faye regretted having jumped to conclusions about Ryan being with a mistress at the inn. She'd never felt jealous wondering what Peter might be up to when not with her. She'd always trusted him and was sure she still did, despite Ryan Kavanagh's heavy hints that perhaps she should not.

'It is an Irish title, passed down originally from his grandfather,' Valerie resumed talking about her paternal ancestry. 'Our papa would be sad that his son isn't more proud of the peerage he inherited. If anything, Ryan favours our maternal relations.'

As her brother closed the lid of the piano and stood up Valerie indicated with a shrug that she couldn't continue with their private talk in his hearing.

Faye watched him absently drumming his long fin-

gers on the piano's polished top. She knew that he was
as aware of her as she was of him and had been all evening, although they had kept a seemly distance from one
another and their eyes had only fleetingly grappled. But
a moment had been all that was required for her to notice the heat in his eyes as they devoured her face and
figure. She had worn the best gown she possessed for
her outing to the manor. Though purchased some years
ago its classic empire style and fine turquoise silk still
suited her as well now as it had then. She had dressed
her hair elegantly, with Mrs Gideon's help, and the loose
blonde ringlets swept on her bare shoulders like strok-
ing fingertips. On the last occasion that they had dined
together her fiancé had caressed her nape…but it was
never his touch she sensed branding her flesh.

'So, I understand you are engaged to be married, Miss
Shawcross.'

'Oh…indeed…I am. My fiancé is overseas at present,'
Faye replied, shaking herself again from a sensual stupor.

'He serves in the navy, Ryan tells me. Have you set
the date for your wedding?'

'When Peter returns we will attend to it…perhaps
next spring might suit,' Faye rattled off. 'Is Mr Mornington at home in Ireland?' She turned the focus of attention on to her hostess.

'My husband has taken the children to visit his elder
brother in Waterford.' Valerie sighed. 'My daughter is
quite a madam and not yet twelve. She swore she would
not go to her uncle's and be bored stiff, but I imagine her
father persuaded her to do as she was told. He wouldn't
have left her at home with the servants…I hope.'

The ladies watched the two young women cavorting
on the rug and their wry smiles spoke for them.

'Your brother is remarkably tolerant of his boisterous ward,' Faye said.

'His ward? Oh, indeed, he adores Ruby.' Valerie seemed a trifle flustered and reluctant to say more on the subject. 'The girls seem to have taken a shine to one another, don't they?' she burst out. 'Perhaps I ought to tinkle a sedate tune; it might make them dance a little more prettily.' Valerie got up to seat herself at the piano.

Ryan had an opportunity to talk to her now the coast was clear, but he remained propped on a fist against the marble mantelpiece. From the moment they had arrived he had been the perfect host, Faye realised, ensuring that they had every comfort.

Dinner had been a wonderful meal the like of which the Shawcross family never tasted any more. When her papa had been alive they might have dined well at Christmas and Easter, but other than that they had eaten modestly. Faye had counted eight courses in all and the manor's cook had done a fine job, as had the maids who'd served at the table, removing and replacing luxurious crystal and flatware with more wafer-thin china and glass. If anybody believed that Ryan Kavanagh was an ill-bred rogue, they were mistaken. She imagined that he was impressing on her that, gypsy kin or no, he knew how to behave as a viscount…but whether he chose always to do so, was his own concern.

'Would you like to stroll in the gardens before the light goes, Miss Shawcross?' Ryan had approached the sofa and extended a hand.

'Yes…thank you…' Faye said after a pause that caused his mouth to tug up at a corner. She allowed him to assist her to her feet.

'I'll find some cards; perhaps the girls might like to

play once they've done with wearing out your carpet, Ryan.' Valerie closed the piano lid and got to her feet to rummage in a bureau drawer.

Faye realised the woman was diplomatically letting them know she'd keep the young ladies out of the way while they had a private talk outside.

The gardens were wonderfully laid out with walks terminating in jasmine-scented arbours and flagged terraces bordered by statuary. As they passed by a rose garden delicate blooms nodded in the mild breeze, perfuming balmy evening air. Ryan threaded Faye's hand through the crook of his arm and steered them in the direction of a fountain. The spray reached quite a height before falling in diamond-like droplets to run off into a narrow pond flashing with golden fish.

'You obviously have a very good team of gardeners,' Faye said to break the ice. The frostiness she'd sensed when they'd parted yesterday hadn't completely thawed.

'I brought some of the staff from Dublin with me.'

'Your cook, too? Dinner was delicious; Mrs Gideon would have approved and she is not one easily pleased.' Faye slipped her hand free of his arm and turned to face him as they came to a halt with fountain mist cooling their skin.

'My mother's cousin cooks for me.'

'Oh…I see…'

'She's a Romany.'

'I'm sure that Mrs Gideon would be impressed by her skill.' Faye knew he was watching for her reaction to his abrupt declaration about his gypsy connection through the distaff side. His sister had just told her that favoured those people over their aristocratic relations.

Faye wondered how Valerie got on with her exotic cousins and how her husband did, too.

'We need to clear the air before your sister travels to Ireland next week.'

'I hadn't yet confirmed that she would,' Faye said with a hint of a smile. 'But I expect you can guess from her demeanour that she is very happy to accept your kind offer…and so am I.'

The girls were probably even now whispering about what they would do to amuse themselves in Dublin. But the reason for her sister going away at all was not amusing…not one bit…and Faye knew she couldn't forget that and neither should Claire.

'That's one hurdle out of the way,' Ryan said drily. 'Now for the rest.'

'I don't want you to feel under duress to tell me about your gypsy relations.'

'None of it is a secret.'

'What *is* a secret then, sir?' Faye asked bluntly. 'Ruby describes you as her guardian, not her relation. Is she aware of it?'

'Yes…she knows,' Ryan replied, gazing into the distance.

'Have you banned her from mentioning your relationship?' Faye asked curiously.

'No, but she believes the tie to be very tenuous. It is not. We are as close as kin can be.'

'She is your sister?' Faye ventured. She was aware that she might seem inquisitive, but she was determined to have some relief from puzzles that bedevilled her. Her eyes rose to cling to his intense blue gaze, but as the silence lengthened it seemed he might yet avoid answering her.

'She is my daughter.'

For a full minute Faye digested that stupefying information. Finally she untied her tongue to utter stiffly, 'You are married, sir?'

'No. I've never taken a wife, but I've had a child with a woman.'

'I see…' Faye said faintly and again felt too taken aback to immediately comment further. 'Where is Ruby's mother now?' she eventually blurted. 'She describes herself as an orphan.'

'Shona Adair passed away. It is a long and involved story—' He broke off to drag some fingers through his ebony hair. 'And possibly this is not the time to discuss it.'

'When would be?' Faye returned acerbically.

'*Touché…*' he murmured with equal sour inflection to his voice. 'You're right, of course. When would be a good time to tell you that I didn't know I had fathered a daughter until the child was twelve years old? Or that I believed I had fallen in love and wanted to marry a girl who was deemed unsuitable by my father's family, and some of my mother's side as well…' He grunted a laugh. 'Perhaps now you can understand why I have been reticent in bringing my past to your notice.' He shook his head. 'It is not something I'm proud of and burdening a woman…somebody special like you…with the sordid details of my lechery and lack of judgement…'

'Viscount Kavanagh! You are needed, my lord, at the house.'

Ryan and Faye swung about to see a manservant bearing down on them looking flustered. The fellow was sprinting in short bursts, then slowing to a walk, attempting to retain some dignity and restrain his flapping coat tails.

Ryan strode to meet him and they commenced talking in low urgent tones.

Worried though she was about what might have occurred, Faye cursed in a rather unladylike way that they had again been interrupted. She had heard extraordinary news and she knew that she would have got a fuller explanation...albeit a shocking one...had they been left alone for a short while longer.

Ryan approached Faye, grim faced. 'It seems that Donagh Lee has turned up and is threatening violence if he's not allowed to see your sister.'

That dreadful news drove every other thought from Faye's head. She rushed forward, but Ryan caught her arms, holding her back from headlong flight to the house.

'Hush...calm yourself, Faye. I will deal with him.'

'I feared this would happen!' she cried in a suffocated voice. 'The scandal will not go away and will follow her everywhere...even to London next year.'

'It will not if we manage the situation correctly.' Ryan brushed a finger along her flushed cheek to soothe her. 'I will get rid of Donagh, but then I think it would be best if Valerie accompanies the girls to Ireland without further delay. Donagh might return. The more fuss he makes the more likely it will be that his behaviour starts people prying.'

Faye nodded vigorously. 'You are right; she must be taken away from here immediately. The threat to her future is enormous.'

'And what of your future? Your fiancé doesn't know about any of this, does he?'

Faye winced and shook her head, then started

wards the house. She knew what he meant by asking that pointed question. And he was right in thinking that if Peter found out about what had gone on he would be rightly furious.

Chapter Sixteen

Two footmen had linked arms to bar Donagh from entering the house, but as the youth noticed Ryan he pelted down the steps to confront him.

'I'm not frightened of you. You might be Ruby's guardian, but you're not Claire's.' He pointed a threatening finger. 'If she'll still have me, then I will marry her. And good riddance to you and to my father. I'm not going to let him treat me like a boy. I'm a man and can manage without him telling me what to do.' Donagh pulled some money from a pocket and threw it on the ground. 'There…you've not paid me off even if my father took your pieces of silver.'

'I think you're short by quite some amount.' Ryan cast a jaundiced eye on the coins on the gravel.

Donagh turned red. 'I'll get every penny of it to you, don't worry.'

'I'm not worried. The deal was done and that was the end of it.' Ryan sounded cool and very calm.

'Not as far as I'm concerned.' Donagh turned a hungry look on the house. 'My father doesn't speak for me. I still want her.'

Faye groaned beneath her breath on seeing her sister and Ruby watching the spectacle from the drawing-room window.

'It *is* finished.' Faye hurried up to join forces with Ryan. '*I* am Claire's guardian and I would not consent to her marrying you.' She felt sorry for the youth; Claire should not have encouraged him in the first place, giving him false hope of being his wife. 'I'm sorry for all the upset,' Faye added quietly. 'But you must accept that it is all over now.'

'Pick up your money,' Ryan said quite kindly. 'Get back to your father before he finds out what you've done.' He knew that Bill Lee would never have sanctioned his son breaking the gypsy code. They were hard, but just, people and once money changed hands that was it. Donagh would be punished if his disobedience were known.

A faint shout reached them and Faye pivoted about to see Mr Gideon flicking the reins over Daisy's back as he rattled along at speed on the cart.

'I came to warn you Miss Shawcross that the gypsy's been over bothering us at the house. I didn't say where you'd gone to. But looks like he's found you anyway.'

'It's all right, Mr Gideon,' Faye soothed the old fellow, rushing to meet him. He was florid in the face from exertion and alarm.

'You be off, you villain, or I'll set the law on you.' Gideon shook a fist at Donagh as he sullenly collected his strewn coins.

'Mr Kavanagh has everything under control now, Mr Gideon.' Faye patted her manservant's arm, then turned to Ryan. 'Thank you for a fine dinner,' she said quickly. 'But I think it would be as well if we left now. Mr Gideon can take us back on the cart and my sister can begin to pack her things for the trip to Ireland.'

Ryan nodded. 'I'll escort Donagh off my property and give you a chance to go without harassment. If you could make sure that your sister is ready to travel from here at eight o'clock in the morning, we will be able to make an early start.' He started to move away, then turned back. 'I shall go with them as far as the port just in case Donagh takes it into his head to follow and make a nuisance of himself again. But I will be back as quickly as I can… there is a lot still to tell you.'

Faye's green eyes raised soulfully to meet his fierce blue stare. Indeed, there was a lot left unsaid. But if he had been on the point of telling her that he'd cherished the mother of his child…a woman who had since passed on taking his heart with her…she wasn't sure that she wanted to hear it. And she would do well to concentrate on the man who did love her and who had proved it by asking her to be his wife.

As though sensing her turmoil and the reason for it, Ryan discreetly touched her arm in comfort. 'I swear I'll be back as soon as I'm able,' he promised huskily. 'I want to tell you everything.'

Faye watched Ryan propel Donagh, looking downcast, towards the stables with a controlling hand on his shoulder. When they were out of sight she sped up the steps and into the house.

'I don't mind admitting that it's a relief to see the back of your sister for a while.' Mrs Gideon shook her head. 'We've not had such an upset in the family since that terrible business with your stepmother.' Abruptly Mrs Gideon put down the potato she'd been peeling and craned her neck to see out of the kitchen window. 'Oh, dear…you've got company, miss, and I'm thinking you could probably do without a visit from the Hollys right now.'

Faye had been humming to herself, checking jars and boxes in the larder to make a list of what needed replenishing. With both her siblings now absent she had guessed the grocery order could be reduced this time. She missed their company, but there was no denying that Claire and Michael had hearty appetites that cost a pretty penny to satisfy.

Placing the bag of flour back on the shelf, she wiped her hands on her pinafore. It was early in the day to have visitors so she imagined that something of moment had brought the vicar and his wife to Mulberry House before noon. She prayed that Donagh hadn't been into Wilverton causing trouble by spouting about his infatuation with Claire…or perhaps Peggy had stirred the pot again.

'I'll receive them.' On hearing the vicar's trap creaking to a halt, Faye untied her apron. 'If bad news has brought them, I'd sooner have it than fret about what it might be.'

In the sitting room she paced restlessly, allowing Mrs Gideon to attend the door, and her thoughts turned once more to how Claire was faring on her way to the port. She guessed that the party might already be approaching the halfway point of their journey; Mr Kavanagh was not a fellow likely to dawdle and he had impressed on her his desire to return as quickly as he could. And heaven only knew she wanted him back so she could have answers to the questions that constantly circled her mind.

Faye had sent three pounds with her sister, instructing her to offer up payment for board and lodging taken at inns. Other than that she had doubted Kavanagh would accept a penny for her sister's keep in Ireland and she hadn't wanted to insult him by offering it as he had refused any contribution to Bill Lee's ransom.

As for Donagh causing a commotion at the manor because of her, Claire had looked shamefaced for a while, but Faye was disappointed that her sister hadn't seemed to care more about the hurt she'd caused the youth.

As the Hollys entered the parlour Faye snapped her mind to the present. She approached Anne with outstretched hands. 'How nice to see you.'

'It's a dreadful hour to pay a call, I know,' Anne started by way of apology. 'But Derek has to attend a burial later and I so wanted him to drive me over to speak to you as soon as may be.'

'Has something happened?' Faye asked lightly, although her stomach had tilted in anxiety. 'Is something amiss in town?'

'No…well, not if you mean Wilverton,' Anne replied. 'I had a letter from Derek's sister and she related something perplexing that I must tell you.'

'Well you've whetted my interest.' Faye smiled and indicated that the couple should make themselves comfortable. The Hollys hadn't come with news of Donagh Lee, but with some Mayfair gossip. And she felt quite inclined to relax and have a chat with her friends.

'Might we have a pot of tea, please, Mrs Gideon?'

'I'll bring it,' Mrs Gideon said but, unlike her mistress, her frown hadn't lifted on hearing what had brought the Hollys to Mulberry House.

Neither did the vicar look completely at ease. 'I'm not sure that this is any of our business, my dear,' he started diplomatically. 'I expect that if there is anything to it Mr Collins will bring up the matter himself.'

'Of course we must speak up!' his wife contradicted with an imperious flick of some fingers. 'I told you on the way here that if Faye were in my position I would expect *her* to be a good friend and tell *me*. *I* am a good friend, and even if the rumours prove false, I'm sure any betrothed woman so affected would rather know than not...'

'It would be best if you just spit it out, Anne,' Faye interjected. She'd gleaned few facts from her friend's garbled conversation other than that her relief was to be short-lived.

Anne leant forward on the sofa and blurted, 'A rumour is circulating in London of an imminent jilting where you and Peter are concerned.' She blinked rapidly. 'My sister-in-law wrote and told me as soon as it reached her ears because she knows that we are good friends.' Anne flapped a hand. 'I don't believe it, of course.'

'A *jilting*?' Faye had not been expecting that and alarm set her heart racing. 'Mr Kavanagh has been an attentive neighbour and Claire and I have dined at the manor, but it is very bad of anybody to say I intend to jilt Peter.'

Mrs Gideon brought the tea and as soon as she'd quit the parlour Faye turned her attention to pouring out, conscious of the Hollys' quiet whispers behind her back. She was assaulted by feelings of guilt and anger at those faceless busybodies in town. She wouldn't shun a loyal, steadfast man simply for a love affair...would she? And how had people guessed that she might and then spread the idea that haunted her mind?

Anne gave a cough to draw Faye's attention. 'Ah...

but it is the other way around.' She shot a frown at her husband. 'Mr Collins has been spotted at Vauxhall and also taking a drive in Hyde Park with a Miss Pettifer.' She sniffed. 'I'm sure it is nothing, but I thought you would want to have it from me, my dear, rather than from spiteful people.'

'Of course I would…thank you.' Faye felt shocked to learn that her fiancé had been seen dancing attendance on another woman. But how could he have been? If for some reason he had not yet sailed for Malta, he would surely have informed her of his change of plans. Perhaps he, too, sensed their love had cooled, but from courtesy he would inform her if he remained in England, wouldn't he? But…this was the second time that she'd had word of her fiancé being seen in London. 'Perhaps Peter has a double. I have heard of people looking very much alike yet being no kin whatsoever.' Faye distributed teacups with an unsteady hand.

Another significant look passed between husband and wife. This time the Reverend spoke. 'Mr Collins *was* in London, my dear, just last week. I saw him myself when I was attending a meeting at St Paul's Cathedral.' He added kindly, 'But he was on his own.'

'We wondered if you had decided to detain him in England to assist you through a sticky patch.' Anne gained her feet and gave Faye a comforting hug. 'I know you are quite able to look out for yourself, but you have had a dreadful run of bad luck…what with Westwood mishandling your money and your carriage accident, too…then there was Michael's suspected scarlatina and not forgetting that minx Peggy Miller's lies.' Anne regarded her friend proudly. 'Any other woman would have buckled under the strain of coping with it all.'

'I have not asked Peter for assistance. But if he is still in England…in London…it will be nice to see him soon.' She sat down, feeling uncharitable for hoping that the couple would soon leave. But she desperately wanted to be on her own to unscramble her thoughts.

'Have you heard from Michael?' Anne asked affably.

'I had a letter from him this morning. He is enjoying himself in Scotland.'

'Is Claire not going to join us?' Anne asked, sipping tea.

'Claire has also gone to stay with a friend for a short while.' Faye wasn't going to elaborate or heaven only knew fuller explanations would be needed and she'd enough on her mind as it was. She drained her tea with rather unladylike haste, then rose to deposit the cup and saucer on the tray.

'A good idea, to get your sister away from the bad influence of that Miller girl.' Anne nodded, looking quite settled.

The vicar could take a hint even if his wife couldn't. He stood up. 'It is time we left now, my dear. I have some matters to finalise for the interment this afternoon. I promised the widow I would pop by before the funeral party set out for the church.'

'I hope the service goes well,' Faye said as the Hollys passed into the hallway.

After Faye had closed the door on her visitors she returned to the sitting room and sank to the sofa, staring into space. The shock had diminished and she realised she didn't feel as upset as she should have on learning that her fiancé might break off their engagement. Her pride had taken a knock, but what was making her feel restless and frustrated was the uncertainty of it all. It was unbearable not knowing and there was only one thing to do: go to London herself and speak to Peter. And she knew she must act at once or she would talk herself out of it…or Mrs Gideon would.

There would be no better time to do as she pleased now Claire and Michael were safely out of the way. Faye jumped to her feet and went quickly upstairs to find her carpet bag. She was sure her aunt would accommodate her for the few days necessary to sort things out, if she sent word ahead of her arrival. And then…and then…

Faye stopped her frantic searching in her clothes press and sat down abruptly on the dressing-table stool. She stared at her reflection and though her green eyes looked huge and apprehensive, she smiled. And then…she would decide her future without relying on anybody else's help or advice.

Peter had strived to separate her from her brother and sister so he could have her completely to himself and had, it seemed, grown tired of the tussle; Ryan Kavanagh had warned her that at some time she would be abandoned by those she'd sacrificed her youth to protect. From her sister's recent selfish behaviour she knew that Claire *would* move on, possibly without a backward glance. In a few years' time Michael would begin to lay the foundation for his future career. And she must also act if she were to avoid a lonely old age.

Suddenly Faye felt more alive than she had in a long while. She had tried to convince herself that all might come right with Peter, but perhaps he also needed more than a love that had grown stale. Miss Pettifer might have provided the fun and laughter that had dwindled between them. Although she'd no idea how she would react to Peter's answer when she caught up with him, she *would* ask about Miss Pettifer. All she had to do first was get past Mrs Gideon and get a ride on her husband's cart to catch the mail coach at the White Hart...

She'd not been in town for quite a few years, but the city hadn't changed, Faye thought. The noise and smells were still unpleasantly overpowering and the blend of humanity astonishingly diverse. Ragged urchins darted to and fro, brushing against the silken skirts of fine ladies. Dandies, swinging silver-topped canes, rubbed their shoulders against labourers' coarse jackets as they strutted through the crowds. A coal cart loaded with oily sacks and sooty-faced men jostled for space on the thoroughfare with the mail coach in which Faye sat. On the other side of the vehicle creaked a crested coach and the portly gentleman within stared down his beaky nose at her, tapping his jowls with his snuffbox as he did so. Faye settled back against the lumpy squabs, this time catching the eye of the passenger seated opposite.

The elderly woman sniffed and turned away, doubtless disapproving of her travelling unaccompanied. Faye was glad to see that they were pulling in at the Bull and Mouth Inn where she could alight and escape the stifling atmosphere in which she'd been confined for hours.

As soon as she was set down and her luggage beside her, Faye dashed out of the inn courtyard to the road to find a hackney to take her to her aunt's home in Marylebone.

It seemed that everybody else had the same idea and she was bumped out of the way by a statuesque lady's maid securing for her mistress the passing hackney. Faye scowled at the smirking servant, then returned to her carpet bag, realising it might be best to allow the other travellers to disperse before seeking a ride. She was unsure of the welcome she'd receive after giving her aunt such short notice of being an uninvited guest. The day was warm and a light breeze cooled her perspiring brow. She sat down on a low brick wall, removing her bonnet, then began dabbing her moist skin with a hanky. The linen became still and she pulled it away from obscuring her vision to stare across the road. Having clearly recognised somebody, she jumped up.

Mr Westwood was on the opposite pavement and was aimlessly strolling to and fro as though waiting for somebody.

Faye had grasped her skirts in her hands and set off quickly to cross the road to speak to him, thinking he might have Peter's whereabouts…but she hesitated at the kerb without knowing why she did so.

Soon she was glad that she had stopped herself weaving between vehicles to reach his side. Another man had hove into view and on his arm was a young woman sporting a flashy feathered hat.

Shocked, Faye stumbled back a pace and instinctively shielded her presence in a doorway. Then a grim twist shaped her mouth. Well, she thought, if that is Miss Pettifer I doubt he has any intention of marrying her…

Faye put up her chin. There was only one way to find out about Peter's intentions towards either herself or that floozy and that was to go and ask him. And she would do it! She started forward, but it seemed she had dithered too long.

The trio began climbing aboard a battered phaeton, the feathers in the woman's bonnet nodding as she jiggled for space on the seat. Faye darted looks about, then spontaneously sprang in front of an approaching hackney to halt it. 'I'll pay you a good amount to follow that coach,' she burst out. 'Would you assist me with my luggage? Quickly, please…' she urged, keeping one eye on the vehicle bearing away her fiancé and his friends. And, yes, she knew now that Westwood was Peter's friend as well as his lawyer. And by the look of her, she guessed that the woman with them was a demi-rep.

'You nigh on give me an 'eart attack jumping out on me like that,' the jarvey grumbled, thumping at his chest, but he sprang from his perch and loaded her bag on to his vehicle.

'That one there!' Faye breathlessly said, pointing to the high flyer hemmed in by traffic.

'I've seen it right enough, miss,' the jarvey muttered beneath his breath and urged the nag to catch up with it.

Faye poked her head through the window to keep the phaeton in sight and then the jam of vehicles dispersed and the chase was on. Peter had the reins and the contraption he was driving bounced to and fro as though he was showing off his skill. But no sooner had the jarvey whipped the nag into action, leaving Faye swinging giddily from side to side within his cab, than he was slowing down.

'What is it? Have you lost him?' Faye called.

'He's stopped,' the jarvey answered disappointedly. He'd been enjoying the game and also had expected double the fare he was due. But he was an honest cove and knew he couldn't charge much for such a short journey.

Faye scrambled from the cab, shielding herself with the open door while peering at the phaeton some yards away. Peter had handed over the reins to his friend and dismounted. Westwood and the woman then set off up the road and Peter entered a seedy-looking building.

'Take my luggage on to this place, please.' Faye handed the jarvey a slip of paper on which she'd written her aunt's address. She tipped some coins into the fellow's palm and he brightened on seeing the generous amount, nodding agreement. 'And if you would, sir, please convey a message to Mrs Agatha Banks that I shall be following on shortly.'

The driver tugged on the brim of his hat and moments later he'd set off, leaving Faye standing on the cobbles in an insalubrious area. She avoided the curious eyes of some people hurrying past, keeping the brim of her bonnet low over her eyes. Then she jerked up her chin, bolstering her courage to follow Peter inside the dismal place into which he'd disappeared.

Chapter Seventeen

Faye peered into the open doorway of the lodging house, then took a few hesitant steps within. She glanced about at an uncarpeted staircase and walls with flaking distemper, wrinkling her nose. The place reeked of decay and boiled cabbage.

'What can I do for you then, my dear?'

A skinny little woman had noiselessly come up behind Faye.

'Oh…good day… I am seeking somebody. I believe he is staying here.'

'Well, let me know his name and I'll tell you if he is,' the woman smirked. 'I'm Mrs Gant, the landlady, and I know all of my clients, I assure you. I'm thinking that a genteel young lady such as yourself might have come to the wrong place, though.'

'I'm looking for Mr Peter Collins and I know he's here because I saw him come inside.' Faye's voice was firm and clear.

Sally Gant had been running a lodging house for more than twenty years and in that time had grown used to young gentlemen hiding from the duns or from their irate fathers in her warren of rooms. This young lady looked too wholesome to allow herself to be got into trouble, unlike those other females she'd spotted with Collins. But Sally was aware that both loves and lightskirts figured in some gentlemen's lives.

'And who might you be?' Mrs Gant asked, straightening her mobcap in a businesslike fashion. Whatever she privately thought about Mr Collins's character, she wasn't about to upset a paying customer; he was always on time with his rent.

'I am Miss Shawcross and Mr Collins is my fiancé.'

'Is he now?' the woman said with an ironic inflection.

But no further toing and froing was necessary. There was a sound of boots clattering down the bare stairs and a moment later the man himself unsuspectingly hove into view.

Faye had to choke back a spontaneous giggle at the look of sheer horror and astonishment on Peter's face. He went white, he went red, then he swallowed noisily and blustered, 'What in God's name are *you* doing here?'

'I've come to see you, Peter,' Faye replied flatly. She suddenly realised that it was immaterial whether or not he wanted to jilt her as there was no longer a foregone conclusion that she would marry him. Even without the spectre of Ryan Kavanagh occupying the back of her mind, she knew her trust in Peter had vanished. And without that fundamental element she couldn't be his wife. She could see guilt burning brightly on his face, although she was not completely sure what was causing it. But she *would* know before she travelled back to Hertfordshire, he owed her that much. And she, too, had difficult explanations to make, she reminded herself. 'Aren't you pleased to see your fiancée?' Faye asked quietly.

Mrs Gant batted a sly glance between the couple. 'Well, sir, I'll be off so you can have a nice talk with your intended.' She scurried off, wondering if she had an opportunity to keep her lips sealed on the fellow's shenanigans for a price.

'Of course I'm pleased to see you, my dear.' Finally Peter composed himself. 'I'm surprised...in a nice way, but also confused that you have made an unnecessary trip.'

'How do you know that it is unnecessary, Peter? I haven't yet told you why I'm here.'

He took her arm, propelling her out of the dingy hallway and into the sunshine. 'You look in fine fettle and I am, too...so what problem is so great that you needed to come? Who have you travelled with?' He glanced about as though to locate her companion.

'I came on my own to see you and I have been perfectly safe, never fear.'

'Well, I'd rather you hadn't done so,' he replied curtly. Then his attitude seemed to soften. 'Let me take a look at you.' He tilted up her chin, smiling down at her. 'You look as lovely as ever,' he purred. 'How have you managed to escape the scamps then for a sojourn to town? It's very unlike you to leave that sleepy place you like so much. Has something of note happened in Wilverton?'

'There is a lot for us to talk about, that's for sure,' Faye replied, thinking his voice, though smooth, had retained an undercurrent of annoyance that he couldn't quite control. His eyes were narrowing as he considered her ambiguous comment, so she spoke before he could question her further. 'What have *you* been up to, Peter, since we parted in Wilverton? I believed you had sailed for Malta and had heard nothing from you to the contrary. I sent a letter to Portsmouth for you—'

'There was a delay in my application for the admiralty position,' he fluently interrupted. 'While I wait for it to be dealt with I am kicking my heels here in town and hoping soon to receive encouraging tidings. You had much on your mind when I left, Faye. Your brother was ailing, as I recall. I would have been in touch as soon as I had good news, but didn't want to burden you with my woes.'

'I see...' Faye said, although she didn't really see at all. A man less bedevilled by woes to the one she'd watched cavorting with Westwood and the flashy-looking woman was hard to imagine. And though Peter had recalled her brother's illness he hadn't asked how Michael fared.

'How did you know where to find me?' Peter threaded her arm through his and started to promenade along the street.

'The Reverend Holly spotted you in town. I thought it odd so...'

'So you came to check up on me, did you?' Peter interrupted coldly.

'I am not spying on you; had I been I wouldn't have made my presence known so quickly, would I?' Faye sounded equally short. 'I only arrived on the mail coach a short while ago.' She glanced at his profile, a little of the entrenched feelings she had for him tweaking at her heartstrings. Their lives had been entwined for such a long time that it seemed wrong to give up on trust and affection and hopes for the future.

'London is a big place, yet you knew where I was... how odd...' It sounded a throwaway remark as though he were careless of an explanation.

'Oh, finding you so quickly was sheer luck. I noticed you entering this building when I was travelling in a hackney cab. I hopped off and let the driver carry on with my bag to my aunt's house. I am staying there for a few days before going home.' Faye held back on mentioning that she'd seen him with his friends. If the lawyer's name cropped up then her investments must, too, for she couldn't delay again in telling him about that. She wished she had spoken of it long ago, then her fiancé would not have been so chummy with Westwood; yet she'd like a more private place than a busy street to speak about something so serious.

'I'm sorry if I sounded ungrateful after you've put yourself out to visit me.' Peter gave her a winning smile. 'Tell me all that's happened in Wilverton.'

'Well, I had a carriage accident…but as you can see I'm fine now,' she quickly reassured him, hearing his hiss of concern. 'It was my own fault for being careless. As for the children, Michael is fully recovered and staying with a friend in Scotland and Claire has gone to Ireland.'

'So you managed to find their confounded mother at last, did you?' Peter gave her cheek a rewarding tickle. 'Very well done, my dear,' he praised. 'It is high time that she did her duty and let us finally be married. Have you been languishing at home, all alone, thinking about me? You wanted your fiancé's company, did you?' He suddenly stopped walking and swung her to face him, nuzzling words against her cheek. 'I am glad you did. I've missed you, too.'

'Mr and Mrs Gideon are always around. I'm not lacking company.' Faye took a pace back, feeling uncomfortable with his display of affection in broad daylight. She found herself wondering if he'd acted vulgar because he'd confused her with the hussy in the feathered hat.

As they strolled on she inwardly argued with herself. She owed her fiancé a fair hearing. She'd seen nothing to convince her that Peter was having an affair. Westwood had seemed equally friendly with their female companion and appearances could be deceiving. It might be that she lacked refinement rather than virtue. Faye knew she was not without fault herself; perhaps Peter *had* succumbed to a flirtation…but so had she fallen prey to another's charms. Whether she'd wanted to or not she'd responded to Kavanagh…how she had responded! A surge of blood warmed her throat at the memory of the passion they'd shared.

'Oh, there is no point in waiting for the right time to bring this up,' she burst out, coming to an abrupt halt. 'There is a rumour going around that you might jilt me for a Miss Pettifer. I doubt it is true as you have just spoken of us being married, but in any case you should be aware that we are being tattled over.'

Again a startled look hardened his features and he loosened his cravat with a fidgeting finger.

'You know Miss Pettifer, don't you?' Faye sighed, slipping her hand from his arm.

'Indeed I do know her, but it is utter nonsense to say there is anything between us. If I find out who has spread the dirt I'll have their hides!' Peter's lips had flattened against his teeth. 'She is simply a cousin of a friend of mine. I've shown her no more than courtesy when we've met.'

Faye digested that and came to a conclusion. 'Is she Mr Westwood's cousin?'

Peter's eyes narrowed on her. 'She is... How did you know that?'

'Have you seen her very recently?'

'I have not!' Peter returned forcefully. 'I haven't seen her since we all took a drive in the park earlier in the week.' He frowned. 'Are you jealous, or is it that you don't trust me?'

'I'm not sure what I'm feeling at the moment, other than confused and tired.' Faye gave a mournful chuckle. 'I think I must get to my aunt's or she will worry that some mishap has befallen me.'

'I will accompany you to Mrs Banks, my dear.' Peter patted her hand solicitously.

'You were on your way out somewhere when I ambushed you. I don't want to delay you longer in going about your business.' Faye knew she'd sooner be alone... and after such a time apart from her fiancé she knew that was a worrying sign.

'And a most pleasant interruption it has been. I won't hear of you travelling by yourself! We should spend as much precious time together as we can. I will soon scotch these stupid rumours going about by announcing the date of our wedding in *The Times*. I think early next month might be suitable, don't you?' He clicked his fingers at a passing hackney. 'Come, we can discuss wedding plans on the way to Mrs Banks's house and break the happy news to her when we arrive.'

'I would rather we kept the matter to ourselves for a while longer.'

'If you wish.' He gave her an indulgent smile. 'I expect you'll want to browse the warehouses for wedding finery to take home with you.'

'A shopping trip with Aunt Agatha would be nice,'

Faye said neutrally. She allowed him to help her aboard. As he climbed in to sit beside her, the scent of violets drifted to her, making her turn away to breathe the fresh air blowing in through the window. Miss Pettifer's perfume smelled as cheap as she looked.

Chapter Eighteen

A beam of yellow light infiltrated the curtains, striping warmth on to Faye's cheek, bringing her awake with a start. For a heart-stopping moment she blinked at the ceiling, confused as to where she was. Then memories flooded back and she rubbed a hand over her heavy eyes, pushing herself up on her elbows.

Despite the problems cramming her head she had slept soundly in her bed in Marylebone. In fact, so sweet had her sleep been that she was tempted to sink down beneath the eiderdown and close her eyes to try to recapture the blissful state of unconsciousness.

But how would that help? she chided herself. Hiding from worries was never the way to rid oneself of them. With a sigh she swung a pair of shapely calves off the edge of the mattress and pattered to the window to gaze upon a new day. Pulling back the curtains, she watched the London street coming to life; it was quite different from the sort of morning scene that would have greeted her in her home village. People were going about their business early, much as they did in Wilverton, but here the hubbub was created by smart carriages and liveried servants, rather than by farm vehicles and peasants in smocks.

A tap on the door made Faye drop the brocade into place and turn around.

'I thought I heard you up and about in here, my dear; it is good to see you looking refreshed. I have to say I was quite worried about you yesterday.' Aunt Agatha backed into the room, carrying a tray. 'I thought you might like some tea. And breakfast is ready, if you are.' She placed the crockery on the nightstand, then turned to assess her niece. 'You seemed very tired when you turned up. I dare say the journey took it out of you... amongst other things.' Agatha was still garbed in her dressing gown with her grey hair in curling pins. She poured the tea, then perched on the mattress as though settling in for a chat.

Faye had had no need to worry about her uninvited visit being badly received: Agatha had been delighted to have her stay despite the short notice and her lack of staff. Her aunt had explained that her maid only came in a few times a week now to help with laundry and cleaning so had personally prepared them a supper of cold meats and pickles accompanied by cheese and a freshly baked loaf. Faye hadn't eaten much all day, nevertheless she'd had scant appetite to reward her aunt's efforts. She realised that the woman was making necessary economies. Her husband had been an army officer, killed in action in his prime, and his widow had survived for over a decade on his pension. Faye admired her aunt for being practical and resourceful. She wouldn't baulk either at getting her hands dirty when the need arose. And, following her experience with Westwood, one never knew when it might.

With a husband by her side, of course, things should be easier. Peter had spoken of an imminent marriage, but Faye knew she'd lost faith in him. After she'd bidden her aunt goodnight and gone up to her chamber, she'd spent a long time staring at the moonlit street scene, mulling things over. But concentrating on whether to try to salvage her relationship with Peter had been impossible with memories of Ryan constantly infiltrating her mind.

'I'll understand if you don't want to say why you've come quite suddenly to town.' Agatha had been watching her niece's porcelain brow being pleated by some inner conflict. 'But I can hazard a guess at the reason,' she added helpfully.

Faye took a sip of tea. 'You've heard the rumours about my fiancé's roving eye?'

'Oh, yes,' Agatha declared. 'I didn't want to bring the subject up yesterday. I thought it best to let you have your rest first; as he dropped you off outside I imagined you might be feeling cross with him. I'm glad you didn't invite him in, though. I would have given the fellow a piece of my mind.'

Faye placed down her cup, feeling let down. 'If you *knew*, why did you not write and tell me? I heard about Miss Pettifer from a friend in Wilverton.'

'Why create a mountain out of a molehill and upset you into the bargain? I'm not sure he is guilty of more than an unwise flirtation with the chit. Why…if every betrothed fellow who cast his eyes on other women was jilted by his fiancée, there would be no weddings.'

'I caught a glimpse of her at a distance…she looks rather flashy,' Faye said, matter of fact.

'Indeed she is! She can't hold a candle to your classic beauty, of course, however young she may be.'

'She is *very* young?' Faye asked wryly. The feathers in Miss Pettifer's hat had prevented Faye getting a good look at her face yesterday. She knew that at twenty-five years old, with a lengthy betrothal behind her, people would assume that her fiancé had grown bored with her.

'I imagine she is about nineteen.' Agatha dismissed Miss Pettifer with an idle hand flick. 'If you are still of a mind to marry him, perhaps it might be sensible to finally set the date, my dear. It has been a long wait for you both.' Agatha held a similar opinion of Mr Collins to that of her late brother—she'd never really taken to the man her niece had set her heart on. But now Faye had invested so much of her youth in him it seemed silly not to go ahead.

'Peter told me yesterday he wants us to be married quite soon.'

'Well, there you are then!' Agatha beamed. 'Piffle! is my answer to those chinwaggers who've the sauce to say he's mooning after somebody else.' Agatha got up. 'I'll set the table for breakfast. Come down as soon as you're ready. Then perhaps we ought to sally forth and give the gossips something to really tattle over: we'll browse the warehouses for some white silk suitable for a wedding gown,' she gleefully declared.

Faye had travelled light and had just one change of clothes with her. She gave the light cotton dress a vigorous shaking as she drew it out of the trunk. Then she turned her attention to the jug and pitcher. She was used to washing in unheated water so it was no ordeal to splash her face, then towel her cold complexion to a pink glow. In fact, it was a fillip that jerked her mind into action. Once clothed she sat down at the dressing table, frowning into her own eyes. Yesterday she had deliberately cut short her meeting with Peter, needing time to think. She'd been on the point of accusing him of lying when saying that he'd not been in Miss Pettifer's company. Faye had sensed that she must tread carefully. Now she was glad she *had* held her tongue and slept on it. Most gentlemen would baulk at admitting they'd been in the company of a woman who looked as vulgar as Miss Pettifer. But if she were the cousin of a friend, how could he excuse himself without appearing rude?

Yet something still niggled at Faye, making her believe that there was more to it. Peter had accused her of spying on him and she realised that the only way to discover what *was* going on might be to do just that…

'Oh, dear! You have missed her, Mr Collins. But do come in for a moment.' Agatha permitted the stern-faced fellow into the hallway…but no further.

'Missed her?' Peter enquired. 'Your niece is not here, Mrs Banks?'

'I'm afraid not, sir. She went out earlier to visit a friend.' Agatha felt rather puzzled and a little hurt that her offer to accompany Faye had been rebuffed…politely, of course. But she wasn't going to let this man know that and continued blithely smiling. It was better he believed that his fiancée had plenty to do and no inclination to sit at home moping over him if he chose to pay attention to silly girls.

'And whereabouts is this friend in London?' Peter asked rather curtly.

'My niece didn't say,' Agatha replied truthfully. 'I believe the woman is a relation of the Reverend Holly.'

'I see…'

'I'll tell her you called, Mr Collins, when she returns.'

Agatha opened the door, shutting it behind him as soon as he'd passed over the threshold.

Peter strode to his phaeton, unaware that he was being observed, though he did give the sleek curricle and prime horseflesh a covetous glower. The driver had disembarked and had headed off somewhere; only the liveried tiger occupied the vehicle. Cursing beneath his breath at having been unable to speak to Faye, he clambered aboard his ride and used the whip on the horse.

Ryan stepped out from beneath the branches of a lime tree. He'd arrived in the street just as Collins was knocking on Agatha's door so had loitered in the shade, waiting for him to leave before approaching the house himself. The speed of the fellow's visit indicated that either Faye had refused to see him or she wasn't at home with her aunt. A rueful smile tilted his lips. Knowing her as he did, her courage wouldn't have allowed her to shy away from a difficult meeting, even if she had now found out she was betrothed to a duplicitous character. So, he concluded that she was out somewhere. He watched as the tired old nag pulling the battered phaeton was whipped to a faster speed. He despised Peter Collins just for that—mistreating any animal was a sin in his eyes.

Springing aboard the curricle, he took the reins and turned the equipage to follow Collins in the direction of Cheapside.

As he joined the queue of vehicles he watched his quarry's back, loathing Peter Collins with every fibre of his being. He had no right to have won the heart of a woman like Faye Shawcross.

And neither had he any right to want her the way he did, Ryan thought. She deserved better than both of them.

But he did want her...he did love her...and pretending that a liaison would satisfy him, knowing that he craved so much more, was no use. At first he'd wanted to protect his pride, propositioning her rather than proposing. She'd seemed unshakably loyal to the man she'd agreed to marry and, admirable as that was, Ryan had felt frustrated…and hurt…by her inability, or unwillingness, to see beneath Collins's facade to the cheat beneath. But just lately she'd not championed her fiancé so forcefully and he'd seen something in her eyes…a spark of doubt that had given him hope that her feelings for Collins might be wavering. He'd seen something in her eyes when she looked at him, too, that went beyond that mix of wariness and longing that could set fire to his loins in a way that made it hard for him to keep his hands off her. Once or twice she'd looked at him in a way that warmed his heart, too, with a glimmer of trust and tenderness that persuaded him all was not lost. He had reason to hope that she might not feel disgust when he revealed the truth about himself…that she might understand what had driven him to act with abominable selfishness when he'd been the same age as Donagh Lee.

'Oh, so it's you come back again, Miss Shawcross.'

'Good day, Mrs Gant. Would you take me to my fiancé's lodging, please?'

'I'm afraid he isn't here, my dear. I saw him leave some while ago.'

'He might have returned though as I believe he was expecting me.' Faye felt awkward uttering the fib. But her need to get to the bottom of things overrode her conscience. She'd come with a list of questions to fire at her fiancé. 'I'd be obliged if we might check upstairs to see whether he passed by unbeknown to you.'

Mrs Gant raised her eyebrows. 'If such behaviour does not offend your sensibilities, Miss Shawcross, I'll escort you to his room so you might satisfy yourself that I know what I'm about.' She gave an indignant sniff, then set off up the rickety treads at some speed.

Faye followed closely behind, averting her face as a gentleman squeezed past them, raising his hat and giving her a lecherous look. On the second landing Mrs Gant came to a halt and pointed along a dank corridor.

'Third door on the left. I'll wait here while you see if your fiancé has slipped by me.' With pursed lips, she folded her arms over her chest.

Despite her cheeks smarting in embarrassment, Faye gave Mrs Gant a nod. The landlady now suspected they weren't really betrothed, but were conducting an illicit liaison.

After a couple of bangs on the door that brought no response from within, Faye turned to glance back the way she'd come. Mrs Gant had poked her tongue into a cheek and was giving her an I-told-you-so smirk.

Faye retraced her steps, slowly, although nervous excitement was pumping blood through her veins at an alarming rate at what she intended to do. 'I know Mr Collins would be delighted to return and find me waiting for him, Mrs Gant. Might I ask you to open up, please? And say nothing if you see him…or it will ruin the surprise.'

'I understand, Miss Shawcross…oh, yes, I do understand.' The landlady gave a ribald chuckle. She held out a palm and when it was not immediately crossed with coins she jerked her head at it.

Realisation dawned and Faye pulled some cash from a pocket.

Mrs Gant's fingers snapped shut on the bribe and she

swept past, using one of the keys jangling at her waist to unlock the door. Without a backward glance she then took herself off.

Faye quickly entered and closed the door behind her with her heart trembling in her ribs. There was an unsavoury atmosphere within the room. The air smelled of stale smoke and strong drink. The sight that met her eyes was equally unpleasant. Wedged beneath the window was an unmade bed with candle stumps adorning the floorboards at its base, as were stained tankards and wine glasses. Various items of clothing had been discarded on to the bedcovers and the frayed armchair was home to a pile of newspapers and documents.

Faye felt disappointment ripple through her as she viewed the mess. She knew Peter was only a temporary resident at this lodging house, yet he had always seemed disciplined and his personal standards high. This was not the living quarters of such a person.

She approached the bed, quashing an urge to straighten the covers and fold his clothes. She was not his servant or his wife.

She perched gingerly on the edge of the hard mattress and looked about at discarded shaving equipment and a comb lying on the washstand. She had wanted to gain entry to try to find some clues as to why Peter was still in London; she sensed it was not all to do with his promotion and there was something underhand in it. Now she had got into the lion's den she felt uncomfortable. It was completely foreign behaviour for her to use deception and sneak about. If she was prepared to act so, it could be claimed that she was no better than he was. She sighed, about to leave when her eye landed on the document on the top of the pile on the chair. She went quite still. The red ribbon tied about it had a distinctive ink stain at the very end that she recognised.

Faye jumped to her feet and snatched it up, unfolding it. She had been right to snoop for clues! It was the investment that Mr Westwood had told her he'd had to sell at a loss because the fund was performing badly. Her fingers became insensate with shock and the parchment dropped back to land on top of the others.

'What in damnation do you think you're doing here?'

Faye jerked about, emitting a tiny startled scream. She'd been staring in disbelief at her bond certificate and the thud of blood in her ears had prevented her hearing Peter's arrival.

'Oh…I came to see you,' Faye rattled off breathlessly, forcing a smile to her lips.

'So I see, my dear,' Peter drawled. 'Oddly, I went out to visit you at your aunt's. Had I not, I would have been here to receive you.' He strode closer. 'Mrs Banks told me you were to be found at a friend's, not rifling through my personal belongings.' He scooped up the papers and flung them all on to the washstand.

'*Your* personal belongings?' Faye suddenly felt her temper rising and with it her suspicion that she had been duped. Not only by Westwood, but by the man who had professed to love her. Boldly she picked up the parchment and thrust it towards him. 'I believe that to be mine. Why have you got it in your possession, Peter?'

'Are you accusing me of something?' He turned his back on her and took out his snuff box, using a pinch.

'I believe I am,' Faye said clearly. 'I'm accusing you of being reticent and evasive at the very least. One of the reasons I came to London was to tell you that Westwood had lost half of my money in bad investments. But I get the feeling that I had no need to do so. You already knew of it, didn't you?' Faye tilted up her chin. 'Please explain why you have this bond in your possession. Westwood told me it had been sold at such a loss as to be valueless. Did *you* buy it? How much did you pay?'

'I'll not beg your pardon for some maggot you have in your head about my affair with his cousin.'

'Miss Pettifer is only part of the problem as far as I can see. And I'm not asking for an apology. I want you to explain what you and Westwood have been up to. If I'm wrong in thinking that something bad has gone on behind my back, then *I* will apologise.'

'Do you think I will forgive and forget that my future wife has made it abundantly clear she does not trust me… that in fact she believes me a fraudster?'

'I didn't say that, Peter,' Faye quietly replied, going cold. 'But I know you have a better understanding of the facts than I.' She pivoted away from him and, on heading for the door, realised she'd never before felt nervous in his company…but she did now.

Peter blocked her path in a single stride. 'Where do you think you are off to?'

'I'm going home to Wilverton. It makes no difference whether or not you have a fancy for Miss Pettifer, I'm not going to marry you.' She took the sapphire ring from her finger and put it on the washstand before again attempting to pass him.

Deliberately, and strongly he pushed her back.

'Oh, you *are* going to marry me, my dear,' he drawled through lips flat against his teeth. 'If you think I have waited all these long years for you to walk away now, you are a fool.'

Faye felt prickles of real fear ice her complexion, but

she met his narrowed eyes with a fierce gaze and a bold question. 'Have you waited for me…or my inheritance?'

'Both,' he growled. 'And I *will* have both…' He lunged at her, his mouth swooping down to kiss her with savage demand. 'I've longed to do this,' he whispered against her bruised lips, his fingers plucking at her buttons. 'But I denied myself and treated you with the respect your station deserved. Now, if my desire has wandered to others, it is your own fault for making me endure such a blasted long engagement. A man has needs that must be satisfied.' He thrust his lips against the warm silk of her throat, restraining her fists battering against his chest. 'If it hadn't been for those brats we would have married years ago and no subterfuge would have been necessary. It wouldn't have come to this. Can't you see what you've done…what you've made *me* do?'

Faye was becoming exhausted from attempting to free herself. He was stronger than she was and her hands were firmly pinioned to her sides. With all her might she stamped her small booted foot down on his instep. He howled and his grip loosened, allowing her to wrench free and dash for the door. He was in front of her before she could open it. 'What on earth has got into you?' She spread her trembling hands in appeal. 'Have you no decency at all, Peter? You should calm down and try to regain your senses,' she panted. 'Let me by or I will scream and create a scene. Your landlady will call the Runners, wondering what is going on.'

'You can yell your head off if you want…she won't come,' Peter scoffed. 'If that crone let you in here, then she thinks you're a doxy and the more noise you make the better fun she'll think we're having. You're thoroughly compromised already, my dear.' He laughed harshly. 'And when I've done with you you'll beg me to marry you.'

'What do you mean?' Faye burst out, fists clenched at her sides. Her fear was dissipating beneath her fury. She wouldn't be threatened by any man, especially not the one she'd, for so long, trusted cared for her.

'What I mean, my sweet, is that I'm ready to consummate our nuptials, right now, even though it is a little premature.' He smiled lasciviously. 'I think beneath that dutiful exterior of yours might beat the heart of a fiery wanton...and all it needs is to be released from the constraint of duty and etiquette. You liked me kissing and touching you, didn't you?' He shrugged off his tailcoat, flinging it to the floor. 'Cissy Pettifer will make a fine mistress, but she hasn't the class to be a gentleman's wife. You on the other hand could admirably fulfil both roles once properly schooled to do so. In fact, now you say you no longer want me, I find you quite irresistible.' Peter possessively stroked her cheek.

Angrily, Faye slapped away his fingers. 'I doubt you have told your mistress that she has no class, have you?' she challenged tartly. 'Yes, I've guessed there is more to it than you admit. You have become besotted with Miss Pettifer but, alas, she has no dowry...that is the truth, isn't it?'

'She's not got a bean...but she has some qualities to make up for it,' he growled coarsely, manhandling Faye backwards to the narrow unkempt bed. He pushed her on to the mattress and followed her down, stopping her shout by slamming his mouth on hers.

Faye squirmed towards the edge of the bed, her hand flailing over the side. As it came into contact with a tankard she grabbed the pewter handle and instinctively swung it up at his head. He howled and rolled off her, allowing Faye to scramble to her feet. She sped to the door, blindly pulling it open. Within seconds she'd raced the length of the wonky corridor and hurtled down the stairs. She rushed past an open-mouthed Mrs Gant and straight out into glaring sunlight.

Two large hands were suddenly fastened on her shoulders, gripping tightly, and with a cry of alarm she raised the weapon she'd kept hold of. This time her arm was arrested at the top of its trajectory and the tankard held aloft.

'It's all right…hush…' an accented voice soothed. 'Faye…calm yourself…what in God's name were you doing in there? Has that villain hurt you?' But Ryan could stab a guess at what had happened if Collins had returned to find her waiting for him with awkward questions. He removed the tankard from her rigid fingers and cast it to the gutter, drawing her comfortingly closer. 'Oh, sweetheart, why have you risked meeting him like that?' He sounded anguished. 'Do you know him for the villain he is now?'

Unable to speak, Faye simply nodded her head vigorously against his shoulder.

'You must go home to your aunt's, out of harm's way,' Ryan said urgently. 'I'll deal with Peter Collins.' The savagery in his tone was at odds with the gentle finger that stroked a loose blonde tendril back from her face. Spotting a passing cab, he hailed it, inwardly castigating himself for not having followed Collins inside the lodging house instead of waiting outside for him to reappear.

'I should have listened to you…you tried to warn me about him,' Faye burst out. She tilted her face up to his. 'You said you wanted to destroy a fantasy I had in my head about him; it's true I didn't know him…not really. How could I have been so stupid for so long?' She clenched her fingers tightly, her nails digging into her palms.

Ryan raised her quivering knuckles to his lips. 'We'll speak of it later,' he said, opening the cab door. 'I promise I will sort this out, then come directly to you.'

Still Faye stood where she was, her breathing and her distress coming under control. Suddenly she felt empty and very sad that her betrothal to Peter had finished in such an abrupt and dreadful way. 'You were right about me. I *am* a fool!'

'No… I'm the fool for not saying more when I had the chance. It might not have come to this had I told you sooner of my feelings. My damnable pride's to blame… not anything you've done.' He placed a finger on her lips as she would have questioned him. 'You're trusting and loyal, and those qualities aren't faults, Faye.' Ryan's head drooped forward as he asked a question, dreading to have the answer to it. 'Did he attempt to force himself on you? Is that why you hit him?' he croaked.

Faye gave a nod, gazing up into a pair of intense blue eyes. She could see that he was appalled at what she might have suffered and she wanted to throw her arms about his neck in comfort.

A maelstrom of unpleasant emotions had fractured her mind from the moment that Mrs Gant had let her in to Peter's room; her senses could have been numbed by the onslaught. But a wave of love for this man washed over her. And a wonderful hope was burgeoning within that she was loved in return and she knew if that were true she would be completely blessed and would want no more.

'You must go home, Faye,' Ryan said huskily. 'Please go away so I can deal with him.'

Faye placed her hand in his, letting him know she was ready to get in. Before he closed the cab door, something occurred to her out of the blue. 'Shouldn't you still be escorting your sister and the girls to the port?'

'I turned around at the halfway house and let them journey on. Never fear, the party will now be close to the coast and have plenty of servants accompanying them.' He discreetly touched her flushing cheek. 'I had to come back and speak to you... I couldn't wait. And God knows I'm glad now that I did return.'

'I've wanted to talk to you, too. Please come to my aunt's, she lives at...'

'I know where she is. I'll come, I swear.' Ryan gave the driver Mrs Banks's address and coins to cover the fare.

It was only as Faye was settling her throbbing head back against the squabs that she remembered that she should have begged him not to get into a fight with Peter. Another rumpus was the last thing her family's reputation could stand.

Chapter Nineteen

'Hell's teeth! Who do you think you are, barging in like that?' Peter had been gingerly bathing the gash on his scalp when the door was pushed open. 'What do you want?' he snarled, unsettled by the stranger's cold stare.

'Your head on a platter,' Ryan answered through set teeth as he walked in. His eyes shifted to the sapphire ring on the washstand and a satisfied smile slanted his lips.

Peter threw the bloodied cloth into the bowl. Like an animal confronted by a predator, he grew tense and watchful. Slowly his gaze narrowed in recognition. 'You're Ryan Kavanagh, the new owner of Valeside Manor.' He quickly made an infuriating connection. 'Did you journey from Wilverton with my fiancée? What the devil d'you mean by escorting her without my permission?' He puffed out his chest, hoping Kavanagh was ignorant of the violent scene with Faye moments ago.

'Miss Shawcross travelled to London alone. But I am here because of her and I don't need your permission for any damn thing where she's concerned.'

'Well, I say you do.' Peter jutted his chin. 'She told

me about you moving your whore into the manor. I won't
have my future wife associating with the likes of you,'
Peter sneered. 'I saw your concubine on the day of the
village fair. Dark as sin, ain't she? I'll wager she's an
obliging little thing between the sheets.' Peter's lewd
chuckle was abruptly cut off by a hand savagely closing on his throat.

'You'd be wise to button your lip and just listen.' Ryan
shook Peter as a terrier might treat a rat. Then his hand
stilled and he said, 'You are no longer betrothed to Miss
Shawcross. You will henceforth stay away from her for
if you do not you will have worse wounds to tend than
those got from a crack on the head from a tankard. Do
you understand?'

Peter's bulging eyes glared hatred at his captor, but he
managed to give a nod, gulping in air the moment he was
released. So now he knew that Kavanagh *had* bumped
into Faye fleeing from the building and she'd blabbed.
'You've a fancy for her, have you?' Peter croaked, peering balefully from beneath his brows. It had never occurred to him that he might have a rival. He'd always
thought he had secured Faye's affection…apart from that
she kept in reserve for her dratted kin. 'We've had a tiff,
nothing more than that and none of it is your concern
in any case.' He snatched up the ring and pocketed it.

'Oh, but it is my concern now she is unattached and
I've taken it upon myself to protect her. I know she
gave you that injury and that she'd only lash out in self-
defence.'

'You know nothing about her, or what she'd do!' Peter
roared. 'She's not ripe for the picking, if that's what you
think. She's mine. We'll be married in a few weeks.'

'You'll be approaching foreign shores in a few weeks,

courtesy of a trader sailing on tonight's tide. It's berthed on St Catherine's Dock and the captain will be expecting you.'

Peter threw back his head and guffawed. 'What madness is this? You, my dear fellow, are addled in the attic,' he spluttered, making a show of wiping a mirthful tear from his eye. 'I'll do nothing of the sort.'

'Oh, I think you will…or I'll let it be known that you've not only been ejected from the navy in disgrace, but you're a fraudster, too…and a man guilty of attempted rape.' Ryan took a step closer. He could see in Collins's sly, hooded gaze that he regretted being thwarted in taking Faye's virginity. And he wanted to throttle the blackguard again, this time until he expired. Abruptly Ryan turned away and strode to the door, putting a safe distance between them. 'I've enough against you to put you in gaol… Westwood, too. Perhaps you ought to think of your parents and how they'll feel when they know they've bred a coward and a criminal.'

'I don't give a toss for them since my father sold my estate…' Peter pressed together his lips, inwardly cursing at having let that slip out.

'Fieldcrest House, you mean.' Ryan turned, planting his hands on his hips. 'You had ambitions to buy it back with the money you and Westwood swindled from Miss Shawcross, didn't you?' His top lip curled. 'But you're out of luck.'

'It was no real swindle,' Peter spat. 'As her husband her assets would have been legally mine. I gained a portion of her dowry slightly ahead of time, that's all!' He hesitated, assessing his opponent through close eyelids. 'Why say I'm out of luck? I *have* bought Fieldcrest.'

'I fear you have not. A better offer was received.'

'Nobody else wanted the estate as it is rundown.' Peter made a dismissive gesture.

'Apart from me. It's close to my land and will be of benefit. I'm finalising the purchase this afternoon.'

Peter lunged at his tormentor, fists up, but Ryan neatly sidestepped and put him on his back with a short sharp jab. He strode away, knowing if he remained close to Collins he'd drop to a knee and continue pummelling him.

From his position on the threshold of the room Ryan said through gritted teeth, 'Miss Shawcross is thanking her lucky stars that she avoided being shackled to a wretch who'd lie and cheat and rob her of her inheritance. You, of all people, she'd believed in and you callously used her trust against her, didn't you?' His blue eyes were cold with loathing. 'What did you pay Westwood for his trouble?'

Peter pushed up on to an elbow and his response was an obscene gesture as he knuckled blood from his lips.

'Let me guess…a few pounds and your promise to introduce his cousin to your future wife so the chit might socialise in a better circle.' Ryan snorted contempt. 'Whitening her reputation would have been no mean feat considering Cissy Pettifer was servicing tars dockside from the age of fifteen. She introduced you to Westwood, didn't she?'

'Go to hell…' Peter snarled, pushing to his feet.

'You first,' Ryan drawled. 'If you don't leave for the Indies but remain in town, I'll make sure you're the butt of jokes in every gentleman's club and drawing room, that's the choice you have. Another thing…if you stay you'll meet me Friday at dawn on Clapham Common or I'll come and find you and drag you there.'

Peter licked his lips. There was something about Ryan Kavanagh that made his guts roll in alarm. He didn't boast, or raise his voice or look irate. But he was lethal and best avoided because he meant every threat, Peter knew that as clearly as he knew the game was up with Faye. She wouldn't willingly marry him now. Even before this fellow had turned up he'd seen the puzzlement in her eyes turn to despising when she'd finally comprehended what he'd been up to. 'And Fieldcrest House? What of that? I'll not do your bidding without fair recompense.' Peter brushed his sleeve, glaring at the man who had him squirming, almost begging for a crumb of conciliation.

'We'll talk about that in a few months' time. And don't return any sooner than that or I'll not consider your plea to buy the place.' Ryan lit a cheroot, savouring the first deep inhalation before saying through curling smoke, 'I understand that you'll be busy packing up for your trip this afternoon but spare some time to visit your friend Westwood. Arrange for Miss Shawcross to be sent a banker's draft for two thousand pounds. I believe that is what her fund was worth when you robbed her of it.' He added as an afterthought, 'And add another hundred pounds to it for her inconvenience and interest due.'

'I don't have it. All I have left is the money lodged with Westwood for the purchase of Fieldcrest.'

'Well, borrow what you need from your father; it's what you usually do, isn't it? You go cap in hand to the elderly man you say you dislike and inveigle for money to pay your debts.' The sneer in Ryan's voice was apparent.

'Have you bedded her?' Even the idea of losing the money he'd embezzled and the house he'd longed for couldn't stop Peter tormenting himself with the idea that another man had taken Faye's virginity…a prize he'd anticipated having for so long.

Ryan glanced over his shoulder at Peter, loathing him with his eyes for just a second before leaving without uttering another word.

On returning to Marylebone Faye was relieved to find that Agatha was out. Her aunt's maid had turned up to do the laundry and was toiling in the washhouse set behind the kitchen. Betty Peeble had informed her that Mrs Banks had gone to the circulating library as she usually did on a Monday. Quickly Faye accepted the cup of tea Betty offered her, then she went and sat down in the parlour, wondering why she wasn't tearful. Her eyes felt hot and tired, but self-pity was furthest from her mind even though there was no denying that the best of her youth had been wasted on Peter Collins, a person she now knew to be unworthy of a minute's devotion.

She was still gently trembling from the shock of what had happened, but was determined to buck up before her aunt returned. She didn't want to alert the woman to the magnitude of it all; neither did she want to upset Agatha by telling her the sordid details of Peter Collins's behaviour. She would simply say that she'd fallen out of love with her fiancé and had decided to break her engagement and return home. It was the truth, after all, if abbreviated. Faye deemed Peter deserving of punishment for what he'd done, both in defrauding, and attempting to ravish her; but the uproar that would follow a public accusation would be too much to bear.

Finishing her tea, Faye gazed whimsically into her cup at the pattern of dark leaves on white china. She sank back against the upholstery and her weary eyelids fell. In her mind's eye she saw her uncertain future now as an empty room. She was standing on its threshold, chary of opening the door because she knew she might find within a strange, lonely space. Her long curly lashes still lay on her cheeks, but her full lips curved wistfully as images of those she'd like to invite inside…one gentleman in particular…drifted past her inner vision. A new chapter of her life was about to begin, just as it was for Claire, and he had been instrumental in helping them both turn the first page. But would he soon disappear back to a life in Ireland that suited him better than the one he had in a remote English country house? How could she tell his thoughts when he'd shown her so little of himself…and yet…she'd seen something in his eyes and heard something in his voice just a short while ago that made her hold tight to her hope that Ryan Kavanagh might see her as more than a passing fancy.

She opened her eyes. Jumping up, she went to the window, scouring the street for a sign of a curricle driven by an impossibly handsome man. He'd said he'd sort things out, then come to see her, but he might be unable to do so immediately on parting company with Peter. She hoped they wouldn't fight. Did Ryan have a weapon? Did Peter? Unable to sit and do nothing with that dreadful thought in her head, she went quickly upstairs to start packing.

The rattle of a vehicle approaching at speed made Faye drop the nightgown she'd been folding and rush to the window. By the time she'd peered out there was just a glimpse of a man, broad of shoulder, with hair like a raven's wing, passing out of her line of vision beneath the porch on the way to her aunt's front door. Then, as though sensing her watching him, he took several paces back and looked up at her window. Faye felt the heat

in his gaze scorching her face to a pink glow. She let
the curtain fall and turned around. In seconds she had
darted down the stairs and met Betty, wiping suds on
to her pinafore as she came out of the kitchen to answer
the rap on the door.

'I'll open up, Betty, I believe the visitor is here to see
me,' Faye announced in a gulp, hoping she didn't look
too flushed, or sound too odd.

'Righto, miss,' Betty said cheerfully and disappeared.

'Would you like some tea?' Faye offered as soon as
she'd closed the parlour door. They were facing one another, blue and green eyes locked together.

'Thank you…no, I can't stop for long.'

'Why not?' Faye blurted, then sank her teeth into her
lower lip to prevent herself begging him to stay. She realised she longed for him to always be close by. With
Peter it had been different. She had been distracted by
her family and he had been concentrating on building
his career. She had accepted her fiancé's long absences
without questioning if it were healthy to hardly miss him.
She knew she would have done without his company
quite easily after they were married, too. If Ryan Kavanagh were her husband she would count the hours till he
came back home from shooting pheasant for dinner…

Faye turned away. It was as well she still had some
pride, she told herself wistfully. She'd frighten him away
in a shot if he knew how intense were her feelings for
him.

Discreetly she looked him over, but could see no sign
of any damage to his face or clothes. She had barely
started to relax when the fist he had propped on the mantelpiece uncurled and she spotted grazes on his knuckles.

'Did you fight with Peter?' Her heart seemed to cease pounding while she awaited his answer.

Ryan smiled ruefully. 'I punched him, but on balance you probably inflicted more damage than I did.'

Faye's soft gasp preceded, 'I didn't mean to! I just wanted to get away.'

'Don't fret about it, he got off lightly,' Ryan growled. 'I would have given him the beating he deserved, but…'

'But?' Faye sounded alarmed. 'Were you interrupted? Did somebody see what happened?'

'Nobody was about; I didn't think you'd want me to hurt him badly.'

'No…I certainly didn't, thank you…' Faye sank to perch on the edge of a seat, sensing an explanation of sorts was required from her for drawing him into this mess. 'We were engaged for a long while and I thought I loved him. I thought he loved me…' She gave a sorrowful laugh. 'We spent so little time together yet stupidly I assumed I knew him. It's hardly surprising that eventually we drifted apart. But I wish it had not ended so very badly.'

'Many couples are kept apart by employment or family circumstances and cope with the separation.'

'You sound as though you think I should try to forgive and forget,' Faye said indignantly.

'No!' Ryan hunkered down beside her chair, clasping her hands in his. 'That's the last thing I think you should do. Collins isn't worthy of you, Faye, and I doubt he ever was. Don't speak as though you're responsible for what has happened. He's a duplicitous wretch and a coward who has greatly wronged you. I imagine he has always been at pains to keep his true character hidden.'

'My father never took to him…nor my aunt. I don't

think the Gideons liked him much either. Oh, they were all polite enough in his company, for my sake. But how I wish they had not spared my feelings.' She smiled with a hint of self-mockery. 'Of course, had they told me outright they believed him a nasty piece of work I would not have listened. I would have thought I knew better.'

Ryan used a knuckle under her chin to make her look at him, his eyes twinkling. 'You are quite like your sister then and my daughter and every other young lady, I imagine, who thinks she has fallen in love for the first time and that her beloved can do no wrong.'

Faye smiled into his deep blue eyes, loving him all the more for finding excuses for her credulity. She angled her face into his palm as he tenderly cupped her cheek. 'It's true that at sixteen we think we know our minds and our hearts...though we don't. How can we, when we have experienced so little of the world and the rogues in it?' She gazed at him earnestly while explaining, 'Claire is sixteen and for a short while she believed that she loved and wanted to marry Donagh; now she seems to have forgotten him. I was that age when Peter gave me my first kiss. I was flattered, and excited, thinking myself quite the worldly woman when in fact I was still a child inside. I believed he was the only man I'd ever want... and I remained loyal to that thought and to him for so many years, even though I believe I knew...'

'You knew what...?' Ryan prompted huskily.

A silence throbbed between them, then Faye whispered, 'I knew I was a fraud. Life is not a fairy tale that will promise a happy ending, but I wouldn't let go of a hope that it might be so, if I just stayed true to the fantasy...'

'I felt that way about somebody…when I was young,' Ryan said simply.

'You must have loved her very much…you must miss her very much…' Faye held her breath, desperate to have a crumb of information about the woman who'd won Ryan Kavanagh's heart and given birth to his daughter.

Ryan pinched at the bridge of his nose as though he regretted bringing up the subject of Shona Adair right now.

'Will you tell me about Ruby's mother?' Faye's soulful voice drew his eyes back to hers.

Ryan stood up, raking his fingers through his hair. 'God knows I owe you an explanation and I want to make it. But not now. I have to go and see to something that won't wait.'

Faye was hurt by his evasion, yet believed that he hadn't exaggerated the importance of an appointment he had to keep.

'I shan't detain you then, sir,' she said stiffly. 'My aunt will be back soon, in any case, so you should leave to avoid difficult explanations. Thank you for all your help today.'

Ryan barked a laugh at the ceiling. 'That's it?' he asked sardonically. 'You're shutting me out again because I have to get to St Catherine's Dock and secure your damnable fiancé a passage to the Indies?'

'What?' Faye burst out. 'Why on earth is *that* necessary? He will be gone soon enough of his own accord as he is due to ship out to Malta.'

'Not any more he isn't,' Ryan returned bluntly. 'I'm afraid his crimes extend beyond the fraud perpetrated on you. He has been cashiered from the navy. Some months ago in Gibraltar he was found guilty of stabbing a man following an argument over a gambling debt. His disgrace will eventually leak out and, for your sake, the further he is from England when it does, the better it will be.' Ryan paused. 'People will believe you jilted him over that and sympathise. It's possible it'll come to light that he attempted to cheat you out of your money, too.'

Faye's eyes had widened in shock while she listened. 'I'd sooner that wasn't broadcast,' she said flatly, although she knew it was a vain hope. 'Peter *was* due to sail for Malta...he told me so at the summer fair...' She suddenly realised how gullible that sounded given her recent experience with him.

'He was fortunate to have got away with a dishonourable discharge; he might have faced a noose but for his senior position.' Ryan approached Faye, his fingers massaging along her forearms as he drew her closer to him. 'I know hearing the brutal truth is a shock. I would have spared you it if I could, but I'll not lie to cover up what he's done. He's quite adept at doing that for himself.'

'So on the last occasion that he visited Wilverton he had already lost his career and taken my investment.' She spoke almost to herself. 'How did you find out about all of this?'

'I made it my business to find out and recruited detectives to snoop and ask questions and bribe people to tell what they knew. I'm sorry if you don't like my methods. I want you to be happy, Faye, and that wouldn't be possible with him by your side.' He smiled self-mockingly. 'Of course, I had a selfish reason for getting rid of him: *I* want you. I'll protect you...care for you, you know I will.' He paused, then said with a throb of sincerity, 'I *can* make you happy...'

'I know,' she whispered. 'But how can I ever be content when there is so much about yourself that is puzzling, Viscount Kavanagh?' She used his title as a pertinent reminder of how little she knew of that side of his life. Abruptly she removed herself from his hold and stepped away. It was too difficult to think straight with the scent of him in the air she breathed and the warmth of his hands branding into her bones. 'You should go; please see yourself out as my aunt's maid is up to her elbows in washing water.'

'You don't trust me.'

'How can I when I have little on which to base that trust?' She gestured in frustration. 'I never again want to be involved with a man who keeps a secret side to himself. So shall I hire detectives to snoop on you? What would they tell me, I wonder, about your army career and your gypsy roots? Then there is your past involvement with the mother of your beautiful daughter, who doesn't even know that she is your daughter. Will they report a scandal concerning Ryan Kavanagh and the mother of his illegitimate daughter? Are there more secret daughters…or sons?'

'I've one child. And you don't need to check up on me at all—' his accent and his expression had hardened in frustration '—I'm not like your fiancé. But I'll admit I regret not having found the courage to tell you all about myself sooner.' He prowled towards her, cornering her when she backed away from him. Slowly he smoothed a thumb along her jaw. 'I'll tell you everything you want to know, I swear, but right now isn't the time. Peter Collins must be on that ship leaving on tonight's tide. If he stays, he'll concoct lies about you to justify what he has done. The scandal you anticipated following Claire's misconduct will be nothing as to what will mire you.'

Their eyes held, strained, and for a moment Faye felt

ready to forget about caution. She was tempted to throw her arms about him, trusting fate would be kind and her instinct right. He was a good man who was trying to do what was right for her, she was sure of it. What had observing duty and etiquette for all her adult life got her? Disintegrating dreams and wasted years. When she returned to Wilverton she was sure the master of Valeside would ask her again to be his mistress. Why not go with him, wherever that might be and for however long the adventure might endure? He wanted them to be happy, he'd said. He'd not mentioned love, but he desired her. And he cared for her and had proved it many times in his actions. Even her father had not always shown her such attention or generosity. She'd seen affection and tenderness in his eyes when he looked at her. Who was to say that in time it might not deepen into true love?

Faye started to attention on hearing a hum of conversation. She identified her aunt's voice, realising that the woman had come in through the garden door, and was talking to Betty in the washhouse.

'My aunt is home,' she hissed a warning. 'As you are in a rush it might be prudent to go now before introductions and explanations are required.'

Ryan gave a single nod, then, without warning, he suddenly pressed his mouth hard to hers. 'I swear I will come back this evening and tell you everything you want to know…and more besides,' he murmured against her pulsating lips. 'And forget about Collins. He's in the past.'

He had gone from the house before Faye had properly surfaced from the sensual bliss that had exploded in her at the strength of his kiss. But her aunt's sudden appearance soon brought her to her senses.

'Betty tells me you had a visitor.' Aunt Agatha had spotted her niece hovering on the parlour threshold. 'Oh…who was it? Have I missed them?' She sounded disappointed.

'It was a gentleman called Mr Kavanagh.' Faye had referred to him as she usually did, knowing any mention of a viscount having been in the house would give rise to excited questions. 'He is a neighbour in Wilverton and called to say hello as he is in town, too,' she rattled off. 'As Betty was here I didn't think there'd be any harm in receiving him.'

'Of course there would not! You're hardly a young debutante in need of a chaperon,' Agatha said rather tactlessly. 'I would have liked to meet him. So, did you have a nice time with your friend who is related to the vicar?'

'I didn't get that far…' Faye had intended to see Anne's relations, after she'd been to Peter's lodgings. In the event she'd not had a chance to do so. 'I bumped into my fiancé and we…that is, things came to a head between us.'

Aunt Agatha heard the gravity in her niece's voice. She quickly approached, taking Faye's hands and giving them a little squeeze. 'That sounds ominous, my dear. Do you want to talk about it? I'll not badger you to do so.'

'I'd like to have a talk as I've decided to go home tomorrow now I have jilted Peter.'

'Let's sit in the parlour,' Aunt Agatha said, patting her niece's arm. 'And I expect some tea is in order to keep our tongues oiled. I can see that there's much to chew over. You settle down and I'll go and ask Betty to put the kettle on.'

Chapter Twenty

The supper things had been cleared away to the kitchen and Faye had helped her aunt with the washing up. Now the two women sat companionably in the parlour, but Faye couldn't relax. Many hours had passed since Ryan had left the house and as the clock on the mantelshelf continued to tick away the minutes her imagination started to twist hither and thither and all manner of disasters began tormenting her.

Had Peter refused after all to go abroad? Had he turned violent, perhaps with knife or gun, wanting to get his own back on Ryan for punching him and meddling in his affairs? Perhaps one or other of them…or, heaven forfend, both…lay unconscious and bleeding on a pitch-black wharf. Then there was always a chance that the commotion had brought the authorities to investigate and they were both under arrest.

Faye might not have known her fiancé as well as she ought, but one thing she *was* certain of: he wouldn't bow down easily to another man's dictate…unless he had a vested interest to do so.

'I think I will retire.' Aunt Agatha broke into her

niece's feverish thoughts, gathering up the playing cards from the table where she'd had a game of solitaire. 'I hadn't realised it was almost ten o'clock.' She glanced at her knitting, discarded by her side. 'These old eyes feel too tired to do a few more rows.'

Faye put down the Gothic novel that she'd made a show of reading. It was a warm August evening, close and sticky; hardly a breath of air stirred the velvet draping the open casement.

Agatha was in the process of stretching her weary limbs when a bang on the door sounded, causing her to thump a hand to her breast. 'Who in heaven's name is that calling at this hour?' She turned up the oil lamp on the table, frowning at her niece.

Faye had got swiftly to her feet, her heart drumming in a mixture of excitement and uncertainty—surely Ryan wouldn't call so late? 'Wait here, Aunt Agatha. I'll see who it is.' Picking up a candle from the mantel, she shielded the flame with a hand as she hurried to the door.

'Keep that chain firmly in place!' Agatha instructed, hovering on the parlour threshold. She had few friends and even fewer relatives. She rarely got calls, even during social hours.

Faye opened the door, just a little. She might be a country girl, but she knew that the city after dark was a dangerous place. Her aunt lived alone and was a prime target for a felon prepared to barge in and purloin what he could lay his hands to. Lifting the candle, she peeped out.

'Miss Shawcross?' A stranger with a drooping moustache raised his hat.

'Yes... I am Miss Shawcross...'

'I have a letter for you, special delivery.' The man slid

the parchment through the aperture then, doffing his hat again, scuttled on his way.

'What is it?' Agatha asked, pattering forward and drawing her shawl about her shoulders. She stared at the letter in her niece's hand.

'It is a note from Peter Collins.' Faye had examined the script by candlelight and recognised the writing. Disappointment rippled through her. Although she'd known it was unlikely Ryan would outrage her aunt by visiting at such an hour, she'd hoped to see him. With Agatha in attendance, not much of import could have been said, but she would have read from his eyes if all had not gone as planned in his confrontation with Peter.

'I expect your Mr Collins is feeling sorry for himself now you have jilted him and is trying to win you back. I have to say I think you have done the right thing... but it is a shame.' Agatha cocked her head at her niece, noting the way she had thrust the letter into her pocket as though wishing herself rid of it. Faye's agitation was proof that the poor girl needed more time to sort out her feelings and her future. At twenty-five years old she was mature enough to know that suitors for a woman past her prime would be thin on the ground. And Faye Shaw-cross was too sweet and beautiful to live out her life as an old maid. Faye had been a kind and dutiful soul to her father and her siblings and had paid too dear a price in Agatha's opinion.

'Come back into the parlour,' she urged, steering her niece by the elbow. She gathered up her knitting from the chair she'd sat in. 'I shall be off to bed and let you read your letter in peace. Then in the morning you might want to have a chat about it all. If you decide you wish to stay for a few more days rather than head straight home, then you are very welcome, my dear.' Agatha approached her niece to give her a peck on the cheek. 'Goodnight.'

'Goodnight...' Faye murmured. When the door had closed she set down the candle on the mantelshelf and took the letter from her pocket. There was no mistake; it was definitely Peter's writing. She wondered if he had sent her a farewell message, begging her forgiveness. Had the fire been alight she might have tossed the parchment on to the flames. She wanted none of his apologies or explanations after what he'd done to her; whatever he said she'd not think him sincere. Her fingers ran over the paper in agitation and butted against a ridge as though something else were contained within the cover. Curiosity pricked at her and she broke the seal, unfolding one layer to find another note within.

Faye stared in astonishment at a banker's draft for the sum of two thousand and one hundred pounds. Westwood had told her that her fund would have been worth two thousand pounds had it performed as it ought. And, of course, it probably had, because she'd been lied to and cheated out of her bond. She guessed that Peter hadn't willingly returned that money to her after having gone to the trouble of embezzling it. Ryan had forced him to repay her. Once again the master of Valeside had cared for her...and the ache within to see him again, to revel in his strong, warm embrace intensified so unbearably that a small moan rasped in her throat.

Carefully she folded the draft and put it in her pocket. The covering note had just one word scrawled on it... *Sorry*...and Peter hadn't even bothered to sign it. Faye scrunched that in a fist and dropped it into her pocket as well. She realised she was no longer consumed with anger, as earlier. Oddly, she felt more pity for Peter Collins than she did for herself. She had hopes and dreams for her future, and a family home to go to. What had he? Nowhere to call his own other than a seedy room to lodge in and no career either. She wondered if his parents might take him in, but the idea was soon nudged aside by thoughts of Ryan.

She glanced at the clock as it chimed ten. She hoped that the night would pass quickly. In the morning she would wait indoors to see him; she was sure if no disaster had befallen that he would come before she set off for the coach station at noon. With a sigh she took the candle sconce to light her way up to bed.

It was only a dream, her subconscious mind reassured her, there was nothing in the room and she could sleep on. She'd dreamt of monsters and goblins when little and remembered her mother soothing her with words and touches while she drowsed with fantastical beasts leaping behind her eyelids. Nothing malign was close by…nothing to harm her…an inner voice murmured.

A soft sigh escaped her lips and she rolled over towards a source of warmth, her limbs stretching languidly.

'Faye…wake up, sweetheart…'

The command was felt as a misty breath against her ear and, angling her head closer to it, she sensed a redolence of sandalwood and smoke, then masculine skin scraping her cheek. The touch of hard hot lips on her jaw brought her eyelids wide open.

She would have jerked upright with a cry, but a pair of firm hands pinned her shoulders to the bed and a capturing mouth stifled her breath.

'Hush…you're quite safe. I couldn't wait till tomorrow

to come and see you,' was murmured into her mouth. 'I'm sorry I'm so late...'

Ryan placed a long finger where his mouth had been, gently moving the digit over her parted lips. 'You won't scream, will you?'

Panting softly, Faye shook her head. As he got up from the edge of the bed she struggled to a seated position.

He lit the candle stump on the nightstand, holding it up so she could identify him while the flame dappled his face with a devilish hue.

'I'm sorry if I startled you. I promise I won't touch you. You're not frightened, are you?'

She shook her head, her loose blonde hair rippling against her nightgown. Swinging her legs off the bed, she stood up.

Ryan gazed at her, wanting to scoop her up simply to lay her back down and feast on her womanly beauty. Beneath her plain nightgown he could glimpse the thrust of breast and hip contouring cotton. He grunted a laugh and put down the candle, standing before it so she was again hidden in shadow.

'What is it?' Faye realised he'd deliberately cut off the light a second after that sarcastic chuckle rasped in his throat.

'Nothing... I'm just regretting not waiting until morning to see you. Either that or I shouldn't have made that promise.'

'I know you keep your promises.' Her spontaneous joy at seeing him was making her breathing erratic. 'I'm glad you came. I wanted you to. I've been waiting.' The pull of his presence was overwhelming, even in the dark she was helplessly aware of him. Blindly she flew to where she knew he stood, hugging him about the waist. 'How did you get in? Who let you in? I've been so worried,' she whispered against his shoulder as his arm immediately bound her tight to his muscular body. His coat smelled of the docks, salty, tarry wool beneath her cheek.

He gestured at the casement where the brocade curtain billowed gently in the breeze. 'I let myself in. A bad gypsy trick, I know. I haven't shinned up a drainpipe in quite some years.'

'You broke in through the window?' Faye sounded in equal part amused and appalled.

'Be fair…it was open,' he protested. 'I can be imaginative in gaining entry to a lady's bedroom. And then again before quitting it…' he muttered as a dry afterthought. The fingers pressed to the middle of her back slid in a sensual caress, travelling up through a cascade of silken skeins of hair to splay against her nape. 'You're glad to see me, you say, but I'm thinking you're going to tell me to keep other promises, or go.'

'I am…' Faye returned. Her small hand forked over his jaw, turning his face so the candlelight played upon it and she could read his expression. 'You owe me that much before we go any further.'

'Where are we headed?' he asked, his low-lashed eyes watching her mouth.

'I don't know, Mr Kavanagh…but…' She inhaled shakily before throwing caution to the wind. 'I'm willing to go there with you if you stay true to your word and I believe what you say. Tell me what happened with Peter, then tell me about yourself, and about Shona and Ruby; or, if you'd rather, you may leave immediately in the manner in which you arrived.'

Ryan's mouth tugged up at a corner. 'You're throwing me out already?'

'Yes,' Faye said simply with a catch to her voice. 'I've been tricked and lied to by Peter Collins. He's made me feel a fool for trusting him. It won't happen again with any man.'

Ryan removed her soft fingers from his face, controlling their joined hands as he took them down. 'You believe me no better than him?'

'Of course I think you better than him! But you vowed to tell me who you really are. If you go back on your word, then why should I trust you?'

'I'll start by telling you what happened this evening, shall I?'

'Please do…but I've guessed that it has all gone as planned.' A short laugh preceded, 'You are here and seem unharmed. You get what you want, don't you, Mr Kavanagh?' Faye freed her hand from his and went to perch on the edge of the mattress. 'For a while this evening I fretted over what might occur between you two. Then I received a letter from Peter and guessed you had removed the risks. How did you coerce him to return my investment money and go quietly?'

'By dangling his childhood home…that is now in my possession.'

'Fieldcrest House?' Faye sounded disbelieving. 'I know it's for sale.'

'I found out he was attached to it so made sure I acquired it as a bargaining tool. You're right…he went quietly…no violence erupted on either side.'

'I'm glad about that, and, yes, he was attached to it.' Faye briskly turned her mind away from the finality of her betrothal and to the matter of Peter's estate. 'I think he was fonder of that place than of me.'

'Are you pining for him already?'

'No!' Faye jumped up and faced him. 'I will never pine for him, only for a future I expected to have.'

'He'd hoped to reclaim the property with what he stole from you. He almost did.'

'I know he spoke of one day getting it back.' Faye pressed her fingers to a throb in her temple. 'I must thank you for making him return my money. Perhaps I should have taken his need for his inheritance more seriously. He never asked me to help him buy it…perhaps if he had—'

'He didn't need to ask, did he?' Ryan bluntly interrupted. 'He took what he wanted and would have taken you, too, without consent. If you'd married him, would you have turned a blind eye to his philandering?'

'I wasn't aware he had a mistress; I suppose that was very naive of me,' Faye said quietly. She gave Ryan an old-fashioned glance. 'In any case, a man who keeps two paramours, one each end of town, shouldn't moralise.'

Ryan grunted a laugh, rubbing the bridge of his nose in something akin to embarrassment. 'I'm no angel, I'll admit it. But I don't keep two women…and haven't for a long time. I don't even keep one any more.' He sounded self-mocking. 'Who told you that tale?'

'The same people who told me you had a concubine at the manor. Or, in other words, the rumour might have come from any number of people in Wilverton.'

'They were all wrong about Ruby, weren't they?' he drawled.

'*You* were wrong, too, sir, for withholding the truth of the matter,' Faye retorted. 'On the whole folk are fair-minded.'

'Are they, now? They'd sooner have a scandal than an innocent answer, it seems; even a little village likes

its gossip. But you're right, I should have spoken out.'
A throb of regret made his voice husky. 'When you've
gypsy blood you learn at a young age to keep things
about your kith and kin private amongst genteel folk.
Honesty can cause a problem.' He gestured abruptly.
'Perhaps I have been naive, too. I believed that Ruby
would be assumed to be my ward as that's how she sees
herself. I thought village folk too prim to come up with
such fantastical interpretations of my domestic arrange-
ments. I wasn't happy when I heard of the vile rumours
swirling about us. But I don't have to explain myself
or my daughter to anybody, or beg their pardon for our
Romany blood.'

Faye had discerned the bitterness and hurt in his voice
and she stretched out a hand to comfort him. 'But surely
by being too proud and sensitive about it you've made
matters worse?'

'I know I have. And I regret not having let you know
a long while ago how I felt about you…really felt. I was
a coward who feared you'd distance yourself from a man
with gypsy blood running in his veins.'

'And what do you think now?' Faye asked softly, feeling that her heart might break from tenderness. She'd
never seen him look so vulnerable.

'Now I know you're too fine a lady to act in a mean
way.'

'You've met prejudice because of your heritage?'

'I've been called a mongrel on occasions because of
my mixed blood. My parents were ostracised by some
people because of their love for one another. It's not just
the gorjas; some Romanies prefer their relatives to marry
their own kind.'

'I…I didn't know, I'm sorry.' Faye kept her voice controlled, but inwardly a rage simmered in her breast at those nameless bigots.

'You didn't want your sister associating with a gypsy boy, did you?'

'I did not,' Faye returned in a voice that held no apology, but a hint of defiance. 'My disapproval wasn't based on Donagh's race; the match was unsuitable.'

'Your sister didn't think so.'

'She does now.' Faye sounded wry. 'It was an infatuation, that's all. She longs to be grown up; riding the country lanes in a caravan and stewing pheasants for dinner seemed wonderfully romantic.' She smiled. 'My sister is a girl who finds it a fag to have to help wash up the dinner plates. She would soon have grown bored with that hard life. In fact, she'd tired of it even before embarking upon it.' Faye gazed earnestly at him. 'Please believe me when I say that I do feel very sorry that she led Donagh on the way she did. In truth, they both have had a lucky escape from a bond that would have made them unhappy.'

'And you...would you grow bored and unhappy with a life on the road, or of being slandered as a gypsy's woman?' His eyes roved her features as though he might read his answer there rather than wait for it.

Faye understood that there was more to his question than simple rhetoric.

'It depends on with whom I would be sharing my journey. I'd sooner spend my days with a gypsy than a fraudster, if that answers you.'

'It does. And it makes me feel a greater fool for not having told you the truth about Ruby much sooner. At first I felt guilty at having drawn the Lees into the neighbourhood, but now... I'm not sure that I do. Donagh

Lee presented us both with a problem and that drew us together and gave me a reason to get to know you better.'

'It seems to me that there must have been more to their pursuit than simply Donagh's infatuation with your daughter.'

Ryan smiled. 'Money is what really brought them.'

'You owed them money?' she frowned.

'They said I did, and I agreed that I did and I paid them. It's the way of things in the clans.'

Faye didn't understand that logic, but didn't want to pry into his private finances. Besides there was something more pressing on her mind that she would know. 'You asked if I would have a life on the road. Are you intending to give up your role as a country noble and go travelling?'

'Maybe…you said you would go with me wherever it might be. If our path doesn't lead to a country house and genteel acquaintances, what then?'

'Then…then the same conditions would apply, Mr Kavanagh,' Faye answered clearly. 'Be you gypsy or gentleman, I will go nowhere with you until you tell me some more about your past and the people who have featured in it. I want to know about Ruby's mother, Shona Adair.'

The quiet between them seemed to pulse with the beat of her heart and when it became unbearable she said softly, 'You should go. I think we both need time to think about things. Come back tomorrow, if you will. I'm not leaving the Bull and Mouth until after twelve noon, so if you want to speak to me before I journey home there will be an opportunity.'

Immediately he strode to the door. Instead of leaving, he turned the key, locking them in.

Chapter Twenty-One

'I want to speak to you now.'

There was an undercurrent of steel in his voice that made a thrill ripple through Faye.

'To say what?' she demanded, equally insistent. 'That you want me to be your mistress and that you will treat me to all manner of luxury while I'm under your protection? I know that, but I won't sleep with a man who is in many ways a stranger. You know of my life and family and comment freely on them, but it seems I'm not allowed to know the important things in your background.'

'I want to tell you everything about my past and I've already said I wish I had done so sooner. But I couldn't find the courage or the right words then…and I'm struggling now. I don't know how to tell you what I've done. I don't want you to think badly of me.'

'Is it something criminal or immoral?' Even as Faye demanded that answer she was inwardly denying that it could be true. She intuitively knew that he was a decent man…but then she'd thought that of Peter Collins, she soberly reminded herself.

'Some might think me immoral for having got Shona

pregnant out of wedlock, although I knew nothing of the baby until many years later. In my defence I believed we had gone our separate ways with nothing binding us.'

'Shona didn't tell you that you were a father?' Faye sounded astonished.

'She didn't have a chance to…by then I was a young officer serving overseas in the army. But my feelings for her were sincere, it was no callous seduction. We spoke of some day settling down together. But it was wrong, I know that now, to have spoken of a wedding when I was barely old enough to understand what marriage vows were about.'

'Your parents disapproved…' Faye guessed, giving him a soft smile.

'My mother was hopeful that our aristocratic relations would react well should I decide to make a wild gypsy girl my wife. My father held a different view… pessimistic, or perhaps practical, might be a more accurate word,' he continued sourly. 'He thought I should marry somebody of my own station when the time came for me to take that step.'

'But *he* chose to marry a Romany rather than somebody of his own station.'

'He did,' Ryan said with a hint of pride. 'My father went after what he wanted despite ostracism from some of his kin. He'd spotted Elizabeth Walsh when out riding and he pursued her. And I'm happy to say that she loved him equally. On the whole they were happy together. My father was an eligible bachelor and apparently many debutantes were disappointed when he wed a woman many thought undeserving of his attention.' Ryan smiled sourly. 'They'd experienced a lot of prejudice and didn't want me to follow in their footsteps. My

love affair with Shona caused friction between them and
I deeply regretted that. But my mother didn't try to stop
us meeting by using her clan connections; she rightly
predicted that my infatuation with Shona Adair would
run its course.' Ryan's mouth curved in a nostalgic smile.
'She knew me better than I knew myself. I was a youth of
seventeen besotted with his first sweetheart. I was also
a viscount's heir. My mother loved her birth family, but
she took her role as Viscountess, and her loyalty to my
father, very seriously.' He paused. 'She impressed on
me that she didn't want me to suffer the discrimination
that had made her life difficult. She told me all this im-
partially, without trying to turn me away from Shona.'

He prowled to and fro in the candlelit gloom and Faye
intuitively stayed quiet, allowing him the time he needed
to dwell on his memories.

'Our affair endured during my absence at an English
university,' he resumed. 'Although I was no longer faithful to her I always looked forward to returning to Ireland
so we could be together. But I never proposed marriage.'

'Did she die before you had a chance to wed and be a
family with your baby?' Faye asked solemnly.

'Shona passed away two years after Ruby was born.
By then she was another man's wife.' He roamed to the
window to stare up at the sky. 'I loved Shona when I
was a boy and I love my daughter now I know her…but
whether I would have willingly done the decent thing
at an age when I was immature and incapable of being
constant… I think I would not.'

'Hindsight is never kind,' Faye said gently.

'Quite so,' Ryan ruefully concurred over a shoulder.
'In the end I was glad I had allowed my father to persuade me to take a commission in the army after I grad-

uated. I grew to love, and hate, the military life. The brutality that goes hand in hand with the valour finally killed my soldiering spirit at Quatre Bras.'

'I expect you saw some dreadful things…'

'I did some dreadful things. It was the only way to survive and get my men off that battlefield. But whatever colours we wore we were all human beings, deserving of some dignity and pity. Those things can't be present in a melee of hand-to-hand fighting.' He continued staring into the night, a shimmering brightness in his eyes. 'Major Kavanagh no longer exists now, so no matter on that score,' he said quietly. 'The point is that my parents were wise enough to agree that the discipline of a career would benefit me. They just each took a different approach to the problem of Shona.'

Faye moistened her lips and sat down again on the bed, feeling troubled. 'Surely you didn't just go away and abandon Shona, did you? You had a child with her by then.'

'I never knew about Ruby. If my parents suspected Shona's firstborn was mine, they kept it to themselves. There was no mention of it in letters they sent, although they let me know that she had married and become a mother.' Ryan turned from the window. 'The Adairs knew that Shona was increasing and found her a willing husband. Donagh's uncle married her and got her pregnant again. She died in childbed within two years of the wedding taking place. The infant perished, too.'

'Oh…what a dreadful shame,' Faye said with genuine sorrow. 'How did you eventually find out about your daughter? Did your mother tell you?'

'If my parents discovered they had a granddaughter, they took that information to their graves. In the end Ru-

by's maternal grandmother broke the news. My daughter
has a wild streak. She gets that from Shona.' He smiled
ruefully. 'Shona's husband turned his back on Ruby. I'd
like to believe it was due to his grief over losing his wife
and baby, because apparently they had all been happy
together for those few short years. But it is more likely
that he no longer felt obliged to rear another man's child.
Shona's family took Ruby in and brought her up until
she was twelve.' Ryan thrust his hands into his pockets
and began to prowl aimlessly in the flickering candlelight. 'Ruby's grandmother was finding my daughter
too spirited to handle. She summoned me...told me all
about it and said Ruby's stars promised her riches, not
a travelling life. The woman was heartbroken because
she wanted to keep Ruby, but knew that I could give her
things that she needed to fulfil her destiny.' Ryan's smile
was ironic. 'Romanies might be superstitious, but perhaps I am, too. We rarely meet, yet I feel close to them.
A bond that is never tightened or nurtured is always present between us.' He looked at her. 'Does that shock you?
That I feel an affinity to the people who entertain you
at village fairs with their gimcrack and lucky charms?'

'I think it is quite wonderful that you have such a
strong attachment to your mother's folk.' She smiled. 'I
had my fortune told by a gypsy.'

'And what did she say?' Ryan walked slowly back
towards her.

'The truth...I hope...' Faye whispered, remembering
the old woman's words that she'd enjoy a happy marriage
with a good man who was close by. Ryan had been just
yards away at the time...

Ryan removed a hand from his pocket to stroke her
warm cheek. 'I have another side to me...the one my

father built. And I am not as averse to using my title as people think. I just don't always see a necessity for it. Neither did I see the point in pinning medals to my redcoat and parading in front of the King for his good opinion.' He paused and touched the scar on his face. 'This is the decoration I don't mind bearing. But there is one obligation I acknowledge above all else. My duty to protect and provide for my daughter will never waver. And I do love her, trial that she is at times.'

Faye imagined that a good deal of young men might try to wriggle out of such responsibilities by any means possible. But not Ryan Kavanagh; she guessed he'd been about twenty-eight when his daughter was abruptly foisted on to him. She'd thought Ruby was too young to be his sister…but…he looked too young to be a sixteen-year-old girl's father. 'You readily accepted that Ruby was yours?'

'I knew the moment I looked at her. My mother was a Walsh and the Adairs and Walshes and Lees have feuds that stretch back over generations. Yet they have married one another along the way. Ruby is the image of my mother. I wish she could have met her, but they were kept apart, so I learned from Shona's kin.'

'How cruel… I expect they would have adored to know one another.'

'The Adairs didn't want Ruby being claimed by the rich and powerful Kavanaghs. They are proud people who live by their own codes. They could have approached my parents for money. They didn't and neither would they take payment from me for rearing my daughter for all those years.' He chuckled. 'Thus, I would be a heartless landlord indeed if after all that I charged them to shoot and fish on the Kavanagh estate they trespass on.' He paused. 'But the Lees saw things differently. As head of the clan Bill Lee took it on himself to demand recompense for having allowed Shona and her daughter shelter within the Lee family. Bill's first demand was that Ruby should marry Donagh and bring some of the Kavanagh riches with her.' He leant a fist against the wall, gazing at it before resuming, 'When I made it clear that my daughter was marrying no man for some years hence, he followed me to England to settle for the cash I'd previously offered him.'

'Was it a lot of money?' Faye asked in awe.

'It was…and she's worth every penny. I don't begrudge paying the Lees. It has salved my conscience in a way; they cared for Shona and Ruby, treating them well, and it was my job to do that.' He paused. 'And now it is time to move on.' He wiped a hand across his jaw. 'But I wish my mother had known her granddaughter.'

'And will Ruby know her father?' Faye asked gently. 'Your daughter believes she is an orphan.'

Ryan thrust his fingers through his hair. 'I know I must tell her…when the time is right.' He paced aimlessly to the window, bracing two hands against the frame. 'She knows her mother passed away when she was little and she believes her father died soldiering. I don't blame Shona's people for embellishing the truth. I was introduced to her as her guardian when she was just twelve. At the time it seemed right to prevaricate and leave a difficult explanation until she was more mature.'

'She's now on the verge of womanhood. She deserves to know that you are alive and love her as a father should.'

'I want to tell her but, as with you, I've never found the words or the courage to do it.' He turned towards

Faye, frowning. 'Will she hate me, do you think, and accuse me of abandoning her mother?'

Faye rushed to him, cupped his face in comfort. 'Of course she won't hate you! It isn't your fault that you were kept in ignorance of her birth for so long. And she'll appreciate your honesty more than any mealy-mouthed half-truths.' Faye gently grazed her palms back and forth on his abrasive jaw. 'What I *do* feel certain of is that your daughter will be overjoyed that a noble man sired her.' She smiled. 'And she'll know where she got her beautiful brunette looks from.'

Ryan jerked Faye closer, smiling as he burrowed his face against her willowy, lavender-scented neck. 'And I think you quite beautiful, too; with your golden hair and green eyes you attract me like a moth to a flame.' He caressed her cheek with loving fingers. 'I'm burning for you now,' he mouthed against her temple. 'But your beauty isn't simply skin deep…my daughter needs you in her life: a strong and principled woman such as you can show her how to be a refined young lady.'

'I'd not pin your hopes on that,' Faye said with mordant amusement. 'Claire has managed to ignore my good example, if indeed good it is.' She sighed contentedly in his embrace. She utterly believed everything that he had told her. 'Both our girls will find their way. They are their own people, as we are, and trying to change them too much would spoil their characters and make them unhappy. I'd willingly spend more time with Ruby, though; I like her very much. But…'

'But…?' Ryan prompted, his eyes black as obsidian and flaring with candle flame as they searched her face.

Faye felt a blush warm her cheeks. 'If we…that is…' She faltered and drew a breath. 'Our future relationship might prevent my becoming close to your daughter. It would not be seemly for Ruby to associate with a woman suspected to be your mistress.' She felt his arms tighten about her and she struggled free to say rather crossly, 'Oh, you know it *will* be suspected. As you have rightly said, even in a little village people love to spy and gossip. We *will* be found out.'

'We must remove the risk then of giving anybody the chance to create a scandal.' Ryan lay sensual fingers against her throat where her nightgown's ribbons had loosened. Dipping his head, he pressed his lips to the pulse bobbing beneath pearly skin.

'I will not move to Ireland and be put in a remote house where you might visit me once or twice a week at your leisure.' Faye stepped back out of his reach in case the magic of his touch swayed her into agreeing to such a thing.

'You said you'd go anywhere with me,' Ryan reminded her, a hint of laughter in his voice.

'Within reason, sir, and within easy reach of my brother and sister until I am sure they no longer need me.' Faye backed away, needing to put a distance between herself and his overpowering virility. This is the reality of being a mistress, she thought. Loving him, wanting him and yet all the time there will be the uncertainty and the loneliness and the waiting… I can imagine it all and hate it before it has even begun.

'Will you go to church with me tomorrow?'

'Church?' Faye smothered a hysterical laugh. 'Are you quite religious, Viscount Kavanagh?'

'Not at all. I've been called a heathen in my time… an abuse that is possibly justified. But I believe in the sanctity of marriage. I believe in those wedding vows and that's why I couldn't propose to Shona. I knew I'd break them and we'd end up hating one another.' Ryan approached her, slid his arm about her waist and rested his forehead against hers. 'But then there's you…' He caressed her cheek with his own. 'There is something else I should have done a while ago, but didn't. Those words wouldn't come easily either; I'm not as brave as those damnable medals I've got in a drawer would have me be. I know your heart's been broken by Collins, but I pray that in time you might forget about him…and love me.'

'What words don't come easily?' Faye breathed, her insides tightening in anticipation of soon hearing something wonderful…something that might make her trust in gypsy lore for ever.

'Come…sit down.' Ryan led her to the bed, then he dropped to a knee in front of her. 'I love you, Faye Shawcross, and have done so since almost the first time I saw you. On the day you came to the manor to fetch the doctor I watched you running for some while before making my presence known. You were graceful as a hind, lovely as an earthly angel with your flaxen hair streaming on the wind. I knew quite simply that I had finally met the woman I wanted as my wife. But as luck would have it, she was promised to another.' He gave a dry chuckle. 'For a gorja you have a gypsy quality about you. Not this, though…' He forked his fingers through her untidy locks, savouring the feel of the corn-coloured silk sweeping across his palm. 'You are everything I want and God knows you've put a fire in my blood like no other. Even Shona couldn't arouse me the way you do and for a while I was at her feet.' He bowed his head. 'The fact that you were Collins's betrothed was agony for me. I wanted to take you from him even before I knew him corrupt and that made me hate myself.' He paused, rubbed a hand across his mouth in a boyish gesture. 'I know you don't love me and that at times you have hated yourself for responding to my lovemaking. But I don't regret showing you how I can make you feel because I love you and want to marry you. I swear I will remain faithful and cherish you and our children. And though I have no betrothal ring to give you right now, I'll lavish on you every fine jewel and gown you deserve as Viscountess Kavanagh.'

Faye could listen to no more of his torment, enchanting though it had been to hear of his devotion to her. Abruptly she sank down beside him on the rug. 'Hush… I need no fancy jewels or dresses and if you think I do, you don't know me at all, Ryan Kavanagh. I love *you*, not Peter Collins. Why else would I even consider travelling along country lanes with you in a draughty caravan, plucking pheasants?' She flung her arms around his neck and he swayed backwards to the rug, holding her on top of him.

'And I always loved what you did to me…how you made me feel, even if I did know that it was wrong to want you when I was engaged to another man,' she whispered, pressing her lips shyly to his.

'Will you marry me tomorrow, before we return to Wilverton? I'll get a special licence. Your aunt can attend you, if you like.' Ryan pushed back a tangle of blonde locks from her flushed face to gaze earnestly into her eyes. Slowly he manoeuvred them, rolling so she was beneath him.

'I've nothing to wear,' Faye protested even though she was smiling in joyful agreement.

'You can wear that nightgown for all I care. Don't

make me wait for the sake of a dress, please, Faye.' His mouth touched hers, sweetly wooing, then the kiss deepened to a demanding, slow-moving seduction. His arms slid beneath her, lifting her up and positioning her so she was straddling him on her knees.

With a little moan of anguish Faye wriggled her fingers between their faces, parting their lips. 'You love me and want to marry me, but I have to care for my family still.' There were still obstacles to overcome and no amount of sensual delight could erase that from her mind. 'My sister and brother are very important to me... and I cannot abandon them, even for you.'

'And neither would I expect you to,' Ryan said, raising their joined fingers to his lips. 'Whatever is important to you is important to me. They may live with us in England or Ireland for as long as you, or they, wish.' He chuckled. 'I cannot predict, though, how long we will be able to endure my daughter and your sister beneath the same roof.'

'They would be up to mischief, that's for sure.' Faye felt choked with emotion. 'You will really allow us all to live as a family, even though you barely know Michael and Claire?'

'I know you... I want you and while I breathe I'll do anything to keep you safe and happy. Your family are my family...even your servants.'

'Oh, Ryan...' Faye clasped him around the neck, smothering his stubbly cheek with little kisses. 'You asked me once why I had been engaged to Peter for so long. I could have told you then that he wouldn't tolerate my siblings living beneath his roof. Now I believe there was more than *just* that making me constantly delay. I had sensed *you* were out there somewhere and I was waiting for you to come and love me.'

'And now I am here can I love you? *Really* love you? Do you trust me that much, Faye?'

'Yes,' she said simply, gazing deep into his velvety eyes. 'I trust you with my life and that of my brother and sister. I trust you with my heart and my body…'

Ryan swept her up into his arms and slowly pivoted about on the spot before placing her on the bed. He braced two sinewy arms over her and for a long moment their eyes remained entangled. 'I'll go now…come back in the morning with the licence and take you to church, if that's what you want. We can wait until our wedding night…' He dropped his head to his arm, rubbing his face on his sleeve. 'Hell's teeth! My big mouth again…' he groaned.

'Don't you *dare* go.' Faye folded upright and plunged her arms about his neck. 'You will love me now, please, Gypsy Kavanagh…' She nuzzled his cheek. 'But ruffian that you are, you must love me quietly…my aunt is not far away.'

'Oh, I can be quiet…' He seemed about to add something, but instead smiled wickedly.

His eyes dropped to her gauzy nightgown and Faye felt the blue flame of his gaze scorching her skin, stirring her to her feminine core. She felt her breathing becoming slow as he gathered the hem of her garment in one large dark hand. She was barely aware of the whisper of cotton on her skin as the material floated away from her body. The throb in her breasts picked up tempo as his ravening eyes wandered from their full beauty to her slender waist and over the flare of her hips. Her breathing became slow, then slower still until she felt quite giddy. The first touch of his hand was firm and possessive, his long fingers sliding beneath the weight of a breast, curving upwards so the nipple was grazed within his palm. She arched into his touch, her naked torso rubbing against the wool of his coat.

'Lie down…' Ryan ordered huskily, throwing off his jacket. His hands were next at his trouser buttons, then his boots were lobbed softly aside to land on the discarded garments.

When he slipped on to the mattress beside her Faye immediately turned towards him. Stripped of a veneer of civilisation bestowed by his expensive tailoring, he seemed bigger, more powerful and disturbingly masculine. Even in low light she could see the thick ridges of muscle in his abdomen and arms. 'I…I know I was engaged for a long time, but we didn't do more than kiss really. That is to say…I don't know exactly what to do to please you—'

'Yes, you do,' Ryan gently interrupted, caressing her cheek with his mouth. 'Just lying beside you pleases me, just kissing you like this and this…' He slid his lips over hers, carrying on so his mouth moistened her throat and the swell of her breasts. 'All of that pleases me… do you like it?'

Faye nodded, swallowing, unable to articulate how blissfully excited he made her feel.

'Whatever pleases you, will please me,' he murmured, moving her hand to lay against his chest. 'Just touch me…in any way… I'll like it,' he groaned on a half-laugh.

Faye started to smooth and explore the satin-sheathed muscle and bone with her palms, revelling in the power she held on hearing his breath catch in his throat. She drew her fingers back to splay over his nipples and he immediately growled an appreciative laugh.

'You see…you do know…' he murmured hoarsely.

He dropped his head to hers, claiming her lips in a sweetly seductive kiss, while his hands lowered to tantalise her breasts with touches that became tender torture as the mewling in her throat increased. He shimmied down her, drawing a rigid little nipple to his lips and lavishing it with licks and pulls until her thighs instinctively parted and her knees drew up.

He went down lower, trailing fire with his mouth on her belly, then his hands clasped her inner thighs, gently spreading them to expose the apex of her femininity to his artful tongue.

'Ryan…' Faye cried, bucking her hips as white light shot behind her eyelids.

'Hush now…no noise, you said,' he growled, capturing her lips to quieten her. He nibbled musky kisses against her mouth, her ears until she became sinuous and cat-like beneath him. Then he shifted to cover her body with his, gently easing into her with nudges of a knuckle, rocking a thumb against the little nub until he heard her pants grow guttural and her arousal slickened his hand. He put his manhood against the dewy opening, rocking forward then withdrawing until he felt her natural rhythm increase and her hands grasped his hips. With a smooth shallow plunge he broke through, stifling her little squeal of surprise and pain with a long, drugging kiss.

'Are you all right?' he asked, as his hips swayed side to side on her groin in a rhythm that made her gasp and curl her calves over his. Too sensually dazed to speak, she answered him with a sigh and by thrusting up her pelvis to graze away the excruciating throb of need writhing in her belly. Every command he mouthed against her skin she obeyed, doing exactly as he asked, trusting him, until her shoulders were all that supported her and her hips were elevated and as one with his. Slowly he increased his movement and the excitement within her grew, layer on layer, drawing her higher and tighter until she felt that a coiled spring had replaced her innards. He ground against her faster and harder, tipping her over the edge and the tension within her burst into starlight and an animal cry of ecstasy.

Ryan's whole body had shaken with the restraint of touching gradually and tenderly when what he'd really wanted to do was plunge headlong into her and drive every thought of Collins completely out of her head. The moment he felt her climax undulating around him he rammed home in long hard strokes, smothering her sobs of pleasure with an erotic kiss until he shed his seed. Gradually he became still and they lay entangled and exhausted.

Faye felt another heart thundering against her breast and the wonder of it made her curve her mouth into a smile against his shoulder. 'So that is what couples do on a wedding night?'

'It's what we do every night,' he said in a voice of velvety amusement.

'Are you all right, my dear? Are you having a nightmare?' Aunt Agatha rapped on the panels. 'I heard you call out. Let me in to comfort you. That beast Collins has caused your torment…he is no good for you…' The door knob rattled.

Faye's eyes widened and she thrust a fist to her bruised and pulsating mouth to stifle a horrified squeal. She ignored Ryan's silent laugh and panted out, 'I'm quite all right, Aunt Aggie; it wasn't a nightmare about Collins…it was a dream…something wonderful.' Her eyes tangled with Ryan's. 'And now I'm feeling quite ready to fall off to sleep again.' Faye heard her aunt's mumble and then her footsteps receding.

Ryan dipped his head and kissed her before springing noiselessly from the bed and swiftly getting dressed.

Faye sat up, keeping the sheet modestly to her breasts in a way that made him smile as he shrugged into his tailcoat. He sat down on the edge of the bed and pulled on his boots, then turned to her.

'Will you tell your aunt we're to be married tomorrow afternoon?'

Faye shook her head. 'She's an astute woman. I'm not brave enough to risk her questions…after what she heard just now.'

'Are you brave enough to risk a life with me?'

'I am indeed,' Faye vowed with a note of soft wonderment. 'And if you're a minute later than twelve o'clock I shall come and find you for I can't wait for it all to begin.'

A shimmer of dawn was putting a glow in the sky, drawing her eyes to the window. 'You must go; it's getting light and somebody might see you leave.'

'I love you…trust me?'

She nodded firmly. 'I do…and I love you.'

Faye sat tensely with her knuckles supporting her chin, but no noise was discernible even though she strained her ears as he disappeared over the sill. She jumped from her bed, wondering if he'd got stuck on the drainpipe, but as she peeped out from the edge of the curtain she saw him strolling past a gas lamp.

He pivoted, walked back a pace into its glow as though knowing she was watching him, then he bowed, slowly blew her a wicked kiss and carried on.

Epilogue

Faye placed down her novel and went to the window to gaze out as it seemed about the right time for them all to come home. A savoury aroma was issuing from the kitchens, heralding dinner time. As though indeed lured by the scent of the succulent beef and onions roasting in Valeside Manor's ovens, two ladies hove into view against a russet-skied backdrop. They strolled sedately, side by side, along the shingle path littered with fallen golden leaves.

Faye watched them, a quietly contented curve to her mouth. If a person didn't know about the rift that had gone before they might think that Deborah Shawcross and Agatha Banks were the best of friends. They weren't, of course, but both women were determined to be civil for their hostess's sake. And perhaps, in the fullness of time, the bitter memories of a family fractured by infidelity would dwindle to shadows. Faye hoped the two widows might find companionship together in their twilight years; her surfeit of happiness made her want to see others happy, too.

Deborah's children had not completely forgiven her

either. Claire's head was crammed with exciting plans for a wonderful double debut with Ruby, so she was happy enough to be charitable towards the woman who had abandoned her.

On finding out that they were to be related by marriage the girls had been delighted and Claire much amused to realise she was her friend's aunt. But for the sake of peace and quiet it had been decided that they could think of themselves as sisters. The girls had grown closer and, in the way of sisters, bickered as well as played together.

As for Michael, he was where he loved to be: back at school with his chums, but he'd written his mother a short note welcoming her home.

A sound of squealing laughter outside drew Faye's eyes to the younger ladies. They were chasing around the corner of the building with their pretty pastel skirts held up about their knees. Ruby and Claire had said they'd gather some Michaelmas daisies to decorate their dressing tables. They had their posies gripped carelessly in their hands. Faye wondered wryly whether any petals would remain on the stalks by the time they were put in vases.

The party of women disappeared towards the courtyard that led to the back of the house, but Faye remained where she was, her green eyes roving the glorious colours of the wooded parkland for a glimpse of the person she really sought. Her vision stilled and she watched him, quietly fascinated as always by her husband's lithe masculine splendour. The light breeze caught at his hair, ribboning his face with jet-black strands. Over one shoulder was slung a gun, over the other three brace of pheasant. At his heels loped his wolfhound, keeping pace with him.

As Ryan drew closer, his eyes drifted to the drawing-room window and tangled with hers. He gave her that subtle smile that put a thrill of excitement low in her belly.

Turning from the window, Faye quit the room, knowing he would head towards the study for some solitude while their female relatives filled the house with loud chatter about their social plans.

She found him as always poring over architects' drawings for a new wing to the manor. 'You brought us home some pheasant.'

'Are you going to pluck them?' he asked with a sideways smile.

'Will you teach me how, Gypsy Kavanagh?' She perched on his lap, kissing his lean, abrasive cheek, loving that he smelled of wood smoke from the bonfire; the gardeners had started cutting back for the autumn already.

Ryan shoved back his chair and encircled her waist with his strong brown hands. Lovingly he smoothed a thumb over the tiny bump beneath her skirt.

'Are you going to tell them the news today?'

'Not yet,' Faye whispered, covering his hands with hers. 'I want to keep our early wedding-night baby just for us, for now.'

Shrill female voices drifted along the corridor.

'One minute they are hugging, the next shouting.' Ryan sighed, sitting back in the chair and pulling Faye against his chest.

'Girls of that age thrive on rivalry, you know,' Faye said, snuggling against him. 'They will constantly think that the other has the prettier gown, or the finer hat. This is nothing to what we might expect when they go to London. I would suggest dressing them identically to be scrupulously fair, but I doubt that would be acceptable to them either.' She chuckled wryly. 'There is nothing for it,' she sighed. 'We must prepare for tantrums.'

'We could ask your aunt and stepmother to take them under their wings, then sneak back here to enjoy the solitude. I'm sure the ladies wouldn't mind chaperoning them if I rent them a nice house for the Season.'

'That wouldn't be fair, Ryan,' Faye chided. 'You know they wouldn't say no, even should they baulk at the responsibility of those two minxes. Aunt Aggie and Deborah are falling over themselves to show gratitude to you. You've been so kind and generous...especially to Deborah.'

Ryan had said, if she was in agreement, he would allow her stepmother the chance to leave her squalid life behind and return to Mulberry House to live there, rent free. Faye had been eager to accept his offer, sensing her father would want the mother of his children to be allowed shelter and dignity in her latter years.

Ryan had also provided both her aunt and Deborah with an allowance so they might live comfortably in their own homes. Faye knew he would sooner they had some privacy than a houseful of her relatives. But he tolerated their long visits, to prove he loved her.

'We are all so thankful to you, especially me.' Faye brushed a slow kiss on the musky skin of his brow. 'You have been wonderfully generous and considerate...'

'As you have been to me...' Desire roughened his voice. 'There is never a night you're too tired to welcome me into your bed and exhaust myself...'

'Ryan!' Faye scolded, blushing furiously.

'Well...enough of your talk of gratitude and generosity, or I will match you like for like with reasons for being greatly obliged to you.' He drew her face down to his, tasting her lips. 'I don't mind doing anything that makes you happy. And I can't get enough of you, you know that.' His amusement held an undercurrent of rueful gravity. 'Even now…before dinner is even served, I long for the evening to be over so we might retire and…'

Faye smothered his throaty words with her fingers for such talk from him always made her feel hot and restless. His raw passion, some nights exquisitely slow and gentle, at other times short and rough and repeated over and over, was a gift that she never tired of receiving. In a way she was glad that she was pregnant simply so her menses would not stop him from loving her the way he did. But he was alert to their need for discretion while they had other people…especially the girls… beneath their roof.

'Thank God we might soon be able to marry Ruby and Claire off, and have more time to ourselves,' Ryan murmured against his wife's cheek, as though his thoughts had tracked hers.

'I meant to say to you about that…' Faye began. 'Do you think it is too soon for them? They are just girls at heart and next Season they will still only be seventeen. Perhaps another year at home might benefit them.'

Ryan gave a rueful sigh. 'I have to admit that I was thinking along those lines while watching them haring around outside.'

'I only wanted Claire wed because I had little money to keep us all. Then after the business with Donagh and the threat to her reputation it seemed the only way.'

'Donagh and his people are now far away,' Ryan

soothed. 'I heard that they are heading towards York and might not come back this way, but return to Ireland.'

'You are relieved about that, too, because of Ruby, aren't you? You think she might fall for him again and go travelling.'

'She is at an impressionable age, as is Claire,' Ryan said soberly. 'Ruby might want to make long visits to her mother's people and I wouldn't stop her from doing so. I understand the pull of the clans for those with gypsy blood. But it is not romantic…it is a primitive life and riven by feuds. I brought Ruby to England not only to distance her from Donagh, but so she might experience a more sophisticated way of life.' He sighed. 'I don't want her to risk giving birth in the back of a caravan, as her mother did.' He shoved a hand through his hair. 'I know the hazards of childbed face women of every class, but I want to protect my daughter if I can.' He gazed earnestly at Faye. 'And I want to protect you, Viscountess Kavanagh. The best physician must attend you when the time comes for your confinement. And he must stay in the house until you are up on your feet again.'

'I'm as strong as an ox and need no mollycoddling,' Faye reassured him and quickly changed the subject. 'So we will have another year to put some polish on those two hoydens before we let them loose on society. Even then I believe you won't allow any poor fellow near your daughter unless he is a paragon. And as I have already netted the only one of those in existence…' Faye teased him. 'She will want somebody as fine as her father. I knew she'd be overjoyed to find out who you really were.'

Ryan looked abashed. 'I wish I'd told her before…it was foolish not to. Any longer delay and it might have been too late.'

'I understand why you acted that way,' Faye said solemnly. 'It was hard for me to find the courage to make changes to my life rather than keep the status quo.'

'Are you thinking of Collins?'

Faye stared at the architects' plans, tracing the new nursery with a shapely fingernail. 'Yes… I am thinking of him.'

'Are you jealous?' Ryan asked bluntly.

'Jealous?' Faye frowned. Ryan had returned from London earlier in the week with news that Peter Collins was back from the Indies.

'Are you jealous that he has married Cissy Pettifer?'

Faye cupped his face with her hands. 'Of course not… she is very welcome to him. In fact, I feel sorry for her. She is young by all accounts and I wonder if she knows what she has let herself in for.' She paused. 'He has made himself a hard bed to lie on…and his wife will suffer alongside him.'

Faye had heard from her aunt that the consensus of opinion in town was that Peter Collins was lucky to have escaped gaol and unlucky to have lost the best thing he'd had: namely, her. Of course it had leaked out that he had stolen from her and that he'd been cashiered from the navy. He was a risible figure and his wife, too, her aunt Aggie had told her, whereas Faye Shawcross was now envied by every young lady who'd never had a chance to meet and attempt to charm the newly arrived Irish viscount with sinfully good looks.

'I feel sorry for his parents, too,' Faye continued. 'But I don't pity him,' she ended flatly. 'I think Peter Collins has been given more chances than he ever deserved.' She gazed at her husband's profile. 'Which brings me to ask…will you sell him back his estate?'

Ryan gave a slight smile. 'I'll consider doing so, if he ever manages to raise the money to pay for it. My attorney tells me he has been in touch because he still wants it. I've got what I want and Collins is of no consequence now. I'm not a vindictive man.'

'You're an extraordinary man,' Faye said simply. The dinner gong sounded and she tutted. 'Oh…I've not even changed yet.' Faye twitched her day dress, making to rise.

'Nor I…' Ryan said, holding her on his lap with two firm hands. 'I'll tell the servants to delay for a short while so we can go upstairs, shall I?'

Faye glanced over her shoulder. His low-lashed eyes were hungrily roving her rounded bosom, making a pulse beat beneath her bodice.

'Yes… I'd like that,' she said, starting to giggle.

Ryan stood up with her in his arms, spinning about with her as he travelled towards the door.

'What am I going to do with you, though, when you've still not learned to be silent and we've a houseful of people?' he teased.

'Kiss me quiet, sir… I beg of you,' Faye whispered against his lips and immediately got her wish.

* * * * *

If you enjoyed this story, you won't want to miss these other great reads by Mary Brendan:

COMPROMISING THE DUKE'S DAUGHTER
TARNISHED, TEMPTED AND TAMED
THE RAKE'S RUINED LADY
A DATE WITH DISHONOUR